A Certain Cast of Light

of Light

Jonathan B. Walker

ISBN: 1543151671
ISBN-13: 9781543151671

Cover Design by Dan Long

DEDICATION

This novel is dedicated to the Bennett family of Connecticut and all of its descendants, past, present and future.

A Certain Cast of Light is a work of historical fiction. While the characters and general historical background are based upon documented source materials, certain incidents, the motivations of the characters, their actions, their writings and their dialogues, are all products of the author's imagination.

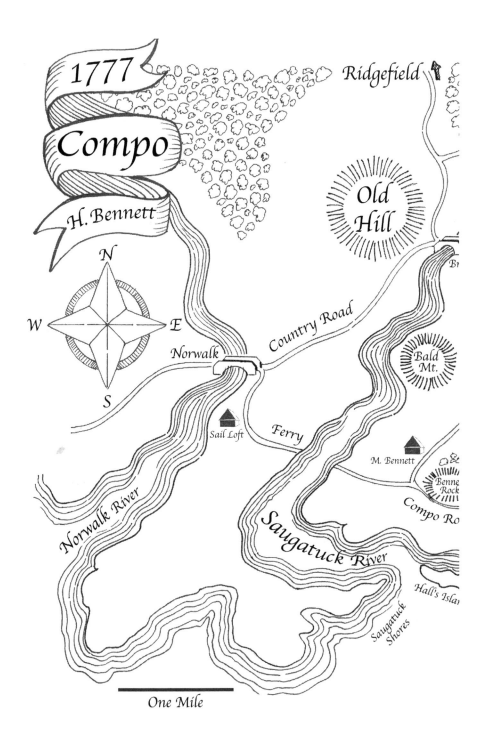

Danbury

Ford

Sipperly
Hill

Fairfield

ridge Saugatuck

Country Road

West Parish

Disbrow's

D. Bennett

Green's Farm Road

J. Bennett

Mill
Pond

Sherwood Island

Compo
Hill

Compo
Beach

Long Island
Sound

Cedar Point

ad

South Beach

Cockenoe
Island

British Fleet

Jonathan B. Walker

Everybody's Humble Servant and Nobody's Friend

April 28, 1827:

On the chestnut beam that spans the window at my writing table, you can still see tally marks chiseled into the grain. Happy's Broom must have put them there, a long time ago. The little clusters of hash marks snake above the window, tumbling over the various ridges and indentations left by the framer's adze before curving down the post on he other side where they stop abruptly at number two hundred and forty-nine, the final four marks left to stand alone, still waiting expectantly to be crossed. I wonder what Broom could have been counting? Could he have been aching for his promised day of manumission? Marking a loved one's jail sentence? It is impossible to know for certain. The number two hundred and forty-nine holds no meaning for me. They are notches from a past that seems so distant, so far removed from our present day I can only guess what they might signify. I'm just glad that Broom left them behind. For reasons I can't explain, running my fingers across their timeworn furrows every now and again makes me ever hopeful. They are a wistful numbering.

As I, Haynes Bennett, begin this epistle it is one of the first warm sunny days of spring with a fresh nor'westerly wind blowing through the elms. It has been an especially harsh winter but the earth finally smells of thaw. Feathery white clouds are coursing across a dome of blue sky, and the air puffing confidently at the curtains feels as if it has a mind of its own. From my writing table in the corner of the kitchen I can look out the open window past Jesse's sheds and the barn and see the road where the Redcoats went racing by – fifty years ago to the day – on their panicked dash to their ships. It's easy to forget that the awful tumult and violence of that distant afternoon took place in such bright sunshine, beneath the same peaceful blue sky that I see today, with the pastures greening on the sides of Bald Mountain, and the buds on the apple trees swelled and ready to open. On days such as this I almost wish that, like my father, I had spent my life as a farmer, close to the earth, carried along by the passing of the seasons. The soil is ready to work and Kessie has gone out to our kitchen patch to plant potatoes. In my condition I can at least cut and dust the eyes and have promised to join her soon. Even Jesse may pitch in. Won't that be a miracle!

Jesse may show an occasional aversion to hoe and spade, but what a long and loyal friend my dear cousin has been! How grateful we are to him for allowing us to refurbish this humble dwelling, the old servant's quarters, on what was once his father's thriving farm. We're survivors, old Jesse and I. We have been haunting these rocky fields and mossy woodlands for years. We've seen people come and seen them go and have lived through many changes. It's been quite the journey, marked like I suspect most lives are marked, by a few feverish hours of triumphs and tragedies receding beneath a long span of middling days with all their ordinary weights and worries and simple pleasures.

So, how did Kessie and I end up living in this modest, rough-hewn domicile? You might well wonder. I just know that when all was toted, the final proceeds for my sail maker's business – the loft, the tools, my Gore Book, plus the inventory of cloths and bolt rope didn't bring enough cash to allow Kessie and me to build or buy our own house in which to live out our days. We thus find ourselves settled here. It took a long time for Norwalk to recover from the calamity of '79, but with the town well on the road to full prosperity these past few decades, I expected a far better return. Could it be the advent of steam? Perhaps, but there will be ships under sail for many years to come. Could it be my association with the Anti-Slavery

Society? I'd hate to think so, but then again, I of all people should not be surprised to discover that there were at least a few so-called respectable citizens – those shadowy men of influence not wishing to see any advancements afforded to the Negro race – who may have operated behind the howling Mobocracy, putting troublesome ideas into the heads of potential buyers. I try not to dwell on these unpleasant speculations. What would be the point? I can only control that which I can control, and if you forgive me for saying so, my reputation as one of the best sail makers in Connecticut remains undisputed. From the moment I began sewing reef points as Mr. Gilbert's apprentice, to the day I fell from the square rigger and hung up my stitching palm, the sails I sewed and the sail plans I configured and saw hoisted were as good as any you will find. I daresay I never received a single complaint about one of my sails either ripping or bagging. Mind you, most of the ships I fitted or re-fitted over the years – including my brother Isaac's sloop – only needed to withstand the winds of our coastal waters and perhaps the West Indie trades, but I fitted my share of tall ships too, the ones requiring the finest grade of Baltic cloth; sails stout enough to round both Horns and survive the furies of the far China seas. I could sew them all.

With one blind eye, scaling the riggings of tall ships was never an easy task. Lacking in the depth perception that two good eyes normally provide, it's a miracle I hadn't ever slipped before – a dreadful misstep that turned my back into a weak and twisted ruin for going on two years now. It is with great reluctance, and with all hope lost of ever fully overcoming my bodily incapacities, that I have put down the yardstick and taken up the quill. I have come more suddenly than I would have liked to that age when it is time to reflect, to do what one can to make sense of life, to tell one's story. My thoughts of late seem to drift naturally to the days of my youth, to a time when not only I, but the world at large were pulled in all directions, torn nearly to pieces. I can think of no better place to begin this story than by recounting what the boys of our parish used to call the "Battle of Beacon Street," a skirmish in the first months of the war for independence that in spite of all the enemy glass we shattered, one could only conclude ended in a draw.

Our company commanders were my older brother William and Jesse's older brother Jabe. Gabriel Allen was naturally among the enlistees, as were Josh Green, Tom Morehouse and Wake Burritt. Our cousin Trowbridge Crossman, who tended to be one of your more "fair weather" Patriots, may have been there that day too. It's hard after all this time to remember every detail. Jesse and I, only thirteen, and younger than the others by two years, had managed to attach ourselves to this little invading force, and were reluctantly given permission to hang onto the sides of the overly laden dinghy as the older boys paddled across the Saugatuck. Just like the others in the boat that day, we two stowaways had a small red ribbon attached to our hats, a secret signal (or so we foolishly believed) to fellow young lads who didn't want their parents, and particularly their mothers, to know the full extent of their military aspirations. The boys of our parish weren't the only ones to adorn their hats in this way. This simple show of camaraderie was not only employed to arouse the young patriotic hearts of Compo, the custom had spread, or so we had heard, to like-minded boys in Norwalk and Stratfield. Wearing the red ribbon made us feel part of the Revolution. Seeing them all in a line on the hats of the boys in the boat that day was a fine sight to behold, and helped to give Jesse and me that extra margin of strength we needed to cling to the gunnels against the swirls and pulls of a particularly strong outgoing tide. When we made it to the far shore we secured our transport to a rotting pylon of an old dock no longer in use. With two miles between the muddy riverbank and the center of Norwalk, our betters feared the two of us would slow them down – especially when taking into account the layers of heavy black muck yet clinging to our stockings and boots – but we kept up valiantly. We proceeded at a trot down the country lane, and when we got to the corner of East Avenue and Beacon Street, Jesse and I clutched our stones and were ready to stand and fire along with the rest of our band of red-ribboned Minute-men. That much I remember well.

Through the pickets of the wrought iron fence we could see the big windows, defended from the stones we held in our hands by nothing more than a few boxwood topiaries. Our targets were a good distance away, looming just beyond the leaping stags and panthers, but well within range. And what inviting targets they were! So unsuspecting and vulnerable: four double hung windows on the side of the house directly opposite our battle lines – two upstairs and two downstairs – framed by freshly painted black shutters with row upon row of sparkling windowpanes. Most parts of the windows shined brightly – mirrored by the late afternoon sky preventing us from seeing inside the house. In other places though – those few parts where the glass was shaded by the elm trees whose trunks we were hiding behind – we could make out the backsides of the lush draperies that hinted at all the fineries we imagined were heaped like pirate treasure inside the stately home that stood on the most fashionable turn of East Avenue in Norwalk. There was no activity in the gardens, but we heard a door slam from somewhere deep inside the house. The enemy outpost was occupied. We would need to strike quickly.

The person who owned the house we were about to attack was a gentleman by the name of Thatcher Sears, a seldom seen yet much reviled Tory. He was one of the wealthiest merchants of Norwalk, an entirely vainglorious man who first attained his riches as a privateer during the French and Indian War, and soon thereafter compounded his gains by insinuating himself with the Crown's Superintendent for Indian Affairs in northern New York. Under the patronage of this influential Baronet, Sears established a large and highly profitable fur trading enterprise in the Mohawk Valley, which he later parlayed into various other successful business ventures, much to the benefit of the entire cabal of wealthy patrons, both here and abroad, with which he was so favorably aligned.

Of course, we boys knew very little of this on the afternoon we found ourselves arrayed behind that fancy iron fence. All we surely knew about the past life of Mr. Sears was that he was once a privateer and that he lost the top digit of his pinky finger – sent spinning to the fishes in Lake Champlain by a Frenchman's cutlass – and that he now kept his disfigured appendage covered with an embossed leather thimble held in place with a blue velvet ribbon tied daintily to his wrist. We were too young to either know or especially care how Mr. Sears rose to eminence. In the fall of 1775 we were just children, too young to earn our own living, much less fully grasp the ins and outs of British mercantilism. Although worldwide conflicts were reaching down to our local parish and had pushed our parents and neighbors to the breaking point, we had only a childlike understanding of current affairs. If anyone had ever asked us to describe the difference between a corrupted tyrant and a visible saint, we could have hardly answered. We simply regarded Mr. Sears as a powerful man who, according to the toddy-headed wags at Disbrow's, was an enemy of our natural rights and a prig who needed to be cut down to size. We couldn't stand the way he comported himself with his assortment of powdered wigs and enameled snuffboxes, or the way he habitually presented himself to his business associates and various other members of his entourage as "your humble servant," an old-fashioned term of address delivered, no less, with an affected aristocratic lisp. What an ass! Especially in those heady months following the battles at Lexington and the defense of Bunker Hill, when Aunt Neesy and Aunt Sarah were knitting socks and scarves for our besieged friends and relatives in Boston, the mere thought of a man like Mr. Sears set our young hearts militating with great throbs of patriotic fervor!

We emerged from behind the towering trees and spread out along the fence. William barked his final orders about which man was to aim at which sash, and on his count of three we sent our missiles flying. Most of the rocks banged harmlessly against the clapboards – I think the rock I threw only managed to pierce the breast of one of the leaping reindeers – but there were some that struck true. We let out a war whoop and by the time the sound of the shattered glass had tinkled to an end, we were halfway down East Avenue and on our way back to Saugatuck.

To this day, I have no idea how word of our foray had gotten back to Father so quickly, or who might have identified us as the combatants. William and I were out in one of the fields the next morning and hadn't even stopped for dinner when we were called into the kitchen by the tolling of the cowbell.

"It is a wicked thing you have done," Father said sternly once he had deftly squeezed our confessions from us, "and you must go immediately to both apologize and square things with Mr. Sears."

He called Cesar in from the barn and wrote him out a pass. He next beckoned William and me to his side, whereupon he unceremoniously tore the red ribbons from our hats, and before you could say "give me liberty or give me death," the three of us were in a rowboat with a dozen squares of window glass wrapped in padding and at our feet. When we got to the house on Beacon Street, William and I sidled up to the front door and knocked. At first nobody answered. We wanted to turn and leave, but Cesar, standing out by the gate with his bag of tools slung over his shoulder, told us to knock again and louder this time, which we did, and the big heavy door creaked open. A man in a maroon coat with a disheveled shock of tightly curled red hair emerged and stood on the stoop, his fists planted on his hips.

"State your business," he barked, as we stood bowed before him, our hats in hand.

"We've come, sir, to apologize to Mr. Sears," William replied. "Is he in?"

"Nay," answered the man.

"Well then," William continued meekly, his voice quavering with nervousness, "would you be so kind as to tell him that William and Haynes Bennett of Fairfield were among the lads who broke his windows yesterday? We've come prepared to replace them, and with your permission we'll set straight to work."

The man looked over our shoulders and nodded at Cesar. "All right then," he said. "I've already gone and swept up the mess you made inside. You'll find a ladder in the garden shed." And with that, he slammed the door in our faces.

Cesar measured and cut the glass while William and I mixed the glaze. The two of us were in equal parts disappointed and relieved to discover that we had only managed to break three window panes – two downstairs and one up – so it only took us an hour or so to make good our repairs. After putting the ladder back in the shed we returned to the front door in order to let the man inside the house know we were finished and to ask if there was anything else we could do for Mr. Sears.

"Yes," the man said when he appeared, "you can swear to never set foot on these premises ever again!" whereupon he slammed the door in our faces – even harder this time – without even a murmur of any of the usual parting pleasantries.

When we joined Cesar at the gate we asked if he knew who that decidedly unpleasant man was.

"Dat's John French," Cesar informed us, whistling through his teeth. He checked to make sure the front door was still closed and that there was nobody out in the yard or on the street that might overhear what he was about to say and beckoned us to come closer. "An lemme tella," he whispered, "he nuttin but trouble. Da Commity ben tryin ta pin sommin on him fer months!"

We had turned to leave when Cesar noticed something out of the corner of his eye and stopped. He walked back to the iron fence and took down the sign we had hung on one of the pickets the day before.

"Wha dis?" he asked and held out the wooden board, reading what Gabriel had carefully printed in charcoal. A hint of a smile appeared on his face.

In big capital letters the sign read, EVERYBODY'S HUMBLE SERVANT, AND NOBODY'S FRIEND.

The Committee Meeting

I remember those drunken Patriots leaning on their elbows at the corner
table of Disbrow's as plain as the scar on my eyebrow. So passionate and
angry they were, spoiling for a fight. It was only an hour or so after lunch
sometime in October of 1776 and already they were as blathered as beggars,
enshrouded in a thick fog of pipe smoke and surrounded by a sea of half
empty tankards – remnants of the Committee of Safety meeting that had
only recently adjourned. These few who remained at the meeting's head
table were squinting through the grimy windowpanes of the tavern at the
newly erected Liberty Pole standing on the green, festooned in ribbons and
topped by a red ensign fluttering lazily in the warm autumn breeze. Long
and rambling toasts were proffered to this much-revered symbol; each man
taking his turn to blather a rum-soaked treacle about the merits of liberty
accompanied by bitter oaths directed towards tea smugglers, Episcopalians,
and every other stripe of Tory scoundrel they could imagine. While they
blithered on, William and I went quietly about our business, delivering
baskets of Father's apples to Mr. Disbrow, making a neat pile of them by
the side of his bar. As our mound of apple baskets grew it became
increasingly apparent that a long morning spent consuming hard spirits and
too many trenchers of Disbrow's infamously greasy potted chicken was
about to hit bottom. Even we boys could tell that the men around the table

were collectively drifting towards a dangerous bend of mind. We feared they might at any moment devolve into a mob of angry and perhaps even violent drunks, and did our best to remain unnoticed.

That's how William and I so often conducted ourselves in the early years of the war: cleaving stealthily through troubled waters whilst keeping to our own affairs, creating as little wake as possible. Tacking through a rip tide, however, is never easy. Joining our friends as they roamed about breaking windows and knocking down fences – delicious mischief and a patriotic duty we loved to partake in – invited the sting of Father's wrath. At the same time, not joining with these boys put our hides at risk too. Indeed, the blows from our own fellows were often far worse than Father's switch. William and I were constantly struggling against the opposing currents of those years, not because Father had joined the wrong side in the fight – nobody was able to pin that particular crime on his chest – but for his stubborn refusal to join the fight at all. This was the sin we'd been coping with then, and for as long as I could remember.

I recall riding home from church one Sunday in our open wagon. I must have been around five or six years old. Father and Gaylee were in the front seat, with Grandfather William wedged between them, wrapped in a blanket. Mother sat in the back with us, with Nate, not yet a year old, swathed and clutched tightly in her arms. It was a few weeks after the British soldiers, billeted in Boston, had fired on the crowd of civilians, and people couldn't stop talking about it, including our pastor. The Reverend Ripley's rousing sermon that morning was yet ringing in our ears: "The voice of thy brother's blood crieth unto God from the ground!" I may not have understood everything he was saying, but found his sermon enthralling nonetheless. I believe even Mother, the most mildly mannered, peaceable person you will ever find, was ready to hop a coach to Boston that very afternoon and skewer some Redcoats, and yet Father was not moved. He stuck to his principles. It was the first warm day of April following on the heels of a long winter and we were anxious for spring. Had it not been for the massacre in Boston we would have thought of nothing except for cleaning out our barns and planting early wheat. When we crested the final hill to home, Bald Mountain and our pastures and freshly harrowed fields came into view. The pink buds of the apple trees lying in the hollows looked ready to burst. "Let them be consumed by their passions," Father said quietly as the wagon jostled and heaved over the ruts. "We will tend to our orchard."

I recognized a number of the men in the tavern that afternoon. There was that usually very kindly man, Hezekiah Hubble, dressed in silks, and a study in contrasts. His old fashioned peruke was impressive but ratty. He projected an air of elegant propriety, and yet you'd often catch him at Disbrow's slyly sopping up the last of the goose grease with his fingers. There was also the fact of his ever-present pet dog, a mangy hound of some indiscriminate breed that on this afternoon was contentedly gnawing a knuckle of ham at his master's feet beneath the table. Sitting at Mr. Hubble's elbow was Increase Bradley, a permanently red-nosed man with a large family including some friendly children about our age. I liked Mr. Bradley. He once called in to see how Grandfather William was faring and didn't bat an eye when Gaylee served him tea – that detested commodity he and his fellow committeemen had only recently prohibited. There was also gathered among them a younger man – a firebrand I knew by reputation quite well, Elijah Abel, who had just been made a Freeman. Although small in stature, Mr. Abel was often combative, dangerously impulsive, and completely impressed with himself. Mother said he may indeed have enough influence and property to be accepted into the community, but in her mind he was nothing more than a town tough. It was an open secret – one of the many whispered from flagon to flagon at Disbrow's in those years – that this very same Mr. Abel was among the crowd of rowdies who after a night of drinking accosted Joshua Betts and accused him of Toryism. All the poor man had actually done was visit his Tory nephews in Westchester, but the mob was undeterred and chased him all the way to the edge of town and hung him to an oak tree, cutting him down only after he begged for his life and swore to take the Oath. This was the fellow I kept my eye on, the one to be wariest of, and sure enough, just as William and I were bringing in the last of our baskets, he called to us from across the room.

"You there, lads!" he cried, waving us over to his side. "Come see what we have here."

Not wishing to disrespect our betters, William and I wended around the empty chairs and over to their table. We saw that Mr. Abel held a leather folio containing what looked to be several dozen sheets of paper.

He rose upright in his chair as we approached and placed both hands on the table to steady his balance. "As I'm sure bright lads such as yourselves know," he began while sifting through his stack of papers, his voice both officious and slurred with drink, "these are Oaths of Fidelity. Nearly all the Freemen of Greens Farms have pledged their loyalty ... but let me see ... I can't for the life of me find the one with your father's signature. Surely it must be in this pile somewhere!"

With our attention fully in hand, he looked up from the papers feigning an expression of shock and surprise. "What's that you say? He hasn't signed? Did you hear that gentlemen? Deliverance Bennett has not signed!"

The gentlemen by then had all turned from the window. Each one of them, including old man Hubble's dog, sat slack-jawed. After a moment of bemused silence, they went wheeling about in their chairs, elbowing one another whilst clanging their tankards on the table. "No! No!" they cried mockingly over the tumult. "Not Dell!"

The noise brought patrons out from the other rooms of the tavern and a crowd soon gathered behind us. A few aproned boys emerged from the kitchen and stood to the side waiting with the others to see where all of this might lead.

Without breaking his gaze upon us, Mr. Abel raised his arm for silence, his expression softening, almost solicitous. "I'm sure there's a simple explanation," he purred. "After all, I hand-delivered one of these to your door not a fortnight ago. Your father took it from me himself ... do you suppose he misplaced it? Perhaps one of your little brothers and sisters accidentally threw it to the fire or spilt their cups of milk upon it?"

With that, the Committeemen began again with their racket, spits of laughter now mixing with their derisive cries. It felt as though the entire room was lurching out of control. Adults I had known and trusted all my life were behaving in a way I had never before seen. William and I stood quietly before the table, all a-mort. We both knew Father had received the Oath, and were, in truth, angry with him for not signing. William was too young to serve in Uncle Joseph's Company, but was planning to enlist the moment he came of age. Mother and Gaylee had been urging Father to sign for months, just to get the neighbors off our backs. We knew all of this, and everybody in the tavern that day knew we knew it too, and yet in that awful moment there was nothing we could say or do. We merely stood there mute. A pair of wooden Indians.

"Look at me, son," Mr. Abel said, glaring directly now at William. He waited for the men around him to quieten down. The entire tavern grew silent. Somebody pushed back in his chair. A man in the crowd behind us tapped ash from his pipe. From under the table came a low growl from Mr. Hubble's dog.

"Look at me," he repeated. "You are old enough to understand that we are reasonable men. You needn't worry. We are not about to take your father to court, or find a rail, or warm a kettle of tar. Surely," he continued, "none of that will be necessary."

He picked up a second folio that was lying beside him on the table. "Take this," he snarled, perusing the fresh piece of paper he was holding in his hands, his face now a deadly black. "Bring this Oath home to your father. Tell him the Committee says it is long past time. Our patience is wearing thin. He must choose sides!"

William stepped forward and just as he was reaching out for the paper, Mr. Hubble's dog barked ferociously and went for his legs. Luckily, the enraged feist was tied to his master's chair and was only able to hurl himself to the front side of the table where he twisted his neck against the rope, snapping his teeth. With some quick footwork William managed to grab the paper without getting bitten. He was unhurt, but his sudden and rather elaborate pirouette made the men erupt into peals of laughter.

I wanted to yell "Stop it!" at the top of my lungs and felt like bounding across the table to throttle the entire drunken lot of them, and I'm sure William felt that way too, but given the circumstances, we had no choice but to simply turn around and push our way through the crowd. Many of those we shuttled past were laughing as well, adding to our humiliation. It seemed to take forever to get outside where Cesar was waiting on tenterhooks for us in the wagon. We jumped into the bed just as he snapped at the reins and pulled away.

As our carthorse Timothy climbed the hill towards Compo Road, we were met with a flurry of thwacks hitting the sides of the wagon. Cesar shouted for us to stay down. I peered over the planks and saw that the aproned boys from Disbrow's kitchen, along with some others including our friends Gabriel and Trow, had positioned themselves on the steep embankments on either side of the lane. They had some of our baskets and were throwing Father's apples at us. With no room to turn around, Cesar had no choice but to shunt through the gap as fast as the old horse could take us. All of us were getting struck, including Timothy, who was wild eyed and screaming. When we arrived to a point just below the boys, their aim improved. We were now being completely pummeled and did our best to cover our heads with our arms, but it was hopeless. My lip was split open and William was bleeding from a small cut beneath his eye. I shuddered to think what was happening to Cesar who needed to keep both hands on the reins and couldn't protect himself at all. The fusillade intensified. Timothy reared and lurched so violently we heard a loud crack and then another as the weight of his twisting body broke both shafts of the rig. I thought for a moment we were going to bog down, but Cesar remained steady on the reins, talking slowly and calmly to the panicked animal in spite of the apples hailing down and got us through the ambush.

That autumn afternoon remains locked in my memory. It was the day the war began in earnest for me, the day when first blood was drawn. The Battle of Beacon Street had been nothing more than a lark. William and I only needed to mend those broken windows and could then go about our business, as delicate as that may have become, attending to our chores while sneaking off with our Patriot friends every now and again to knock down a Tory fence or two when Father wasn't looking. But when those apples came hurtling down upon our wagon, I knew the stakes had risen. The violence we felt against us was as real as it was bewildering. My little corner of the world seemed suddenly to be teetering on a thin shoal of ever-shifting sands. The rage I felt against those fellows pelting us with apples could hardly be contained, and yet in a few short years some of those very same hooligans would be counted among my closest comrades, fellow Privates in Uncle Joseph's Company of Home Guards. We were to spend long hours together on midnight patrols down at the beach, by the gristmill, and through the tidal marshes on the lookout for smugglers and Tory raiders, alert for signs of British warships. Crunching single file over drifts of broken mussel shells, working our way through the dew-soaked stands of salt grass, and afterwards, as the morning sun would be fingering up over the Sound, we'd sit around the last embers of our fires drinking gills of Disbrow's watered rum. Bonded for life.

From the brow of the hill William and I looked back from our seat on the wagon and saw the boys raising their arms in triumph, and could hear the taunting sounds of their laughter. They next took up a chant, their fists shaking in rhythm, repeating the words just spoken by Mr. Abel. We could hear their voices echoing yet through the trees even after we had turned onto our road and they were out of sight:

"Choose sides! Choose sides! Choose sides!" they called.

Dear Rachel, and any others who may be someday reading this. This is yer Uncle Jess, yer old Henny's cousin an true an lifelong compatriot. It's March the first or thereabouts of eighteen hundred an thirty six, an he's been gone now for nearly ten years. Kessie's just washed up drowned, an I figger Henny would a-trusted me with this diary a his, or whatever it is he calls it. I finally got round to reading what he wrote, an if I knows him, which I sorely do, I know he won't object to me scribbling down my own views here along the margins — or on the backs a the pages too, iffen I ever run out a room. So anyways, if I could shout up to heaven and Haynes could hear me, this is what I would now confess, an you all might as well hear what I has to say as any other: I was there that day old friend, with them other raskils bombadeering you with them tarnal apples. I allus meant a tell ye when you was yet alive but never got round to it an hope it ain't too late to say that I'm sorely ashamed of myself an that I'm ever so sorry for what I done although to be honest I had no choice in the matter. Them boys were in the sourest mood and taking no prisners and I saw right away that it were coming down to a simple matter of either me or you, an I figgered better to go along with the general flow a things an have it be you that gets it this time around an live to fight another day, standing shoulder to shoulder like we allus done it. So there is the truth of it and how it were that day. Can you ever forgive me? -- JB

Pope's Day

My older brother William was tall and strong of body like our father with his same prominent jaw and even facial features. Although he lacked the usual Bennett swarthiness and was instead fair with blue eyes like Mother and the Benedict cousins, no one ever questioned whether he and Father were cut from the same jib. They moved the same. When seeing one of them at a distance – walking across a field or carrying a bag of grain to the dock – it was difficult to tell them apart. William was never a deep thinker nor particularly bookish, but he had a fast and nimble brain and showed an interest at an early age for enlightened agriculture. He shared Father's desire to stay abreast of all the latest views on land cultivation and animal husbandry. It was a given that William would be the one to carry on with the farm and to expand the ambitious apple orchard Father had long been planning. Like Father, he was the quiet sort, only speaking when spoken to. Had he chosen a motto it would have been 'Well done is better than well said.' As a boy during those years when I knew him the best, he was generally compliant and ready to please, which was why, I think, both my parents and Gaylee were caught so unawares when he came out so strongly on the side of the Patriots. Until that point, my parents often set him as an example for me to follow, wishing I might show the same good character and steady soundness of mind as demonstrated by my virtuous older brother.

It is often said that care should be taken lest you get exactly what you wish for, and when it came to my feelings toward William, my parent's wishes redounded to them in twisted spades. I did indeed look up to my brother, studying his every move. I copied his speech, his dress, his mannerisms. If he wore his hat down over his eyes one day and then decided for whatever reason to place it at an angle, I was sure to tilt my hat in kind. If he were to be given the chore of splitting firewood or cutting hay, all I wanted was to wield the same man-sized axe or scythe. This of course sent him straight around the bend, and he did his best to swat me away, to leave me in the dust. In almost every single picture that comes to mind when I think back to our childhood together, I see William and Jabe on the run to somewhere grand and exciting, with Jesse and me trailing along behind them in hot pursuit.

This was never truer than on Pope's Day, 1776. As was our family custom, I think in order to steer the two of us away from the hooliganism that was known to break out on that Holiday, the entire Bennett clan was gathered at the beach for our own private bonfire, and our own spirited dressing-down of Guy Fawkes and all things Catholic. Bundled warmly to ward off the November wind, we dug out our baking pit on South Beach and lined it with stones to roast our clams, mussels, and oysters. Mother, Aunt Sarah, and Aunt Neesy set out the breads, pies, and sweetmeats on a blanket while Gaylee wrapped the last of the sweet corn and squash in seaweed to be roasted alongside the shellfish. Father and my uncles, Moses and Joseph, went out on the point to smoke their pipes and talk politics. Grandfather William stayed back with the women, wrapped like a Papoose in a blanket. A few of the older cousins helped to set up the meal while the wee ones – there must have been half a dozen – played in the sand or ran about the rocks collecting shells and feathers and a multitude of colored pebbles.

William and Jabe – with Jesse and I tagging behind – went off in search of the other boys that were sure to be gathered nearby to bake their own clams and light their own bonfires. The long-standing families of Compo still flourishing in those years were all duly represented that afternoon: the Greens, Allens, Godfreys, Meekers, the Hills and the Hales, the Sherwoods, Disbrows, the Greys and Crossmans, and in no time a force of twenty or more of the neighborhood ruffians had been collected. We got ourselves organized on the big pasture, choosing sides for a game of Darebase or as some had begun calling it, 'New York and Boston.' No matter its name, our version of the contest was rough, and as usual, we elected to play it tackle instead of touch. No mere slap on the back would do for us. We preferred bringing our opponents down to the cold hard ground in order to dispatch them to jail. The battle that day was evenly matched, rumbling back and forth across the pasture from Grey's Creek to Slate's Corner and, as often happened, it wasn't long before it devolved from a friendly game into something more akin to a general melee.

The trouble broke out when I was caught in the Boston camp acting as a spy. Gabriel Allen tackled me to the ground a little harder than called for. I took exception to this and must have said something that struck a nerve because the next thing I knew, Gabe, who outweighed me by a stone or more, called me a rotten Tory and fell upon my chest, battering me with his fists. He had my shoulders pinned to the turf with his knees and was giving my face and ears a merciless boxing, putting me in desperate need of rescue. Mind you, it had hardly been a week earlier when William, for whatever reason, was the one pinning me to the ground and turning my ears to mush, but seeing someone else giving me hell was more than he could bear, and to my great relief, my good brother came crashing through the crowd and sprung me loose by slamming his shoulder at full speed into Gabe's ribs.

An all-out riot ensued. For several minutes the fighting was fierce with fists and boots flying in all directions. We were trapped in a vortex of thrashing arms and legs from which there was no escaping. Eventually the entire mass of bodies more or less wrestled itself to the ground and began to lose its fervor. Jesse, who had an uncanny knack for knowing the most opportune moment to join a fray, which is to say when he was certain the worst of it was over, let out an Indian war whoop and dove on top of the heap just as William and I were wriggling out from the bottom of it. For reasons known only to our hale and hearty cousin, instead of throwing punches, or putting one of the Allen brothers in a headlock when he landed on the pile, he started to laugh. My first thought was that's the end of him, but to my surprise, his display of tomfoolery had the exact opposite effect and we were soon all laughing with hard feelings coming, at least for the time being, to an end. We dusted off our coats and licked our wounds and after bidding one another a happy Pope's Day, we sauntered off in our separate ways.

Back at South Beach the Bennett bonfire was already going with the whole clan huddled around it digging into their meals, happily throwing empty shells and corncobs into the flames. Soon it was fully dark, and we sat listening to the firewood snap, watching dreamily as the sparks disappeared into the night sky. Uncle Joseph was deep into his cups with Uncle Moses not far behind. Gaylee glared as the two of them raised their tankards to their fellow Sons of Liberty, offering toasts to General Washington and all his brave and loyal men in arms. In spite of their promise to Gaylee to dispense with any talk of the war whilst the family was enjoying dinner, it wasn't long before they and my father were deep into their usual harangue. The tide had irrevocably turned, they reminded him. "You can wish for royal rule all you want, and your calls for calm and for reason may indeed have some merit, but none of that," they continued, with their voices rising, "can erase the fact that the General Assembly in New Haven and Hartford are in the hands of the Patriots. There is now a new law of the land, with a local Committee of Safety more than capable of enforcing it. These new leaders are ambitious men," my uncles insisted, "full of patriotic zeal and determined to advance themselves. Those that dare to speak out against them are being kept under careful surveillance. Men refusing to sign their Oaths risk losing their right to own property. Men found committing acts deemed inimical to the cause are being sent to the Mines. Properties have been seized right here in Fairfield! Come now, Deliverance," they bellowed, "you are not only putting your own family at risk, you are, by association, putting each of us at risk as well!"

Gaylee finally had enough. "Stop it you boys!" she commanded at the top of her lungs, which silenced them at once. We were all stunned and quieted. We sat watching the fire not knowing what to do or say until Uncle Joseph and Uncle Moses re-filled their tankards and commenced to slurp and slur their way through some popular ballads of the day.

Before long we were once again a happy party although I noticed after a while that Father had stepped away. I went to see where he had gone and espied the glow of his pipe on the spit of rocks that jutted into the cove towards Hall's Island. As I got closer I saw that William was there too, and

19

the three of us sat on the rocks looking out across the Sound. Although we had no way of knowing so then, it was the last Pope's Day any of us would ever celebrate.

With collars raised to ward off the cold, we lingered a few moments without speaking. The bonfires on the shores of Long Island were pinpricks on the horizon. A concentration of these specks created a single yellow glow at a point directly opposite us, a light we had never seen before, and at the place where we knew General Howe had established his headquarters. It was a large luminescence, completely out of proportion compared to the other lights around it, and only a few hours away by whaleboat. Father, William, and I sat considering what this new and ominous light might mean to our town and to our family. A small part of me longed to believe that Father was right, that the Redcoats were here in America to restore order, and we could soon go back to living as we had done before, before all the strife, back to the golden days when, as Cesar used to say, the farm was "running on all bays." The larger part of me though, was firmly on the side of my uncles and the Reverend Ripley. In my own boyish way, I felt innately inclined towards the arguments put forth by Thomas Paine, and thought of the Redcoats sitting in their camps on this night across the Sound at Fort Franklin as invaders, a chilling threat to our natural liberties. I know that my brother, in his quiet and simmering way, was similarly aligned to the Patriot's cause, perhaps even more fervently than I. He couldn't wait to turn sixteen, when he'd be free to join the militia even without Father's consent. So the three of us sat on the spit of rocks, lost in our own thoughts. William leaned down and picked up a flat stone and skimmed it across the water and I silently counted out the skips trailing away unseen in the darkness, whilst from over our shoulders, our drunken uncles sang:

"From the east to the west blow the trumpet to arms,

Thro' the land let the sound of it flee.

Let the far and the near, all unite with a cheer,

In defense of our Liberty Tree!"

A Sail!

The stone fence we were building up the southern face of Bald Mountain never went anywhere. It pains me. To this day I hate the sight of it. Yes, there was the war, and yes, the future in its particulars seemed no more reliable than chaff forked into the wind. And yes, my father and all of us were being tossed and pitched by this very same storm. Even still, the future in its generalities felt as certain as ever that spring. I could conceive of no force strong enough to throw us off our course. After all, the farmland up and down Compo Road had been sustaining the Bennetts for over a hundred years, and had I ever paused to think of it, I would have said that the stone boundary to the large orchard Father was planning would be finished and would stand for at least a hundred years more. My father was the kind of man to keep everything around him in good order. He was ever mindful of traditions yet was also a forward-thinker, a planner, and as steady as they come. When he started a job it was sure to get done, and yet that mound of fieldstones and the first few rows of the stone fence we started, remain spilled across the ground just where we left them fifty years ago at the base of the hill. The Blacks and Reds grazing on that pasture today continue to pick those stones clean. It is as if the cows – some few generations of them by now – have all agreed to honor those granite markers, to keep moss or lichen from ever taking hold on them, like Druids bleaching a cairn.

This promised to be one fine apple orchard, eventually twenty-five acres all around. It would more than treble our annual yield, leaving us with as many as 3,000 bushels of apples to take to market every year. Father's new orchard was to have apples for every purpose, some varieties of which we had already grafted to our rootstock in the little quarter acre enclosure just north of the house: Rhode Island Greenings and Cranberry Pippins for cooking, Harrisons, Styres and Hewe's Crabs for cider, Siberian Crabs for jellies and preserves, Calville Blancs for tarts and pies, Toleman's for livestock, and of course, plenty of the always prized Roxbury Russets and Newtown Pippins. The contours of Bald Mountain were ideal for apple production. It was high enough to minimize the danger of late spring frosts, sloped just right for both good drainage and soil retention, and with exposures on all points of the compass, variable enough to protect against the vagaries of our New England climate. Those varieties particularly susceptible to harsh winter winds could be grown in protected enclaves on the southern slope, while varieties bothered by the summer's heat and humidity could be tucked into cool corners on the northern side. Father thought through all of this. He had the entire twenty-five acres carefully mapped.

In those days, most farmers were still relying upon apple seeds to improve and expand their orchards. Not Father. He understood the virtues of grafting and took the time to gather only those scions from the most productive trees of the most desirous varieties that could be found in nearby orchards. The other farmers, although a bit bemused whenever Father showed up at their door in late summer with his budding knife, were always happy enough to give him a shoot or two from their trees in return for a bushel or two of our apples later in the fall. I'd often go with Father on these pomological sojourns, following him down the rows of trees with my ball of soaked yarn, bundling together the bud sticks he handed to me.

"This is the perfect spot for Northern Spies," Father thought aloud as he stood to stretch his back after he and my older brother William placed a large stone onto the dirt ledge we had dug into the side of the hill. Ezra Weed, our hired hand, further nestled it into place with a crowbar. My job was to fill in the gaps with smaller rocks.

The stone fence was going to trace along Bald Mountain's eastern perimeter and run roughly parallel to the road, so we not only wanted the wall high enough to keep out the livestock, it needed to look smart. Father had the section we were meant to finish that morning staked with plum lines and twine to keep us level. As we bent to our work, the morning sun went darting in and out of clouds, changing the pasture rising above us from vivid green to cold grey and back again as suddenly as the opening and closing of a shutter. The pile of fieldstones over Father's shoulder looked formidable. It had grown larger by the day since the first true thaw. Fieldstones grow like potatoes in Connecticut farm fields. You think you've got them all out of the ground in a certain spot one year only to find that by next year's thaw another half dozen have heaved to the surface. It is a never-ending process adding a great deal of toil and sweat to our annual labors. Good for fence making, but hard on our sledges.

As the morning wore on, it became impossible to ignore what had been pressing upon our minds since dawn. "Better run up and see what you can see," Father said to me. He and Ezra and William were leaning against the completed part of the wall mopping sweat from their necks, ready for a break. I pushed past and scampered up the steep incline of the pasture. From the top of Bald Mountain I gazed first to the north where I could see the freshly turned farrows in a corner of the field Cesar was harrowing, and waited to see if he and Seth and Ham would come into view down their next row. As long as Cesar was in the field I could rest assured that no alarming news had reached the house. He'd be the first person Mother would run to if there were any reasons to call us in. After a moment, I was relieved to see the jets of steam shooting from the noses of the team emerging from behind a stand of trees, followed by Cesar's familiar green slouched hat and beneath it, the thumbprint of his face, which at that distance looked as black as India ink.

Beyond our field I could see where the Saugatuck River cleaved through the village. The tide was an hour or so past dead low. A boy in a checkered shirt was walking through the waves of salt grass towards the mudflats just below me over the brow of the hill, likely on the hunt for shrimp or early blue crabs. A little further upriver a man was intent upon loading bundles onto a skiff tied to Jessup's dock. He showed no signs of distress, and nothing about the activity on the wharfs and vessels on the opposite bank appeared to be amiss either. Further north of the village, a farmer was slowly crossing the Country Road Bridge in his mule and cart, and beyond him, in the hills that stretched endlessly inland, the wide scattering of farmhouse chimneys sent up curls of smoke into the alternating streams of white and grey clouds. It was a bustling spring day in Compo no different than any other.

I looked next to the south, where the river empties into its shallow bay, about a mile distant. The curved finger of Saugatuck Shores lying flat above an iron-blue patch of the bay was bracketed by the letter 'V' made by Burritt's Landing and Bennett's Rocks which rose abruptly from their opposing riverbanks. In the skies beyond the Shores, dark clouds were about to engulf Long Island, barely discernable on the far horizon. Hidden between these two ribbons of land was the open Sound. I was about to return to the others when a large two-masted sloop entered into the frame. All I could see from my vantage point were its top gans'ls, caught just then by a shaft of sunlight, two brilliant canvases billowing sharply against the blackened skies beyond them. My breath stopped as they slowly glided eastwards behind the Shores, floating above the dunes and the rooftops of the oystermen shacks like a pair of half-mooned ghosts.

"A sail!" I shouted and careened back down the hill like a madman.

The Light Dragoon

Father had good reasons to be expecting trouble – it is easy to know this now in hindsight – and yet, as always, he cautioned us to remain steady. British war ships had become a regular sight out on Long Island Sound – especially since they had taken occupation of New York City and set up their headquarters just across the Sound from us in Huntington. A lone ship, even one as large as I had just seen, meant little. So after brushing the clumps of cold mud that had stuck to my britches on my tumble down the pasture, I joined with the others, lowering my shoulder yet again to our task at hand, doing my best to contain my agitations – a mix of fear and, I must admit, a goodly dose of excitement at the prospects of an adventure. We continued at our chore as best we could, and were soon lost in a productive working rhythm. After about an hour or so, the idea of a British invasion seemed as remote a possibility as it had all spring. Even after some day laborers, just off the ferry from Norwalk, scuttled by with word that they had seen more than just the one large ship sailing eastwards from New York, we hardly looked up from the piles of stones at our feet.

Our finished wall was nearly two rods long when we paused for lunch. That was when Gabriel Allen came galloping up the road with news that couldn't be brushed aside. "There aint just one or two British war ships out on the Sound" he exclaimed, "but an entire flotilla of them!" The leading sloop-of-war had come-about just east of Cockenoe Island, leaving no doubt that they weren't just passing by and that the beach at Compo was to be their landing point. "The enemy is at our doorstep!" he cried and reported that his family as well as the Greys and the Hills were already loading valuables and provisions onto wagons to make good their escape and urged us to do the same. I had never seen Gabe so wildly animated – nearly out of his wits, he was. Naturally, we were desperate to learn more from him. We wanted to know, how many ships? What of troop transports? Are any of our own gunships a-sea and ready to meet the threat? Any sign of the Home Guards? But before we could ask these and other critical questions pressing upon our minds, Gabe heeled his horse and was off.

I realize that my children and grandchildren, who may someday read this, only knew their grandfather and great grandfather as a man stooped and gray, a fixture on his rocking chair on the porch of his bungalow – the place where his own younger brother had banished him. It's hard even for me not to remember my father as that broken old man watching the world passing him by, but on that earlier April afternoon, on the eve of those four tumultuous days that changed forever the course of our lives, he was young and vital – a commanding presence in his calm way, with dark, deep set eyes and a firm, squared jaw. His hair was the color of rubbed iron, and was kept neatly tied in a queue that fell below his collar. He never put on airs. During the week, the sleeves of his homespun shirt were rolled up tightly as he lent his hand to even the dirtiest of work on the farm, while on the Sabbath he powdered his hair and entered church respectfully, wearing his finest coat and blue silk vest. Even in those days when Father and I were at such odds with one another, I thought of him as a strong and confident man, comfortable with his given nature, not one to ever speak idly or out of turn.

He nodded toward the cattle grazing nearby and told Will to run for cousin Jabez.

The cattle had only a week earlier been let out of their winter barns to graze on the newly greening pasture and would be in plain view of anyone passing on Compo Road. William and Jabe were to take them across the Country Road Bridge to Aunt Sara and Uncle Jabez's farm in Norfield where they'd be safely hidden away from a hungry army.

"Go first to the house," Father said to William. "Your mother will have a letter waiting for you there." As William dashed up the road, I stood spooling the twine around the plumb bob in full knowledge of what he and Jabe had secretly planned in anticipation of this very turn of events, desperately wishing I could be going with them.

Father turned next to Ezra. The man who held Ezra's indenture was a Mr. Nash, who never seemed to have much use for him and was always lending him out. Because Nash also happened to be a Captain in the Norwalk militia and was an ardent Patriot, we always suspected Ezra might be a spy for the Committee, although Father never worried much about him. His lack of industriousness as a laborer didn't speak well for an ability to gather any sort of useful intelligence one way or another.

"What of you?" Father asked of the indolent man who was sitting on the pile of unplaced rocks picking breadcrumbs from his smock. "I suppose the Captain will be gathering up his men and will want you anon for his Waiter."

After successfully guiding the last of the crumbs from his shirt into his mouth Ezra looked up at Father, his face as expressionless as ever. You'd never know by looking at him that we had just received such stunning news. "I'm not keen for soldiering," he said at last.

"I can see that," Father replied, "but Mr. Nash and I have an agreement."

"But sir –"

"Here," Father continued, reaching for the lunch satchel. "Take another biscuit and get yourself to the ferry. We've got work to do here."

My parents had long agreed that should an invasion ever come, we would not flee. Why should an army bother to plunder our farm – or any other farm for that matter – along the Connecticut coast? Why send an entire invasion force to do us harm when marauding Cowboys were already in our midst, skulking in the dark of night over the roads from Westchester, or drifting in on their whaleboats from across the Sound, supplying their billeted agents with whatever provisions they could pilfer from us? Why would the Redcoats tarry here at all, my parents reasoned further, when a far more valuable prize was sitting in the Continental's depot seventeen miles away in Danbury? And most of all, why send children and valuables out onto the roads in a time of crisis only to become easy prey for Cowboys and Skinners and all manner of banditti? Scoundrels like these would be sure to follow in the wake of a large invasion force, ready to seize upon the confusion and panic that would inevitably ensue. If anything, my father assured us, the British Regulars would protect the lives and property of peaceable British subjects such as us from any and all that would do us harm.

No, Father didn't even need to say it. He would take a few prudent measures to protect our livestock, but the family was staying put. That left me, too young to help with the cattle and too old to be huddled with my younger brothers and sisters, free to investigate. Mother and Gaylee would be worried sick when I didn't show up for supper, and Father may come looking for me, but no matter. Here was the opportunity of a lifetime, and one I wasn't about to miss! Thinking it best not to be seen out on the road where assorted aunts and uncles had their farmhouses, I stole away up to the rocks beyond our cow barn where there were still plenty of trees to provide cover and began working my way down the ridgeline until I neared Bennett's Rocks. Safely hidden beneath the freshly greening canopy, I knelt behind some stones to consider my options. The familiar sound of Uncle Mosy's voice, barking urgent orders to Broom, drifted up from the road. I knew I must stay well clear of them. I could hear my young cousin, Tabitha, weeping. It sounded as if her cries were coming from near their kitchen door, and I could picture her, standing in her yellow dress, puling among the blue hyacinths crowding the pathway that curved through their yard.

Meanwhile, I couldn't wait to see what lay behind the trees at the top of the hill before me. The thought of finally laying eyes upon a large body of Redcoats, the very same vaunted army my father and uncles had once so proudly been attached to, was almost too much for me to bear. I wanted to burst over the brow, but knew a little circumspection was in order and looked to find a suitable tree to climb.

'Too much to for me to bear' says he! What a tarnal Chesterfielder! I'd a-been knee deep in dilberries right about then an I tell you what, if I know you Haynes you was britches-full of them too. Yer just too persnickiddy to say so. Look here, we played our 'Whites and Reds' ever since we was wee. Sometimes we'd play it running across a

28

field or down through the marshes. Other times, we'd plunk ourselves down in the middle of that gravel bank that run between yer house and the river. We'd make us a flat mound like an arrowhead. Laying at the tip was the citadel of Quebec and back by one of the corners was the cliff where Colonel Howe led his bayonet charge against them French picketers. We'd use red pebbles for the Redcoats and white ones for the Frenchmen and once we had them all properly assembled the bloody charges and counter charges on the Plains of Abraham would commence. We'd get us some of the famous Regments a Foots, and some of them Grenadiers and a handful of Highlanders and roll them all down against the Frenchies who was lined up in their horseshoe and we'd fire our guns and push them tarnal Whitecoats back towards the river. We licked them ever time!

I can just picture it, cousin Haynes all arsey-varsy, knowing full well that once over the brim of Bennett's Rocks he'd see with his very own living eyes an invading army sent by the very same William Howe in our game, that hero what hollered "See how they run" atop our mound of gravel.

My kin an airs can thank their lucky stars it were you and not me scampering along the ridge that day, because I'd a flewn right over them rocks. I'd a nary bothered to climb no tree. I'd a flewn right over happy as a grig and likely been bagged and shipped off to the Jersey where I'd a sat in the cold and the damp and lived on rats with the rest of them sorry fellers if I ever lived at all. – JB

It was drawing towards the middle of the afternoon, and as I squeezed my way up through the branches of a tall hemlock, I could see the sun approaching a bank of clouds off to the west and felt a breeze that hinted of heavy rain. Straddling a branch a few feet from the top of the tree gave me an unencumbered view of Cedar Point and the Sound. Off to my left, the pastures of Compo Hill, which normally would have been dotted by sheep and dairy cows, were vacant. Straight before me, the two-masted British Sloop-of-War whose topsails I had spied earlier lay at anchor, with twelve six-pounders bristling from its decks. It had cleared east of Cockenoe Island and had weighed anchor barely ten rods off our stony beach. Another large warship was in full sail and about to pass behind the Norwalk Islands, with the sails of smaller gunships and transports popping up from over the horizon by the minute.

This wasn't just a feint or another rumor of a British invasion. The calamity Uncle Joseph had been warning about for months was surely set to unfold. The actual war, which until then had been only read about in gazettes or heard about from neighbors who had a brother or a son or nephew who had seen action in far off sounding places like Bunker Hill or Brooklyn Heights, was about to come to Fairfield, and with any luck I thought, I would be a witness to its opening salvos.

Within an hour or so most of the ships had dropped their anchors, over twenty sails in all. A shot was sounded and soldiers suddenly appeared on the decks of the transports, with waves of crimson spilling over the sides as the longboats were lowered. On two of the longboats, about a dozen horses stamped nervously until they were guided over the sides and reined ashore, splashing over the shallows. Another longboat delivered heavy field pieces that teams of men in white smocks were struggling to haul up the beach. The soldiers began forming into companies up and down the shoreline while drummers tapped out the orders of their officers.

With all the excitement and activity, I almost forgot to seek out what I was most anxiously looking for, what Mother and Father would want most to know. And then the unmistakable hunter green coats of the Prince of Wales American Volunteers began assembling on the deck of the last transport in the line, and my heart sank. These were Tories – most of whom were recruited from Fairfield County – committed and angry men willing to take up arms against their neighbors, some of whom were almost certainly greedily anticipating their measure of revenge, and my cousin Jabez Lockwood whose father owned the very house in Norfield where Will and Jabe were currently headed with the livestock, was certain to be among them.

I remained in my crow's nest – safely hidden, or so I thought – until the sun lay hovering just above the trees on Saugatuck Shores, a pale presence obscured behind a bank of thickening clouds. I was completely enthralled by the activity on the beach. Never had I seen so many men massed together, a hiving nest of crimson and green that slowly organized itself into a column that stretched nearly a mile, from the edges of Cedar Point until it disappeared behind the wild tangle of vines and trees just below me at the foot of Bennett's Rocks. I was about to climb down and run for home when a voice boomed up from the ground. "You there! Boy!"

came the cry. It was not the accent of a local man and I froze, my heart pounding fiercely in my chest. "Come down ere a King's man shoots ye down like a pigeon!" My first instinct was to scramble yet higher into the tree, but I was already perilously close to the flimsy tops of the hemlock. There was no option but to comply, and I began to make my way down, expecting at any moment to receive a blast from his gun, my legs and arms trembling so uncontrollably I could barely keep from falling. Through the branches, the outline of a man on horseback began to emerge. "Steady there … let me see you," the voice intoned. I looked down between my legs to see a mounted Light Dragoon looking up from his saddle. The carbine he shouldered was locked and trained directly at my heart.

The soldier was dressed in a bright red coat with a white sash draped across his chest. A sword swung by the side of his yellow breeches and polished black knee boots. On his head he wore not a tri-cornered hat, but a kind of a helmet, from the crown of which a chestnut-colored plume fell back towards his shoulders. From the front of the helmet a bright silver skull and cross bones stared up at me, and emblazoned below this ominous death mask were the words "Or Glory."

I jumped to the ground. The horseman loomed above me, his mount taller than any I had ever seen. Tethered behind it were horses I immediately recognized – two sorrels, and I noted, not the black. "Those are my Uncle Mosy's mares," I managed to say.

"Is that so?" the man replied. "They shall be paid for in due course, now off with you!" And with that, he holstered his firearm and spurred his horse. Night was ready to fall. A blast of wind blew through the tops of the trees, and with it came the first spatters of rain. Before disappearing into the dark tunnel that cleaved Bennett's Rocks in two, the Dragoon reined his horse and looked back over his shoulder.

"You'd be wise to stay clear of the road!" he cried after me, and I turned and bolted into the woods.

The Spring House

I ran with such unbridled speed from the helmeted soldier I tripped and somersaulted down the hill. I landed hard and remained for a moment on the ground to regain my air and check my limbs, relieved to discover I was still in one piece. With one hand I felt for my hat, which had fallen among the sodden leaves beside me. I was splayed at the bottom of a small gully. Water trickled unseen beneath rocks blanketed with moss and liverwort. The sky behind the ceiling of early-budding tree limbs above me was as grey as pewter. I blinked away the few pinpricks of rain alighting upon my face. As I clambered back up to the ridgeline, I heard voices – or thought I did – coming through the gloaming. It could have been a whippoorwill, far away, or a nighthawk hunting down by the river. My ears were playing tricks. Fearful of what I might encounter, I paused, turning my head from one side to the next before venturing on.

After a moment, I heard the sounds again – and they were indeed voices, closer now, coming from the shadows ahead. One of the voices sounded like a woman's. Stepping cautiously from tree to tree, I could make out the light of a lantern blinking through the understory. I started to skirt around it when I recognized the shrill voice of my Aunt Neesy. She was calling for Broom. I ran towards her and saw she was standing by the door of their springhouse, holding the lantern over her head with one arm while clutching her one-year old daughter, Rachel, with the other. Her other children, Tabitha, David, Rhoda, and my dear friend Jesse, were clinging to either side of her skirts.

"Don't be alarmed!" I called just before bounding into the circle of light, whereupon my normally composed aunt let fly with a bloodcurdling scream causing her children to commence with an awful wailing.

"Hush, Aunt Neesy! It is but me, Haynes! Hush Jesse!" I called, walking towards them with arms spread wide. "There are Redcoats about. You should be in the springhouse!"

It was cold and crowded inside the small fieldstone structure. Aunt Neesy sat down on a trunk, which looked to have been hastily placed while my cousins pressed close around her. A few jugs of milk and butter were scattered about them on the dirt floor, with the remnants of the lamb they had been picking away at since Easter pegged to the wall behind them. A pistol lay at her feet just beyond the stones that lined the wellspring.

"I was calling for that damned Broom," she cried. "He was meant to hide the goats and our milk cows. Not far from here. Why didn't he answer when I called? Do you think he's scarpered?"

"No, not Broom – "

"Your Uncle Mosy is gone," she continued without drawing breath over the halting gasps of her children. "Off with that fool brother of his to round up the militia, casting Broom into the woods with the animals. Leaving me with the children. We must now fend for ourselves! To escape from that butcher Tryon – Oh, Haynes! They will burn our house for certain!"

"You'd better turn down the lantern –"

"Your Uncle Mosy is no soldier! He is but a simple farmer. Why is he so taken with that popinjay – that miscreant firebrand with his incessant talk of liberty and his so-called New Israel?" She paused to take a few deep breaths and hush the children.

"What of Aunt Sarah and the girls?" I asked.

"Off to the safety of friends, I suspect. Or perhaps seeking refuge in the meeting house – any haven they can find, away from the roads to Danbury."

"For certain? Is that where the Redcoats are heading?"

"Your uncle believes it so – they both do. They will be after the military stores there … Tents and pork barrels for the invaders," she continued, a little quieter than before, "death and destruction for lovers of liberty!"

It distressed me to see my aunt in such a state of panic. And yet, I wasn't surprised, and remember thinking that she was now getting precisely what she deserved. From the moment Gabriel came roaring up the lane to spread the alarm I knew that for many like her, the compendium of long-growing animosities were coming home to roost. Especially in the households of my aunts and uncles who had so boldly joined with other Patriots, agitating loudly for armed conflict. My two uncles, Joseph and Mosy, who lived on adjoining farms on either side of us along Compo Road, had Father good and bookended. When they weren't badgering him about signing his Oath, they were out raising rum toddies to the Sons of Liberty at Disbrow's. Their views were passionate and widely known, and as Gabriel so aptly put it, the enemy was now at their doorsteps. Their moment of reckoning had arrived.

I looked over and saw Jesse, his face lit by the lantern and gazing back at me from behind his mother's skirts. "What is to become of us tonight?" cried Aunt Neesy, not yet finished with her tirade. "They say Tryon is wont to prey upon young boys. Boys like you and Jesse, ere you grow up to become rebels. And what of Jabe, and William? I pray they've made good their start … Oh, I fear our farm will be plundered. I fear our beloved house will be burnt to the ground! Of course, *your Father* needn't worry," she added looking at me with a raised eyebrow.

From the dark corner of the springhouse Aunt Neesy sat shushing her children while the flickering light cast eerie shadows on the walls behind them. She gathered her youngsters into her arms, and after a few moments their crying subsided. Baby Rachel looked to be asleep on her mother's lap. Nothing stirred.

"Round up the militia indeed," Aunt Neesy said quietly while looking again over at me, her chin pressing upon the top of Rachel's nightcap. "The only thing Joseph knows how to round up is rum. Rum and a bad case of bottle ache."

"Aunt Neesy," I said rising to my feet, "the Regulars will surely be on the march soon. I must get home. I pray you will be safe here."

Once outside I peered down the path in both directions. Night had fallen completely, and I felt a sudden pang of longing. I wished to be sitting around our kitchen hearth surrounded by my own family, with the fire warming us, while high through the trees came the sound of drums from the beach. First one muffled tattoo answered by a second drifting in the wind, like the distant call of owls.

"I have a good notion where Broom and your stock will be," I called in a loud whisper through the keyhole of the springhouse door. "Behind the big ledge, but two swales away. When I pass I'll tell him to listen for a pistol shot."

"What pistol?" Aunt Neesy asked.

"The one Uncle Moses gave you. Should the Lobsterbacks find you, cock the hammer and fire into the air!"

From behind the door I could hear Jesse and the others beginning to wail yet again, and with their muffled cries ringing in my ears, I turned and ran for home.

Alright alright, I might a been hiding behind her skirts, but as I recall, yer face weren't exactly flushed with military valor right bout then neither. It were white as clay!

And need I remind you, we spent a long cold night confined in that tarnal place? But that ain't all. Tis a miracle we made it there in the first place, an ahead of them dragoons. When Gabe rode by our door Da was in the kitchen, his feet stuck in a roasting pan soaking the blisters his new riding boots had give him. A fine pair a boots they was, fit for the officer that they voted him, but they was stiff as steel, an once all the tarnal excitement commenced, he neglects to put them on an goes a-sliding about the barnyard rounding up the livestock in his stocking feet. He orders Broom to untie our collie dog Lucy to help drive the beasts into the woods. Jabe! cries he, give me a hand with Violet (she was our ornery sow and set to farrow) whereupon Mother reminds him that Jabe was already gone with William to round up the Reds and Blacks. All right fine, declares he, we all know Broom lacks the brass anyways, so I'll do the deed me-self and the old fool promptly leaps into the pen, whereupon his lack a proper footwear puts him at a distinct disadvantage compared to a mean old sow whats in full flower, a fact that Violet of course immediately divines, so when he approaches her with his noose she charges for the gate an crashes straight through, but not afore dispatching the old Ensign to the mud — down he goes upon his backsides with the grand lady biting him for good measure on his forearm as she passes. A nasty wound, it was. Two deep punctures.

Mother hastily applied some bandages an suggests in no uncertain terms that he was too old for this sort of nonsense an suggested further that if'n he insists upon acting the soldier then donning his soldiering boots might improve his military bearing. Fair point, he meekly allows, and after squeezing his muddy stockings into his brand new shiny black boots he rushes to let the horses out of the barn an throws a rein around Thor, his favored steed, an with that spirited beast safely in hand an the trunk secured to the saddle, we was finally ready to head to the springhouse. Broom and the goats and the sheep and the milk cows (Violet did not return until a few weeks later, trundling back to troff with a dozen piglets in tow) had gone on ahead to hunker down even deeper in the woods for the night. When we got to the springhouse we knelt by the door and joins hands in prayer, asking for God's forgiveness and protection. I've left the pottage on the fire, Mother suddenly remembers. It must be a-boiling over! Don't fret about the damned soup! curses me old man whilst handing over his pistol, and after patiently reminding her how to load an fire it, he spurs Thor for Disbrow's. The war was now begun! — JB

Our Safe Haven

I crept as quietly as I could into the kitchen and found Father sitting in his usual place by the fireplace wearing his red velvet banyan and smoking his favorite clay pipe, struggling as best he could, it seemed to me, to look calm and relaxed, to project a sense of normalcy on an evening that was anything but normal. Grandfather William was in his rocker on the other side of the fireplace, slouched in deep slumber, as he nearly always was in those days. Mother and Gaylee were sitting at the table with their backs turned to the door, absorbed in a conversation with young Nate, while my sisters, Mary and Esther, sat off to the side, busying themselves with a skein of yarn. Betty, who was not yet three, was climbing around on the floor beneath the table near the cradle where John, the baby, lay sleeping. It was Betty who spied me first, racing from around Mother's chair and pointing a finger.

"He's come home!" she shouted.

Mother let out a cry and ran across the room to embrace me, followed closely by my siblings, who crowded around, shouting questions all at once. From over Mother's shoulder I was able to see Father, still sitting at his chair, looking angry but remaining composed. Gaylee, on the other hand, never one to contain her feelings, rose to her feet and slapped her palm down hard on the table.

"Where the devil have you been all these hours?" she snarled through clenched teeth. Standing across the table in her black dress and shawl, the old woman appeared in the diminished light of our kitchen like a piece of charred wood. "Pray, tell us now," she continued with her eyes narrowing, "where has our brave rebel been? Taking on the Royal Inniskillings and the King's Own single handedly? Deliverance! Molly! What are we to do with this one?"

"Calm yourself, Mother," my father urged, angrily knocking the ash from his pipe against the side of the fireplace. He leaned forward in his chair. "The boy is home now. Let's hear his news."

"Yes, Gaylee," I began excitedly, "Royal Regiments of Foot have landed! Plus, companies of Grenadiers. I tell you, Father, there must be thousands of Regulars forming on the beach!"

I sat down at the table to catch my breath. "I counted six field pieces … drawn upon Compo Hill … Twenty-six sails at anchor … Two large sloops-of-war. And Father, I was met by a mounted Dragoon! He had me fixed in his sights!"

"In truth?" my father gasped.

"Oh, you foolish boy!" Gaylee roared from over her shoulder as she poked angrily at the embers in the fireplace. "Don't you know he could have taken you prisoner? Is that what ye want?" She stabbed hard with her poker. "Tis a deadly dangerous game you are playing!"

"He was far too busy rounding up horses to worry about me," I continued, as sparks from Gaylee's poker drew up the chimney like flecks of blood. I stood quietly while she turned to Grandfather William, straightening the addled man in his chair as best she could. It didn't look as if he were taking any of this in, suffering as he was from a fever of the brain, brought on years ago by a series of awful shocks and fed by a rage he was never able to dissipate. Grandfather's malaise started long before I was born, in 1760, when after the span of a few short months his son and namesake died of fever in Quebec City and his parents and sister all perished in a house fire. The conflagration broke out over the same foundation where the new, larger house now stands, and Grandfather William blamed it on a Negro servant girl named Happy.

Nobody in our family ever spoke much about any of this. Gaylee would, from time to time, mention the fire; a tragedy she maintained was linked to a superstitious curse. I remember her stories about a whale lamp in the hallway that mysteriously fell over and about a witch named Mercy, but I can't remember her ever saying anything about Grandfather William selling Happy. Had emancipation not become such a hotly contended issue by the time I was a boy, I believe talk about the house fire would have remained buried in the darkling past of Bennett family lore. Our neighbors, on the other hand, regardless of where they stood on the question of manumission, were more than happy to dig through the ashes in our cellar as if we needed to be reminded of our past, which like all families had its fair share of less-than-honorable episodes. They'd express nothing but deep sympathy directly to our faces, and many would go so far as to say that Grandfather had no choice but to rid his household of such an indolent servant. But behind our backs, when they thought we couldn't hear or weren't watching, I'd see their looks and hear their titters.

Now I ask, how was I to know that yet more skeletons were about to arrive at our doorstep, rattling out there in the wind and rain, seeking interment? How was I to know that these next visitors would alter the course of our lives so irrevocably? How was I to know that all these years later it would be left to me to remain vigilant with the spade, ever-prepared to cast a few more shovelfuls of cleansing dirt whenever another bit of broken bone beckons from the ashes that fill our family cellar?

Lord a mercy Haynes you do go on! Like allus you write pretty, but damn if ye ain't missing some of the finer points. Starting with that bit about Happy and Grandpa William you jest danced round. He blamed that poor Negro servant girl for that tarnal fire. What's that you say he calls it? Willful Negligence? What in hell's that supposed to mean? An then, instead of simply trying, convicting, an hanging her like he says he had ever right to do, that crazy old son-of-a-bitch (God rest his sole) turns round and does something that's far more swift an terrible – he sells her to that Deleware farmer, ripping her away with nary a second thought from our Broom who couldn't a been more'n six. Barely weaned he was!

Ye may be too tippy toed an enlightened-like to even mention the whole true reason for the house a-burning down, but I ain't. It warn't no accident and it warn't no willful crime neither. It were that spell is what it was, that tarnal curse we all still bear, and while it may be too late for you and me old friend (well, you for sure!) it wouldn't do Rachel an Ziba, an Sarah an John Hervey an all the rest a them no harm to remember to stir their gruel pots clockwise an to spit in their fires ever now'n again!

I hears tell she were an awful terrible witch what cursed us Bennetts! Raven-haired an milky skinned an by most accounts not exactly hiding her apple dumpling shop beneath no cloak neither! She were neither tall nor short, thin nor stout, but striking in her manner with lightning bolts a-firing from her hair! Pass her on the lane an she had a way of reading yer secrets, of staring ye down with them tarnal eyes a hers, what Gaylee allus said shined as black as anthersite coal. She was a sharp-tongued old harridin, with a pewling, cat-pawed husband back at home emptying chamber pots and airing laundry. They say she rankled nearly ever man she ever met.

Her name was Mercy Disbrow, and it was Grandpa William's grandfather Thomas Bennett who testified in court against her. The noose was round her neck and she looks to the crowd and shouts I will not hang alone! So they twines her hands a-hind her back, and then, in the whisker before the chair was knocked away a man rides up a-waving a decree from the Governor what sets her free.

So Goody Disbrow walks away free, but that don't mean she were innocent. Not a-tall, Gaylee told us firm, she warn't no more innocent than Satan himself. She kept her familiars – her cats and toads and such – and all her evil woodland ways for the remainder of her days. She finds our Thomas down in the salt grass one day an says there'll come a fire an that yer cupboards will be left bare as a bird's tail an Thomas sees that there's a flame burning right in the palm of her hand an she looks right at him an says seven generations of your seed is now damned an throws the fire into the air where it disappears in a snuff of smoke.

You want proof? Gaylee allus asked we quivering chicks huddled round her skirts in the cellar of yer old house and points to the scorch marks still plainly seen on the foundation stones and tells us, here my children is all the proof ye will ever need. There once was a servant girl living in this very house. She was some parts Negroe, some parts English and some parts Injun an she dies in childbirth. Mercy was the one what wet nursed the little orphan who went by the name of Janet, who grew up and had a baby she named Jenny, who grew up and had a baby she named Happy, and Happy as we all know, was the wicked wench who lit this very place a-fire. So listen here, Haynes. You know as well as I. It warn't no accident! That tarnal fire was a curse plain and simple and we Bennetts, as is true in so many other matters, we Bennetts is what we allus are: guilty as charged with bones a-plenty buried ever whichways! – JB

"The Dragoon had two of Uncle Mosy's mares with him and was intent upon returning to the beach," I said, continuing with my story. With my mother placing a comforting arm across my shoulder, I recounted how the soldier disappeared between the rocks like a specter, and about my encounter with Aunty Neesy and the cousins in the springhouse. I told them also about seeing the Prince of Wales American Volunteers, which especially alarmed my mother who worried her nephew Jabez Lockwood – a favorite of hers – would almost certainly be among them. We all worried that the Tories, those who were driven from their homes, might someday return should the direction of the winds ever return in their favor. We feared that those most aggrieved would surely want to take their measure of revenge, adding to the ravages that had plagued our quiet countryside for so many months. It will only be a matter of time, Father warned, and now here they were, armed and set to march with the most powerful army in the world.

Mother turned to face Father straight in his eyes. "Can you promise me yet again, Deliverance, that there will be no plundering on this night, and no houses put to the torch?"

"Those are General Tryon's orders; of that, Molly, I have been assured. Our house is the safest place for us to be."

Hearing this, Grandfather William stirred unexpectedly in his rocking chair. All eyes turned towards him, surprised to see him sitting up and alert. His voice emerged from the shadows beside the hearth as clear as clapboards snapping from across a dale.

"There will be no safe haven in all of Christendom," he said, "once that soldier boy son of mine takes his poke at the hornet's nest."

Whereupon he fell back into his chair, sending a pall over the entire room.

Hail Cesar!

May 5th, 1827:

Betty and Mother have come down from Weston for the afternoon and we all went to the West Parish burying ground to pay our respects to Father. Mother takes good care of her late beloved husband, and spent her time at his graveside carefully tying back the spent daffodils to make way for the irises, which are coming fast. I took a moment, as I always do on these occasions, to walk around to the other side of the cemetery wall where the unmarked stones and a few wooden crosses were to be found, scattered randomly beneath the trees. If you didn't know that these forlorn markers were there, you might not ever see them. Cesar is interred at the edge of this shadowed patch of ground put aside for the servants, where brambles tend to encroach upon him. I took out the shearers that I brought along to cut back last season's growth. "Shaving your nappy old head," I chuckled to myself, and was reminded of the day after we got pummeled with the apples. That next morning, I recall Father turning to Ezra Weed and asking, "Where in tarnation is Cesar?" who hadn't come to the house for his porridge and beer, which was unlike him. The sun had just risen and we were already in one of the far fields binding and stacking oats while rain threatened, making Father anxious. "He's shaving his nappy head," was all Ezra had to offer in his usual surly tone and with his nose scrunched for good measure, reminding us of the indignity he felt for having to share quarters with a Negro. Father overlooked this show of disrespect as he often did – he'd get no work at all out of Ezra if he had to correct every single show of insolent behavior – and asked me to run back down to the house and check in on Cesar. William and I were both quite bruised and scraped after being barraged by all those apples, and I feared that he might be more hurt than he had let on.

Sure enough, when I knocked on his door and looked in, our beloved servant was standing by the window where the light was better, trying to examine the back of his head reflected in the tiny shard of broken mirror glass he had hanging on the wall. He had somehow managed to shave off a patch of hair on the side of his head behind his ear and I could see he had a nasty cut there, still oozing with blood. "Be a goo lad," he called when he saw me enter, "an han me dat kine peppa." On the table was a bowl containing a red poultice he had made from the hot peppers he grew for himself, and I brought it to him and watched as he dabbed the wound. He winced. "Oooh, dat smats! Look. See wa dem sonabitchies done!"

Even today, in spite of all I know to be true about the dreadful stain of slavery, it's easy to forget that Cesar was as hurt as any of us were by the war with England. He had much less to lose, many claimed, which was most certainly true in a way. He had no property, real or otherwise, and was never able to use the money he saved while Father still owned him. He was a skilled laborer – by all accounts the best joiner in Fairfield – purchased by my grandfather along with Titus, a framer, to help build the house over the foundation of the one Happy burned down. That was where I grew up, and until I found myself years later down at the elbows and moving with my family from one hastily constructed hovel to the next, I never fully appreciated what fine workmanship went into a Cesar window frame, stairwell, or wainscot panel.

These days, Kezzie and I still get out. We receive our invitations now and again for this or that occasion at some of the better homes in town, and if you know how to look, you can see the signs of Cesar's handiwork everywhere. His twins were christened in our parlor, in front of the beautiful walnut mantelpiece that he built. Those baby girls looked as black as charcoal in their white Christening dresses, such wild little things, yet nobody, I would venture to say, who was there to welcome them into our community of faith, and who saw the depth of feeling written on the faces of their two proud parents, would ever suggest that Cesar had any less to lose by Father's stubborn pride and Uncle Joseph's vain ambitions than we did. On the contrary, the only true case that can be made is that compared with us, Cesar and Phyllis and their two babies had everything to lose.

One of my first memories of Cesar was seeing him crouching on the stoop of the servant's quarters, chin resting in his hands. I was but six years old. It was the day Uncle Stephen came for Titus. I was sitting opposite him, leaning back against the trunk of a tree playing with the Cup 'n Ball he had carved for me. The long summer day was coming to its close. Everyone had gone, leaving the two of us alone in the sultry, breathless air, sitting comfortably in our silence save for the occasional 'tink' whenever my tethered wooden marble found its way into its wooden cup. Cesar's expression was melancholic. He had been forced to part with the close companion he had lived with for over ten years, and was no doubt troubled about sharing his quarters with the stranger Father contracted to replace him, due to arrive in the morrow. The replacement was an indentured man from Ireland, the first of a string of such arrangements over the ensuing years with which Cesar was made to cope, always with grace of course, but grace with a touch of stinging nettle, which was Cesar down to his boot buckles.

Cesar was a man of many hats, quite literally so, and with the exception of when he was kneeling in prayer inside the sanctuary, I can't ever remember seeing him bare headed. He remained hatted when working shirtless on scorching hot days, hatted when bent at the waist picking beetles from a long row of potatoes, hatted when drawing water from the well or emerging from the privy. He remained hatted even in our house, which as you can well imagine, irritated Gaylee half to death. The number and variety of the hats and caps that made up his repertoire was endless. Besides the slouchy green farmer's hat that he wore most often, he had a handed-down beaver skin cocked hat with gold embroidering that he wore on special occasions, a couple of brimmed Monmouth caps for cold winter mornings, and an untold number of banyans of various shapes and colors that he'd wear while working at his bench in the barn. Like so many of his race, hats were never merely placed upon his head, but rather perched at whatever rakish angle his temperament at any given moment dictated. It amazed me that such precariously placed chapeaus could stay fastened just where he placed them. No matter the weather or what he was doing, Cesar's hat never flew away, not when he jumped from the hayloft or galloped on a horse or when bent to a stiff sea breeze while working through the salt marshes. How he managed it, I never knew. It's part of his abiding mystery.

His cocked hat was pulled nearly to his nose. I sat gazing into his face, uncharacteristically downturned on this evening, endeavoring to read his thoughts. His skin was as black as any Negro I had ever known or seen, with decorative scars that swirled over his back and chest and up to his face. He had lines etched across his right cheek that looked as if he'd been swiped by a catamount's paw. These were deeply furrowed and almost warlike, but what you noticed first when you encountered him was the delicate half circle of raised droplets around his right eye socket. These raised welts were luminescent in the waning daylight, a string of lovely black pearls shaped like the letter 'C' which, he once told me, was how he received not his given but what he called his "quired" name: Cesar.

Born on a sugar plantation in Jamaica, Cesar came to us via Rhode Island where he learned his trade. He was a kind man, and reticent – what some mistook as surly – and spoke with a dialect that only those who knew him well could easily understand. Many believed his broken English was a sign of inferior intelligence, but they were wrong. Cesar might have been difficult to understand, but he could read and write and cipher and was to my way of thinking at least, far more intelligent than half the people who ever mocked him to his face, or behind his back. Besides performing magic with a chisel and plane, Cesar was invaluable as a farm hand. He could fix anything that was broken in either the house or barn. He could right a breech better than anyone I knew, and shear a lamb faster than it takes to boil an egg. Grandfather William bought him along with Titus as a kind of matched set on the same day he sold Happy at the auction house in Black Rock Harbor, and what he got by jingo, besides his bitter dram of vengeance, was a real bargain.

During the year it took to build the house, the family lived with relatives while Cesar and Titus and Happy's Broom slept and took their meals in the cow barn. Once the big house was done they built the two-room cabin where they all lived for a long time. Broom was only ten or eleven years old when his mother was sold, and Cesar and Titus became like fathers to him. When there was time for me to sit with Cesar at his workbench he'd tell me about those olden days, hard but happy he said they were, the time before I was born, when yields were high and Father had the farm running on all bays. New fields were in constant need of clearing and Father could always count upon wagonloads heaped with flax and wheat to take to market. Those were also the years when Grandfather began lending Cesar out to other houses, allowing him to observe and learn from the wider world. Not only were his joiner and husbandry skills honed by his wanderings, it was while doing some carpentering for Judge Jonathan Sturgis that he met and married Phyllis. Although they could only be together on rare occasions, it was plain to see how much they loved one another. She was his "Norden Staa." After the twins Promise and Gift were born, Father and Cesar made their agreement, sealed with a handshake. Cesar could keep the wages he earned as a joiner, and would be manumitted as soon as he had enough money saved to buy his wife and daughters from the Judge.

Seeing Titus go – and just a year or so after Uncle Moses took possession of Broom – was clearly hard on him. Nobody likes that much change all at once. It leaves an ache.

"Cumma chile," he said to me pushing his hat up to the crown of his head. "Go ta fwar an gemme a 'tail fo da smok, den come set belong side me a wiles."

I did as told and went inside to light one of the cattails he kept in a jar by the stove. I came back and nestled up against him, both of us facing the road while he puffed his pipe to life, encircling us in gauzy smoke that smelled of wood shavings and cinnamon. It was one of those still summer evenings when sounds travel unlikely distances. From somewhere all the way across the river a door slammed and we heard a mother speaking to her child who came back at her with a smart reply … so close they sounded … a pair of parrots perched upon our shoulders. There was hardly anything of Titus's to load onto the wagon, but it was still an awful business, with chores that needed doing in addition to everything else and by the end of the day, we were flat tuckered. There wasn't a breath of air as the sun began to set. Nothing stirred save a few birds flying lazily through the distant treetops. Behind them the eastern sky was barely a whisper, slowly paling to pink.

"We's gwine ta miss dat raskil Tidus," Cesar said after a long draw on his pipe, "ain we chile?"

"Why did he have to go?" I asked. "Isn't there enough work for him here?"

"Dats not fo we feel mices to-a cide. Ba lemme tellah, dis id wudda I says now. Dem Ish patatamen, dey stink bad, lie-a rum an cabbage, oh Lawd, dey sorely do!"

Gaylee called from the porch. It was time for supper and our evening psalmody, a ritual so very important to her. The decrees of the Lord are firm ... they are more precious than gold, than much fine gold ... They are sweeter than honey, than honey from the honeycomb.

Both Cesar and I knew full well it took Gaylee more than one call to get everybody in. We could sit a while longer.

"Ye know wadda I be tinkin?" he wondered aloud, blowing a stream of smoke into the sky. "I be tinkin dat Pommis anna Giff id bofe settin somers rights dis zact minute, an deys a-lookin up at dis zact summa sky."

"Deliverance! William! Haynes!" Gaylee shouted, louder this time.

"Gwoine, chile," Cesar purred, "do as she say." I nestled my face into the side of his knee. "Gwoine now! A-fore she busts!"

Cesar was like a second father to me, and in fact, especially during the difficult war years, I would have said he was my only father. He was ever so gentle and kind. He was warm and affectionate towards all of my brothers and sisters of course, and they thought the world of him, but I believe he took a special shine towards me. Perhaps it was because of my small stature that he was so quick to give me words of encouragement, always there with a hug, or to playfully tousle my hair whenever he thought I needed cheering. And on this morning, the day after the boys had pummeled us with our own apples, it was my chance to show a small kindness towards him. He knelt upon the floor and tilted his head in my direction. "How do it look?" he asked, and I told him the bleeding had stopped but that the wound looked awfully angry and sore. "Betta covva it den," he reasoned, and handed me a piece of cloth. "Hol dis whilst I get me a hat," and I kept the cloth pressed over the bald patch on his head while carefully walking with him across the room where he had his array of hats hanging on pegs. He picked out a woolen Monmouth cap that he knew fit snugly and I kept the patch in place with my fingers until he had it pulled over his ears. From where we were standing he could see his reflection in the shard of mirror and turned his head towards it in order to assure himself that the patch would hold. He whistled through his teeth and smiled approvingly at himself.

"Ooo-eee," he chuckled, his eyes still fixed admiringly on his image in the mirror, "a man ken nevva hammanuff hats!"

Father's Faces

Although my father and I may not have ever been as openly affectionate and tender with one another as were Cesar and I, my memories of him seem to be growing more strongly as time goes by. I remember his many faces, which often come vividly to mind these days. There is what I call his 'predawn face' that would appear at my bedside in the loft at the old homestead. The lamp he holds casts a hard shadow across his features. His countenance suggests neither sternness nor kindliness, nothing more hot or cold than a tacit reminder of the obvious fact that the sun is about to rise and that there is work to be done. Then there is his face that appears in the full light of day, it is a face even more difficult to construe. In this memory, he is walking behind a plow or standing at the other end of the pew. He is absorbed in his own private thoughts, with a face that reveals nothing – no connection whatsoever to the task at hand, or the world circling around him. And there is, of course, the face when he's sitting by the fire of an evening, wearing one of his silk or velvet banyans with his nose buried in one of his beloved books. It's that face that says, dare not speak to me now, with his lips tightly pursed, yet moving slowly side to side as though working on a piece of hard candy, a mannerism Kessie tells me I myself am inclined to exhibit from time to time, an unconscious tic I suppose, which may very well be the only trait I inherited from the man. There is yet another face of his that floats through my memory, and this is one that leaves me unsettled. It is what I call his "grim necessity" face, a cold face that still occasionally emerges in the waking moments of my recurrent dreams, looming in dark silhouette, framed against a patch desolate pale blue sky. And then there is the face that turned towards me not too long ago on the last morning I saw him alive, a face I'd much prefer to forget entirely, but cannot. His cheekbones no longer framed by thick grey hair, but by wispy white filaments, his chin reduced from chiseled to jowly, his eyes from dark and piercing to weak and watery.

Finally, there is the one face of Father's that comes to mind with no troubling complications, stirring an emotion I believe is at least vaguely akin to love. It is also my very first childhood memory. I mustn't have been any more than three or four years old. We are walking towards the brow of Bennett's Rocks, at the place where you can see Cockenoe Island just to the side of Compo Hill, with the ribbon of Long Island lying flat upon the Sound further in the distance. On some days from our Connecticut shore, Long Island looks gauzy, obscured by a summer's haze or a winter's mist. At other times, its profile is all but a faint and distant ghost skulking behind a lowering fog, or lost altogether behind a curtain of murky grey skies. On rare days, however, when the winds shift to northerly, the air becomes so fresh and so crystal clear Long Island looks almost magnified. You can make out farm fields and hedgerows. You can even see the rough outlines and detect the different colors of barns and other buildings, and in a few places at the top edges of the ribbon you can see the tiny points of church steeples poking into the sky.

I have no idea how I could have gotten to this spot at such a young age, or why Father and I would have been there in the middle of a working afternoon. It could have been a Pope's Day or some other special occasion. I seem to be looking down upon him, so perhaps Cesar carried me up from the road and has me perched on his shoulders – we children did, after all, love to take our turn climbing onto Cesar's back – which also explains how I could have gotten to this rocky prominence in the first place. Father is gazing out across the Sound, and I look in that direction too, and become aware of Long Island. Because I am merely a child, I think this is the way Long Island must always appear, so fresh and clear and so close, and when Father turns to catch my eye, all the usual tenseness is missing from his face – he's beaming, and he spreads his arms wide and exclaims, "That's what you call church-steeple clear!" and while I had no way of appreciating how rare a view it was, I surely understood how rare it was to see Father's face so unguardedly animated, so happy, and I have never forgotten how it felt to be so warmly embraced in that wonderful, toothy smile.

Aunt Sarah and Uncle Jabez

June 3rd, 1827:

    I rode up to Ridgefield yesterday to call upon my Aunt Sarah, the rich widow, who has always been rather fond of me – and I of her – in spite of a shared history, which over certain periods of time tended to run, shall we say, a bit cold. She and Uncle Jabez did, after all, make out like brigands during the war, and I continue to believe that there was a moment when they could have stepped in behind the scenes to help facilitate a better outcome for our branch of the family. They could have vouched for Father's many honorable virtues, but chose instead to keep their own heads down. By allowing the rumors of Toryism that had been circulating against Father to go unchecked, and by remaining mum about the true reason why he happened to be traveling on the same road as were the Redcoats on that fateful day, the two of them were able to effectively deflect any suspicions that may have otherwise emerged about their involvement in the illicit London Trade. I feel a certain amount of resentment over this, but time has a way of binding all wounds, and especially when it comes to the blood let by members of one's own family. In the case of Aunt Sarah, our natural filial warmth towards one another was rekindled four or five years ago, when we unexpectedly found ourselves at the same meeting of the Anti-Slavery Society at Keeler's Tavern in Ridgefield. She spoke so eloquently that day, and has proven ever since, in spite of her advanced age, to be a passionate and tireless advocate for ending the scourge of slavery in our state. Having sold their farm after Uncle Jabez passed away, she lives now in a fashionable part of Ridgefield, on West Lane, and in a grand style, with her four-wheeled chaise and a townhouse filled with all manner of imported fineries. We sat in her lovely parlor discussing our effort to establish an academy for Negroes. I had initially wanted to name it The Promise and Gift Academy, thinking that that had a nice ring to it, but was prevailed upon by other committee members to settle for the more prosaic Weston Academy For Free Negro Girls. In any event, Aunt Sarah continues to be very interested in doing all she can to make this dream a reality. She had earlier pledged to donate a building lot in Weston that she still owned, giving us a fine location for our school, and I came away this day with her promise to also contribute money towards construction costs. It was a very propitious meeting indeed. I got more from Aunt Sarah with regard to the school than I had ever expected. I was even able to secure a few more vials of her seemingly endless supply of laudanum that somehow came into her possession upon the death of her other brother (my Uncle Stephen) who had been a physician in life, and a close neighbor of hers in town.

Feeling greatly buoyed by these accomplishments, I couldn't resist taking a slight detour on my journey home to Compo, and steered my nag past the former Lockwood farmhouse on Godfrey Road. The old place has hardly changed a wit, with the two carved stars yet rising over its front doorway and its three-door barn looming off to the side, as imposing as ever. Many unpleasant memories were of course brought to mind as I ambled by, but there were fond remembrances as well. I recall in particular the few days my brother William and I spent there in February 1777, just weeks before the raid. With Jabez Jr. off with the Provincials, and our uncle stricken with one of his flair-ups of gout, the two of us were employed to split and stack the firewood they'd need to see them through the rest of winter. You couldn't ask for more gracious hosts. We were treated as honored guests rather than as the hired hands we actually were. Aunt Sarah teased us after supper, as she always loved to do, about the silly things we did as little boys, and long into the evening, with the candles flickering low, she chatted affably about her days as a girl growing up in Compo: digging for clams, making soap and candles with Gaylee, jousting with her five strapping brothers for the last pork chop on the serving plate.

There was also time to talk about current affairs, and when William broached the subject of the war, and about how the tide had suddenly turned dramatically in favor of the Patriots, I wasn't sure what to expect from our hosts. William was an ardent advocate for American independence, and by 1777, when the conflict had drawn closer to home – with humbling defeats suffered by the Continentals on Long Island and at White Plains – he was no longer the least bit circumspect about expressing his opinions. This could create problems for us in those terribly anxious and divisive months, and on this occasion, there was simply nothing I could have done to stop him from wagging his tongue. General Washington had just a few weeks earlier crossed, and then re-crossed the Delaware, achieving his stunning victories at Trenton and Princeton. The entire country was abuzz with the news, and William, who just a few days earlier had received a first hand account of the glorious events from his close friend Wake Burritt, was even more flushed with rebellious fervor than usual. Wake was a Private in the Connecticut Line, and was there at Assunpink Creek. He told us about the Americans funneling across a narrow bridge to seize the high ground beyond, and how he was carried along by his fellow soldiers like a piece of driftwood on the far edge of the column. Like the rest of them, he was miserably cold, stricken with a raging case of the itch, and at the point of near collapse following days upon days of forced marches through driving gales of sleet and snow, and there, as Wake recounted so vividly, was His Excellency, General Washington himself, looking resplendent upon his enormous white horse. The great general extolled the lads to keep moving, and as Wake left the bridge and began to climb the hill, he was pressed yet again by his compatriots, this time against the shoulder of that magnificent steed, and he felt the hard edge of the general's riding boot digging against his ribcage – a sharp pang which seemed to pass from his body and shoot like a current of electricity throughout the entire mass of his fellow soldiers. From that moment on, any and all depravations from which the men were suffering no longer seemed to matter, and they were suddenly ready to fight like they had never fought before. Four times the Redcoats tried to storm that bridge, and four times they were repulsed by American cannon and musket fire. The British dead piled up like cordwood as the victorious Americans shouted their huzzahs!

"We can win this war!" Wake declared, and I knew from the

fevered look in William's eyes, that in spite of being under sixteen years of age, he would do everything in his power to enlist. He would defy the fierce oppositions set down by our parents and, if necessary, he would find his moment to steal away. Meanwhile, as he was relating the battle at Assunpink to our aunt and uncle, I did my best to read their faces. Uncle Jabez had made a point of telling us earlier in the week that he had just recently signed his Oath of Loyalty to America, but that could have been merely a ruse. After all, his eldest son was at that very moment encamped somewhere on Long Island with the Provincials, so I believed my aunt and uncle were at least leaning King-ward, and half expected them to explode in anger, or to express some sort of rebuke for what they more likely than not, deemed to be William's unseemly show of disloyalty, but to my relief, they merely sat politely and listened to his "liberty mad" speech without so much as saying boo. If they were Tories like I suspected they were, they were most certainly kindly Tories.

When William finished his tale, there was an uncomfortable period of silence until Aunt Sarah stood from her chair and calmly walked around the table to where he was sitting. Even in the dimness of the dying candlelight, it was plain to see that his eyes were fully ablaze with marshal ardor. And yet, Aunt Sarah did not reprove him. No, not in the least. All she did was smile that ever-sweet smile of hers and took my brother's face tenderly in her hands. She sighed in a matronly sort of way, and then bent down to kiss his forehead before bidding us all goodnight.

Uncle Joseph

Unlike Aunt Sarah and Uncle Jabez, Uncle Joseph was an open book of emotions, erratic at times and difficult to predict, but with thoughts and tempers that were ever legible. The man was a complex character, full of contrasts. He was highly pious, inspired in his youth (as he so often reminded us) by the itinerant revivalist George Whitfield. He was proud to call himself a New Light, one of the zealots who saw corruption lurking everywhere. And yet, in spite of being quick to decry the weaknesses of others, he was never much good at managing his own affairs. He reeked of rum by midday, and of Madeira after vespers. His fields were untidy, vines curled up through the limbs of his apple trees, and he was often unable to put enough silage in store to see his livestock through the winter. This was exactly the situation that April 1777. Three of the heifers Will and Jabe were driving to Norfield had been kept alive over the winter in Father's barn. It was a yearly practice that Father accepted willingly and without judgment, but one that Joseph found deeply humiliating even though he did everything in his power never to show it.

I remember once when I was perhaps ten or eleven years old, Mother sent me up the road to Aunt Sarah and Uncle Joseph's house looking to fill a jar of molasses. When I stepped unannounced into their kitchen, I found Uncle Joseph on his knees, sobbing uncontrollably. Aunt Sarah was there to console him and had her arms around his shoulders as he cried out, "It is yet another sign of God's disappointment in me!" Luckily they both had their backs turned and before they had the chance to know of my presence, I made my exit and ran hard for home, empty jar in hand.

I had never before seen a grown man cry, and it unsettled me. Feeling distraught and not sure what to do, I looked for Cesar in his work shed and found him running a molding planer across the edge of a board, his sleeves covered with long curls of sweet-smelling hardwood. "Whassa matta?" he asked, and I told him what I had seen. He listened patiently but kept to his task, adding curly ribbons to the cloud of them at his feet as I explained how I had been sent to fetch the jar of molasses Mother needed to borrow, and described how I had dashed into their house without knocking and how ashamed it made me feel to have barged in upon them and to have seen something I knew no child, much less an uninvited nephew, was ever meant to see.

By that age I was just beginning to be aware of the tensions that existed between my father and his youngest brother; the awkwardness that seemed to permeate the air whenever they met at the market, or stood together after church. I suspected the thickness of the atmosphere that seemed to follow Uncle Joseph wherever he went had something to do with his excessive drinking, along with the little signs of disarray about his farm that even a child's eye could detect, but these were issues only for adults and never openly and fully discussed by anyone. I know now that the weakness of Uncle Joseph's character was not only a problem between him and my father; it was also a point of contention between Father and Mother, and between the two of them and Gaylee.

It's a scene I saw repeated so often as a child: They'd all be at the table talking around and around about something Uncle Joseph had said or done, but never getting to the actual heart of it, and as soon as Mother's and Father's voices rose to the verge of shouting, Father would push back from the table and abruptly leave the room. "You should be more firm with him!" Mother would call to Father's back as he stormed away. Gaylee would then look up from her sewing and fidget in her chair. "It's that devil rum," she'd lament, and lean over to primp Grandfather William's neckerchief or gently scrape a bit of mustard from the corner of his mouth.

As it turned out, the problem tormenting Uncle Joseph that morning was indeed a grave one. His herd of cows had come down with an infectious disease that none of the local farmers had ever seen before. The mysterious murrain began as an abscess and almost always led to the animal's death. We've since had similar outbreaks and have learned more about how the disease progresses. While cows of any age might contract the malady, it hits calves the hardest. They can look hale and hearty at birth and remain healthy even after they're weaned, and it doesn't make a difference whether their mothers are one of the lucky few to contract and survive the disease, or if they are among those even luckier cows that never show any signs of it at all. One morning a calf will feed well, and then within the hour it becomes listless with a sore about the size of your hand appearing on its back, and a day later the beast will almost surely be gone. Within two years of that first outbreak more than half Uncle Joseph's herd was lost. In his mind it was a return of the fifth plague and nothing could be done about it. Father implored him to clean out his barn, to try separating the herd into different fields, to cut out the abscesses and experiment with varying doses of sulfur and jalap – anything that might lead to a reasoned understanding and management of the disease, but all Uncle Joseph could do was throw his hands in the air, leaving his fate as he did on all matters, to Providence.

Hold on a minute Haynes, Uncle Joseph didn't leave ALL matters to Providence an certainly not on this sad occasion. I remember our cows was similarly afflicted, and my old Da had it in his mind to do exactly what that son-of-bitch uncle of ours did, and that is sell all his calves to some hapless young farmer who don't know no better and try and re-coop as much of his investment as possible a-fore the whole lot of them got there blisters and was lost! Uncle Joseph was full of tarnal superstitions no doubt about it, but when it came to tossing his bread in the air an making sure it comes down butter side up, that man's brain went all sharp an enlightened-like!

Moses, Mother says to me Da when he told her bout his plan to sell his herd. Don't give me none of that fifth plague rigamaroll an pretends only God knows what's gointer happen to them cows, she hollers. You knows they's as good as dead unless you do something right by them, so before you go passin em off on some poor sucker, try givin em some medicine … an while your at it clean out the damn barn! – JB

Cesar put down his planer and knocked the shavings from his arm. "Come here, chile," he said to me and I walked over to his bench. With one hand resting atop my head he looked me straight in the face and asked if anybody saw me in the house, and I told him no. He then asked if I still had that jar for the molasses Aunt Sarah needed, and I told him yes. "Well den," he continued, "oona gits rye on back dere and whens ye gits to de doe, starts a-callin' an makin' alotta nwoise an I promise – yer Unka Joe'll be done wid his catawallin, an yer Auntie Sarrah will come dancin' to de doe as swee as candy!"

"Do you think so?" I asked.

"Ize knows so," he replied with a wry smile. "An don't take no mine a yer Unka Joe. Dem tears is what dey calls Crock-dile Tears."

"What are Crocodile Tears?" I asked. Cesar wiped the wood shavings from his sleeves and drew me into his arms. "Go axt yer ma," he replied, "she tella."

With the onset of the war, Uncle Joseph's life took on a renewed sense of purpose. In the years leading up to it, we grew accustomed to seeing him regularly rise from his pew to give impassioned pleas to the cause of liberty. According to my uncle and others like him, the old order of Congregationalists – and of course, all Episcopalians who continued to say a prayer each Sabbath to King George – had grown overly enamored with temporal affairs; wholly corrupted by an insatiable thirst for material gain. Personal salvation could only be attained after overthrowing the tyranny imposed upon the entire community from overseas, and, Uncle Joseph often roared, it was every American's solemn duty to God to rise up against their earthly oppressors!

Within a week after receiving word of the hostilities at Lexington and Concord, Uncle Joseph joined the 6th company of the 4th Regiment in the Connecticut Militia where he was commissioned as an Ensign. In just over a year he rose to the rank of Captain and was placed in command of the Company of Home Guards. While all the Bennett brothers and cousins of Fairfield County dutifully took their turns serving in the trained band in the years immediately preceding the war, and many were serving with distinction now, Joseph took an especially keen interest in military matters. He loved drilling with the men on the green and was a tireless recruiter, never failing to meet his quotas.

Uncle Joseph and Uncle Mosy both saw the future more clearly than my father ever did, and had the good fortune of picking the winning side. "They cast their lot with them Paytrut rascals" is how Jesse always explains the rift that drove the family apart and he is at least partially right, but the enmity that grew between my father and the rest of the family – and most principally Uncle Joseph – wasn't merely created by their views of self-government or their different visions of our country's future. Their differences had far more to do with personal temperament than with their adherence to one political camp or another. Unlike his younger brother, who could be impulsive and quick to anger, Father was a man of reason – I believed at the time cautious to the point of faintheartedness – and feared the savagery of the mob. He was never one to act on impulse and was always one to balance his options after careful consideration of all sides of a question. This bend of mind is what made my father so determined to expand his library and to stay abreast of the agricultural sciences and why in stark contrast to his bothers, he was more comfortable actively obtaining knowledge from one of his beloved books, than by merely receiving it in his pew at church.

He and Uncle Joseph also had very different attitudes about wars in general, and about the necessity of waging them at all. These feelings about the nature of war were strongly held and conceived and hardened decades before the Redcoats landed at Compo.

Now that I'm older, I know just how inescapable events in our past can be, and in the case of the Bennett brothers, there was an earlier war, a formative event in their young lives that I believe made all the difference. And what was it about that Seven Year's War in the past that changed the way they viewed the armed conflict that had erupted in their present? Was there something providential about their involvement in it, or as the case may be, their non-involvement in it? There's always an argument to be made for that sort of Devine intervention, but to my way of thinking, how the Bennett brothers ultimately came to their positions on the Revolutionary War stemmed from their views of that earlier war, and those views were ultimately determined by nothing more significant or providential than the mere accident of the order in which they were born.

Being the eldest, Uncle Moses was called into the Connecticut Line

60

at the very start of the campaign against the French and the Indians. He was mustered and drilled and instead of facing an enemy on a battlefield he was sent up to the New York frontier to build Fort William Henry. The only weapon of war he wielded was an axe to fell trees for parapets. Father, who was born some few years after him, took his tour of duty in the summer of 1757, and experienced a far more gruesome enlistment. He was present at the massacre that followed the surrender of that very same fort Uncle Mosy merely helped to build, and if the legends often told have any truth to them, he must have been witness to scenes of unspeakable carnage. Even though Father never once spoke to us about the massacre at Fort William Henry, he bore witness to it, and I doubt seriously he was ever able to dislodge it from his memory, and certainly not from his dreams.

Uncle Joseph on the other hand, was too young to serve at all. He stayed home playing Ring Taw with his sisters by the fire. Without ever having suffered the depravations of war or without any first-hand knowledge of the hardships of soldiering far away from home, it was easy for a man like him to rattle a sabre when Boston's Committee of Correspondence began to spread its propaganda. I believe Uncle Joseph thought of war similar to the way I did at the time, as a child, with child-like visions of battlefield glory. I realize now that the phrase "Remember William" – a rallying call often made by various members of our family – meant starkly different things to the Bennett brothers. For you see, William was the brother whose birth order caused him to pay the ultimate price. He was born between Father and Uncle Joseph and was therefore called into service towards the end of the war, when the fight had moved to Quebec City, a battle he managed to survive only to succumb to scurvy during the siege that followed it. When Uncle Joseph or Uncle Moses invoked the name of William it was something to be wrapped in honors, whereas when my Father remembered William, he remembered the younger brother made of flesh and blood, and thought of his death as a soldier as nothing more than a tragic loss, a complete waste of a life.

Looking back, I believe Father was amused by his younger brother's ardent patriotism and the silly backwoods military costumes that he donned. He tolerated his brother's antics in spite of the hypocrisy of affecting a "common touch" whilst at the same time angling for his own betterment. That was the aspect of Uncle Joseph's character that must have rankled the most – that uncanny ability of his to turn every situation to his own material advantage, the way he always managed to advance his station in spite of his aversion to honest work, and his professed disdain of corrupt materialism. Mother always said it boiled down to his life-long talent of "marrying well." Three times he improved his holdings, first by his betrothal to a Lyon, and next by marrying a Sherwood, and finally, to assure his creature comforts to the very end of his days, by combining his estate with one of the widowed daughters of the mighty Sturges's.

By the spring of 1777, with the British army stationed just across the Sound, one of the surest routes to a family pew in the front of a church in Connecticut was to rise up the ranks of the militia. Nobody knew this better than Uncle Joseph. And yes, if one was clever enough, there were handy profits to be gained in the business of patriotism. I was there when Father accused him of working a scheme involving willing substitutes for wealthy men who were able to pay their way out of their military obligations. Joseph, of course, took great umbrage at this, and suggested that my father should in the future keep such unfounded suspicions to himself lest, he cautioned, other parishioners and members of the Committee might be freshly reminded that he was yet to sign his Oath of Fidelity.

But here's the odd truth. In spite of all of Uncle Joseph's airs and shortcomings, when that man spoke, people listened. My older brother Will and I surely did. We both secretly vowed to defy Father's wishes and join his Company of Home Guards – or perhaps even the Connecticut Continentals – as soon as we turned sixteen. For William that would be in just a matter of months, while I'd have to wait a few years, a fact I found painful to bear, especially now that I had seen the Redcoats land at Compo. There was something about the sight of those invading soldiers swarming on the beach that stirred me deep inside. Perched there in the hemlock I felt an anger I had never felt before, an emotion so dark and red and primal it defied expression – and it frightened me.

Here's another odd truth. In spite of all the anger and bitterness, the suffering and the loss of life and property during those years, the Christian capacity to forgive (some might say more like the human capacity to forget) is what prevails. At times these days it seems almost as if nothing of consequence ever happened. We returned so readily to the rhythms or our daily lives, accepting whatever fate was left to us. It's almost as if the decade of war never existed. We eventually forgave all those high and mighty Patriots that brought us down. Including Elijah Abel, including Uncle Joseph. Yes, even him, for after all is said and done, who am I to question his motives? I know that the man whose zeal and excesses brought harm to so many, loved his brother; loved the rest of us too. Of that I am quite certain, an opinion keeping me at odds with my brothers and sisters who still contend our uncle was a calculating fiend.

What poppycock! We may a-had no choice but to forgive Uncle Joseph in public, but in private, when it truly counts, we waren't nearly such forgivin Christians, and I mean Haynes waren't neither. Come, Haynes, think of all them nights (or more like all them early mornings) when we stumbled out of the tavern. It was during them heavy drinking years of ourn. We wheezed our way up the hill an turns south towards me humble farm, a route that took us directly past Uncle Joseph's door, at the place where one a his tarnal wives – I can't remember which'n – decided years ago that the entrance to a residence as esteemed as the mighty Bennett homestead ought-a be graced with a fancy rot iron arch. As any passerby could plainly see, this archway is tasteless and out of all proportion, with sad-looking wisteria vines poking up from either side, and as Ol Bacchus would allus have it, the time it took you and me to wend our way from Disbrow's to that tarnal gate was the time it took our bladders to revolt against the awful abuses we had jest inflicted upon them. Thus you have the makings of our secret ritual; a rondy-view we faithfully attended to for decades. With one hand employed for the purpose of taking aim and with the other raised in a fist to shake at the big old darkened house, we unleashed buckets of sour-smelling revenge upon Uncle Joseph's gate and wisteria vines, which now I think of it may explain why they never took fully to root and are yet to blossom.

I don't mean to give no discredit to you my friend, may God rest your loving sole, I wish only to set the record straight. Uncle Joe may a loved us all, and he may a had his politics right in a general sense, but underneath his tarnal deerskin britches he was a scheming son-of-a-bitch, plain and simple. Uncle Joseph forgiven? My arse!

The Sounds on Compo Road

On the night the British marched past our house, I gulped down the supper saved for me in the stew pot before we children were sent forthwith to our beds in the loft. Very little sleep was taken. I was fearful that my uncles, especially Uncle Joseph, might do something untoward that night. Concerned, yet secretly hopeful. Hopeful that they would succeed in rounding up a detachment of willing Patriots and strike a fast and telling blow. Yes, Uncle Joseph looked foolish parading about in his homespun coat and linen hunting shirt, taking on the part of the rugged Minute-man. And yes, I instinctively sided with those who said it would be wiser to wait until a larger force could be properly assembled. A force strong enough and with the experienced leadership needed to make a difference – but even young as I was, I also sensed it would be important to send a message to the occupying army in New York that Connecticut stood ready to fight, and that they could not count on the Loyalists among us to come out in numbers.

In our loft that evening, not long after my parents had raked the fire and gone to bed, my siblings and I – save the littlest ones – found ourselves crowded by the window that faced the road that ran by our door just a few paces below. The night was as dark as ink. A steady light rain was pattering on the roof over our heads. The wind drifting through the opened window had turned colder, so we crowded close.

None of us spoke for the longest time until Esther craned her neck and grabbed hold of my arm. "Is that a storm I hear?" she sputtered.

We leaned forward together and held our breaths, kneeling by the open window, spellbound. It was a rumbling sound unlike anything we had ever heard, so difficult to place within the context of our experience, but whatever it was, it was steadily approaching, growing ever louder. In a few moments, a different sound began to float above the mysterious droning, a sound familiar, the squeaking of wagon wheels, yet so wrong to be heard at such an hour.

"Look!" Esther cried again, craning her neck sharply to the right. "Torches!"

We all looked towards the beach and could see lantern lights flickering behind the trees that lined the road. The sound of the marching was hard upon us now, filling the entire loft. Some muffled voices were starting to be heard too, mingled with the sharp squeaking of the oxcarts, and to our surprise, an occasional peal of laughter.

Just then an officer out on the road shouted "Com-pan-y halt!" a command that was immediately repeated by another officer off to our right, and then by another officer still a bit further down the road, and then by yet another – until an entire string of "halts" could be heard trailing off into the night like the sound of a grouse flushed across a field.

"They stretch for a mile!" Nathan panted as we leapt from the window, and I was suddenly feeling quite certain that our house was about to be set aflame. We started to race towards the stairs to roust our parents, when the rumbling of the boots and the squeaking of the wheels were taken up yet again, and we settled back at the window. After a few minutes we heard the snorts of oxen under the shouts of "Gee!" and more soldiers came, followed by what sounded like horse-drawn wagons. Most of the heaviest rumbling had passed up the road to our north, and just as we were starting to hope that the army and any danger was about to pass us by, a fusillade of musket fire came echoing out of the distance.

Pandemonium ensued.

Drums rolled and whips cracked. Officers were shouting orders in all directions while we children careened about the room, tripping over beds, kicking shoes and pillows as the babies wailed in their cribs. It took us a moment or two to realize that Father was shouting to us from down in the kitchen. "Haynes! Nathan! Ester! Mary! Pick up the babes! Get down here! Hurry!"

Father stood at the bottom of the stairs lighting our steps with a candle. He was fully dressed, his banyan replaced by his cocked hat. Mother was fully dressed too – neither of them had gone to bed. Cesar was also in the house, fully dressed and leading Grandfather William towards the door to the cellar, which was where we were ordered to go. As we passed through the kitchen I caught sight of Father's English fowling piece lying on the table.

Gaylee was already down in the damp dirt cellar sitting on a bench surrounded by a few candles. She scooted over and signaled for Grandfather to sit beside her. We sat in numbed silence on some barrels and crates set in a semi-circle, listening to the footfalls of Father crossing and re-crossing the floor above us. He and Cesar were pulling open the window sashes in the kitchen one by one, and slowly creaking open each of the shutters. Drums continued to roll in the distance, joined now by the sound of fifes.

"That fool Joseph has gotten his wish," Gaylee despaired. "Found his courage, I daresay, after several of his Rattle-Skulls with the lads at Disbrow's."

"Yes," Mother concurred while gazing up at the ceiling, following the crossings of Cesar and Father's footsteps with her eyes. "And may God help us now."

Bones in the Kitchen

There came suddenly a sharp banging at our front door, with a cacophony of voices out in the yard while Father and Cesar's footfalls fell hard on the floor above us. I tore up the cellar steps with Mother clamoring behind me. She was pulling on my nightshirt, grabbing at my arms in a vain attempt to keep me from the cellar door, which I managed to kick open, sending it crashing against the wall just as another loud hammering of fists echoed into the kitchen. The heavy planks of our front door began to shake, its hinges straining violently against the jamb as a man – or men – on the other side repeatedly shouldered up against it.

A voice boomed from out on the porch. "Is this the home of Deliverance Bennett?"

Father stood in the middle of the kitchen with his fowler shouldered. A single candle flickered on the table behind the darkened form of his head and chest. "None other!" the resolute silhouette replied. "Pray, state your business!"

In spite of the noise and confusion, we were soon made to understand that the intruders outside our door were, as we had feared, British soldiers, and that they had with them a number of gravely wounded men in need of immediate attention. At first, Father refused to admit them.

"If I open that door they'll send me to the Mines!" he shouted over the barrel of his musket, whereupon Mother ran to him. Father still shouldered his gun and Mother pushed the barrel aside, stepping directly between him and the door. She took hold of both his shoulders and dipped her head forward, compelling him to look her straight in the eye. "The Committee might send you to the Mines if you take these soldiers in," she said in firm even tones, "but God will surely send you to hell if you turn them away."

"It won't matter what you decide!" Gaylee hollered from the head of the cellar stairs with both hands covering her ears. "Unlock that door, Deliverance, 'ere those red devils knock it down!"

I looked back into the kitchen – at the two silhouettes of my parents now standing between the candle and me. Neither one of them moved for what seemed like a dog's age. Meanwhile, the commotion out on our stoop and in the yard continued unabated, with the door shaking and heaving and my brothers and sisters wailing like banshees in the cellar. Torchlight was by then shining through the windows, sending grotesque shadows cavorting about the walls. Our entire house felt to be spinning out of control. Father, at last, nodded to Cesar who was standing wide-eyed beside the door. "Go ahead," he said to him calmly, his fowler still shouldered. Cesar took a breath and unlatched the bolts, and in spilled a crimson-coated Regular with a lantern in his hand. The soldier immediately began pushing chairs aside and was imploring mother to clear the table when two more Redcoats barged into the kitchen, carrying between them the first of the wounded men on a canvas litter. Next through the door came an officer wielding a pistol.

"Sir," he directed to my father with his pistol raised, "kindly lower your firearm." Father complied and once the fowler was leaning safely against the wall the officer turned to my mother. "Madam," he said in perfect King's English. "I am Lieutenant Digby Soames, and we wish to attend to our wounded. In the comfort of your home, if you please. Out of the cold and the rain."

He then handed his plumed helmet to Cesar who placed it among the assortment of seashells that decorated our mantelpiece. By this time, I had slunk out of the way, back against the far wall. I gazed across the kitchen and there, glinting in the candlelight, was the very same silver skull that beckoned me down from the tree with the same two crossed bones held in its ghastly grimace, its dark sunken eyes holding me fast from across the room.

"Well I'll be blown," the officer chuckled, turning in my direction. "If it isn't our little pigeon spy!"

Painful Ordeals

The first soldier through the door, who turned out to be a company surgeon, took charge of the situation, directing the litter carriers to carefully place the wounded man on our kitchen table. He then motioned to the door, waving in two more Redcoats who were carrying yet another wounded soldier – this one a Private for the Provincials. He signaled that they place the lad, who was moaning piteously, onto the floor directly in front of the fire. Next to appear was a third wounded combatant, this one with a heavily bandaged hand and able to walk without assistance. All three of the wounded were clad in the green coats of the Provincials, which I could see caused Mother great consternation.

"Pray, what of Jabez Lockwood?" she asked fervently of the man with the injured hand just as he was sliding down the wall to take a seat on the floor. "He hails from Norfield. Is he marching with you? Has he been harmed?"

"Ah, yes, Ma'am," the man replied, "Mr. Lockwood is one of the General's guides. I can assure you he is unharmed. I saw him moving forward with the column 'ere I was taken here."

While this conversation was going on Father pushed his way through the small crowd and pivoted Gaylee towards the cellar door, asking her to stay down there with Grandfather and the children. He was about to push me through the cellar door as well until Lt. Soames stopped him, saying that there might soon be a job or two for a fellow of my spit and spirit. After a pause, Father assented and instructed me to stand out of the way, in the far corner. I stood obediently beside Cesar until the wounded man on the table screamed out in pain, whereupon getting a closer look became too difficult to resist. Although Cesar grabbed hold of my arm, I broke free and quietly positioned myself behind one of the soldiers who was standing at the end of the table. The surgeon had just removed one of the wounded man's boots, and after unwinding a temporary bandage, he began cutting through the fabric of his blood-soaked breeches with a pair of shearers. There I saw a jagged black hole just above his knee. Blood began to ooze from the wound, which the surgeon quickly covered with a fresh bandage, instructing one of the soldiers to hold it there with pressure.

"What is your name, Captain?" he inquired of the man who lay on his back on the table. The stricken officer was holding his hat on his chest along with his powdered wig hanging lifelessly from the brim like a rabbit skin. The surgeon took the hat and wig and tossed them towards the wall. Even in the poor light you could see that the man's face was ashen, and that his wounded leg was out of kilter, extending from his upper thigh at a sickening, unnatural angle. His name was Daniel Lyman, and he was imploring the doctor to do all he could to save his leg.

"What about this poor boy?" my mother called from the hearth. She was crouched on the wooden floor by his side, gently stroking the young lad's forehead, holding one of his hands.

"Keep him as warm and comfortable as you can," the surgeon replied and instructed me to put new wood on the fire. "He'll likely be asking soon for water."

The soldier sitting against the wall leaned over and placed his good hand on my mother's shoulder. He introduced himself as Private Israel Beers and told her that the young soldier's name was Stephen Betts, that he was from Norwalk and that he had taken a musket ball in the gut, something we all immediately understood to be a death sentence.

"Daniel," the surgeon said turning again toward his patient on the table. "The ball has broken your thighbone and we will need to set it, but first we are going to roll you over to see if there's an exit wound."

Turning over the wounded man was no easy task. It took all four soldiers to get him on his stomach while the surgeon did his best to hold his leg steady and keep it from jarring. The surgeon waited for a few seconds after they had him on his stomach, allowing Lyman's cries of agony to subside, and then told him that he was a lucky man. The ball hadn't gone clear through which would have been the preferred diagnosis, but was lodged just below the skin and, he assured him, removing it would be as easy as lancing a boil. The entire operation, cutting out the musket ball, returning Lyman to his back and setting his broken leg into a wooden splint, took several minutes plus large quantities of Father's whiskey and all four soldiers to quiet and hold him down. The worst was when the surgeon proceeded to stick his finger deep into the hole, probing for gory bits of clothing that he pulled out and wiped onto the table, saying it was vitally important to get all the pieces out lest they fester and condemn him to a slow and agonizing death in a week or so.

With the worst of Lyman's ordeal finished, the surgeon's attentions turned to the soldier on the floor with Mother. The poor lad was indeed asking for water, and calling also in his delirium for *his* mother, while mine sat on the floor next to him quietly speaking into his ear. "I'm here, Stephen," she gently purred. "Right beside you my dear, brave boy."

The surgeon knelt beside the young Private and felt for a pulse. His face was the color of oyster shells; his lips had turned grey. Mother stared up at the surgeon as he conducted his examination as if hoping against hope that his expression might suddenly brighten and tell her that the Private's condition was better than at first assumed, and that he might pull through. But all the doctor did was gently draw in the lapels of the young soldier's green coat, blanketing the bloody bandage that was wadded on his stomach.

Father and Lt. Soames were at the back of the room, discussing the next steps that needed to be taken. The four Regulars were to make their way back up the road to rejoin the column. The surgeon would return to the beach with the wounded where they could signal for the hospital ship. Soames would accompany that latter party, to scout for it along the road, while we would be supplying a suitable means of conveyance.

"Haynes," Father barked at me, "get yourself dressed and help

Cesar hitch Shem and Ham to the hay wagon."

Cesar and I grabbed one of the soldiers' pine torches and made haste for the barn where we collared the oxen and hitched them to the wain. Out in the yard, the two Reds began pawing nervously at the ground in the circle of our torchlight; enshrouded in a cloud of mist created by their breaths. Lt. Soames mounted his horse as the litter-carriers carefully settled Captain Lyman and Private Betts into the cart. Israel Beers climbed aboard and turned to give a hand up to my mother, who over the loud protestations of my father had insisted upon staying at the side of her young charge for as long as she could. The surgeon covered them all with as many woolen blankets as we were able to supply, while Father sat beside Cesar at the front of the cart. Before they left the yard, he beckoned me to his side.

"My fowler is in the kitchen, primed and loaded," he said. "Everyone but you is to remain in the cellar until we return. We should be back long before morning. There may be Cowboys and Skinners out and about, so remain alert."

Satisfied that I had taken well his instructions, he cracked the whip over the shoulders of the oxen and the cart lurched forward. I started to head back into the kitchen but ran instead to catch them up. When I got even, I fell into a trot.

"Father," I stammered between breaths "... there's something ... I need ... to know ... how is it ... that the soldier ... the one ... out on the steps ... could have known your name?"

"We will talk in the morning," Father replied and cracked the whip once again. I watched them disappearing into the gloom. Only Cesar looked back, raising his hand in a hesitant wave, and in the next moment they were gone. I remained standing out on the road with the rain dripping from the edges of my hat until I could no longer hear the squeaking of the wheels. We were to talk about it in the morning Father promised, although we never did. Not even after thirty years.

An Unwelcome Appearance

"Lord have mercy," was all Gaylee managed to say when she joined us in the kitchen the next morning at daybreak. The place was a frightful mess. We thought we had most of the blood cleaned up the night before, but there was far more of it than we had been able to see by candlelight, and it had gotten everywhere. It was spattered across the table and chairs and was puddled and not yet fully dried here and there on the floor by the hearth. There were ruddy boot prints of it up and down the front steps, with handprints on the walls. If a neighbor had walked in just then we'd have all been sent to the Mines. There was no alternative but to get the kitchen and entranceway back up to tip as quickly as possible. The regular chores would have to be left to Cesar. All our energies were set immediately to scrubbing the floors and the walls and the furniture, while Mother got out a washtub to launder her blood-soaked garments in lye and cold water. She was clearly affected by the fate of Private Betts. He was still clinging to life, she had told us, when the Marines loaded him into the launch. To her thinking, a truly merciful God would have taken him long before then. The cold rain and the lurching of the oxcart over the ruts in the road to Cedar Point only added to his terrible suffering. "No man should have to endure such misery in his final moments," she hissed, while angrily rubbing the soap across the folds of her petticoat, "much less such a youngster, in the flower of his life."

It took an hour or so to get the house in order. Mother was able to remove most of the stains from her shift and linen petticoat, but her gown and quilted skirt were ruined. While the rest of us emptied our buckets out in the yard, she dispatched the worst of her bloodied clothes to the incinerator. All in all, it was a grim business.

Later in the day we found ourselves congregated yet again in the kitchen, this time waiting for Father to return from Disbrow's. We knew he'd come back with the latest news from the patrons gathered there, and were anxious to hear of it. Had the Redcoats reached Danbury? Had they torched houses along the way? Was the Militia gathered in good numbers? Were they able to put up any form of defense before the heavy rains set in? Such were the concerns we were able to give voice to. What we couldn't bear to speak of however, and what we worried about the most, was whether anyone had seen the Redcoats enter our house, or, more unsettling than even that, had any of our neighbors seen Father and Mother drive the wounded men to the beach in the oxcart.

We did our best to occupy ourselves as the day wore on. I sat by the window oiling Father's prized English fowling gun, rubbing down its tiger striped stock, taking extra care to bring out the shine of the brass lock plate with its intricate engraving of a stag surrounded by oak leaves. Gaylee stirred our supper as it heated over the fire while Mother and my younger siblings busied themselves making candles. Grandfather William slouched in his rocker. It had grown late in the day with the light beginning to dim. Each of us was quietly lost in our own thoughts. The only sound was an occasional spit and hiss from the fire, barely discernable above the steady rattling of the wind and the rain at the windows.

Sometime before dusk Esther peered through the shutters and wondered aloud, "Shouldn't William be home by now?" It was a three-hour trek to Aunt Sarah and Uncle Jabez's, perhaps four or five with the cattle. He and Jabe would have arrived in Norfield after nightfall on Friday and were expected to be back home with us well before noontime today. Mother didn't bother to respond to Esther's question. All of us knew the answer, and we could plainly see by the lines dug into her brow that one more worry had been added to her mountain of them. I'm sure she was wishing Father had never sent boys on what could be a dangerous piece of man's work even in the most tranquil of times. I, of course, wasn't the least bit surprised that William hadn't gotten home. I knew what he and Jabe were planning!

Father didn't return from Disbrow's until after dark, and to Mother's great despair, he came through the door without William. He told us that quite a crowd remained at the tavern, but none had seen or heard anything about two boys driving a small herd of cattle up the Newtown Road. Meanwhile, a steady stream of Minute-men had drifted in throughout the day, stopping to dry themselves by the fire and receive refreshment. General Silliman had left orders there for all willing and able men to head to Danbury via the Redding Road. The feeling was that no fighting would be possible in weather as foul as we were having that day, and there wasn't much hope that the Continental stores could be defended, but all agreed a properly organized force of Militia would be able to inflict serious damage upon the Redcoats once they were ready to leave town. And as long as their ships remained at anchor by Cockenoe, the column was more than likely going to return to Compo following roughly the same route as they had just taken. With the help of Providence, it may even be possible to lay a trap and bag the entire invasion force!

Several houses had indeed been torched overnight, Father learned, and the depravations that General Tryon was sure to inflict on the residents of Danbury were being wildly speculated. Patriot blood was running hot enough already, Father relayed, when a courier burst in with word that the house of our cousin Elias Bennett of Easton was among those that had been burned to the ground by the Lobsterbacks, and that his wife had been savagely treated by them. Elias had ridden off at midnight to join Silliman while Anna, who was in a delicate condition, mounted a horse, carrying with her a bag of Spanish dollars and headed for Compo where her mother still resided. As she was crossing through Coley's Flats she happened upon a group of mounted British scouts, the courier reported, who beat her with the backs of their swords, stripped her of her clothing, stealing her horse and the bag of money, leaving the poor woman to die in the cold and the rain. She lost her baby, the messenger cried, and lies herself near death in the home of a kind citizen who found her wandering about his yard and took her in.

"I told anyone who would listen – don't be swayed by such breathless talk," Father declared as he sat down by Grandfather William, patting him gently on the arm.

"Oh you foolish, hard-headed man!" Gaylee cried. "Why enter into it?"

"Because," Father replied with some irritation, "of all people, I would arouse more suspicion by staring silently in my grog. Reasoned objections to speech of that kind are commonly expected of me."

"Yes, but you should have been more guarded! Why not let the lads have fun with their stories?"

"Because, dear Mother, in this particular instance I had just moments earlier received confirmation that the courier's story was a far cry from the truth. Elias's wife did indeed cross into the Redcoat's camp last night, but when the scouts saw her condition they allowed her to pass, and is, at this very moment, safely tucked inside the home of her parents where she delivered her baby. A healthy girl, I hear, named Abigail."

Gaylee's expression softened with this bit of cheerful news, and Mother looked up from her candle molds. "Did anyone listen to your Toryisms?" she asked.

"Nay, I was shouted down by many. But you mustn't worry. A smattering of others spoke in support of me. There were a few other level-headed men at the bar who agreed that if Washington himself didn't consider the stores at Danbury important enough to defend with more than a mere handful of Continentals, why should a collection of farmers, clerks and blacksmiths be expected to risk their all?"

It didn't surprise me to hear that Father had been shouted down. If he weren't my father, I'd have dressed him down myself right then and there in the kitchen. I had grown weary of seeing him so cautious, so hesitant, always the one to advise others to remember who they are and, as he often phrased it, to "apply reason before passion." Here's what I believed at the time: You can't bring "reason" to a brawl, and Tryon was a no-holds barred butcher willing to use whatever means possible to bring ordinary Americans to their knees. Maybe Father had heard from the

Allen's and it was true that the British scouts allowed Anna Bennett to pass through their camp unharmed. I can't be sure of precisely what he had been told. What I can be certain of though – and what I correctly understood even at the tender age of thirteen – is that no matter what bits of gossip were passed along to my father that afternoon, he would have only listened to that which comported with his Loyalist leanings. To Father, old John Bull trumped the upstart Uncle Sam every time. Clinging so strongly to this conviction made him, in the final reckoning, just as unreasonable as those he so readily accused of having been separated from their senses.

Looking back, it's hard to remember what enraged me the most, and made me so determined to seek out and join the Patriots. I suppose it was the accumulation of events: watching the Redcoats swarming on our beach, encountering the Dragoon with the horses he had stolen from Uncle Moses, the report of the craven scouts tearing the clothes from our cousin Anna, a helpless expectant mother, and the mere notion of Stephen Betts. I too, couldn't get that young fellow out of my mind. Through the eyes of the father and grandfather I have now become, it is nigh impossible to fathom how it could be that witnessing a young soldier suffer such unimaginable pain would have done nothing but turn me against the war. Yet even now, as I sit at my table writing this, the sight of the blood spilt upon our kitchen floor is but a dim memory – hardly anything more consequential than a few splashes of incriminating evidence that needed to be scrubbed away. What remains as vivid as yesterday on the other hand, is the picture in my mind of the uniforms the soldiers wore, and of their military kits leaned up against our wall. So smartly trimmed were their coats and vests! So new were their Brown Bess muskets! So brimming with lead were their cartouches! And, to my thinking, so dissolute and evil were their intents. Any invading army as grand, as arrogant and as well equipped as this, needed to be stopped. As the morning and then the long afternoon wore on, I brought to mind the image of General Washington painted so vividly for us by Wake Burritt the year before, and pictured myself marching step-for-step with the brave Patriots who were no doubt gathering at that moment with an aim to repel these evil invaders from our country. While Gaylee stirred our evening's gruel and the others sat making their candles, I quietly plotted to steal away. When the moment was right, I'd take the fowler down from the rack and go find William and Jabe. Once united, we'd swear our oaths and head towards the sounds of battle.

"Yes, fine," Gaylee worried, "but what word of the gunfire so close to our door last night? There must have been many a-glass raised to that brave bit of soldiering!"

"Indeed there was," Father replied. "'The Gallant Seventeen' is what they're calling them, with both Joe and Moses credited as being among their number. According to the denizens of Disbrow's, at least a dozen of the Lobsterbacks were sent straight to hell last night as a result of their sure and deadly aim."

"Where are those two sons of mine now?" Gaylee wanted to know.

"With Silliman in Redding would be my guess –"

"But Dell," Mother began, unable to mask the worry in her voice, "there must have been talk of the casualties. There surely must have been questions directed at you about Redcoats who may have been killed or wounded so near our house."

"None," Father assured her. "From what I could tell, the Redcoats chased our gallant heroes past the wall and into the alder swamp. No patriots were left in the area to make mischief for us."

"Don't be so certain," Gaylee put in. "They may have scarpered, but eventually someone will wonder about the aftermath of their skirmish." She pulled a chair towards the fire and sat beside Grandfather. "Joseph may be intent upon chasing after the Redcoats today," she continued, "but give him time. He'll have questions for ye."

"I don't believe he will," was all Father could think to say.

"Ah, but I know my sons," Gaylee said with a wistful sigh, while leaning in towards her husband. "Joseph is fool enough to ask you about it publicly … and you are fool enough to answer him with the truth."

Just then there was a sharp knocking at our door and we all sat up straight. Father gave Mother a long look before walking over to see who could be out and about in such foul weather. I half expected to see a posse of Aldermen standing out on our porch and believe we all had similar thoughts. The door opened with a rush of wind, and in stepped Ezra Weed.

Father's face darkened as the uninvited guest sidled into the room. "Pray, what brings you here?" he queried, "I sent you back to Captain Nash yesterday afternoon!"

Ezra removed his hat and shook out the rain. His tattered cloak was sodden and dripping onto the floor. He started to run his fingers through the wet tangles of his long black hair until his hand became caught by the snarls. "Yes, indeed sir, but you see, the ferry waren't running with all the fuss about. I was headin' back when I saw the torches comin' through the gap at Bennett's Rocks and decided to duck in'ta Broom's. There waren't nobody home, which I s'pose you knows already. Figgered nobody'd mind a temp'ry boarder."

"Did you see the Redcoats pass?" Father asked.

"More like heard 'em I'd say."

I stood to speak. "Did you — "

Father silenced me with a raise of his hand and faced Weed. "But Nash and I had an agreement!" he protested. "You are meant to be with him now."

"Yessir, but there was a message waitin' for me at Disbrow's. The Cap'n wants me to stay put he does. So, I'm jest here to inform ye," he continued with a bow, "that I'm back in me room now, and at your service."

By this time Gaylee had gotten up from her chair by the hearth and was standing at Father's elbow with a poker grasped tightly in her hand, glowering at Ezra. She appeared ready to burst into flames. "Send the miscreant away!" she spattered with an angry shake of the fire iron. "We have no need for his service!" Father spun around to restrain her, prying the poker loose from her hand and whispered something to quieten her down before turning again to address Ezra.

"You spent last night at Mose and Neesy's farm?" he inquired casually whilst seeing him to the door.

"That's right, sir," he confirmed while turning to survey the room.

His hat was still held obsequiously in his hands as a gush of wind from the open doorway flapped at his begrimed cloak. "'Twas quite the int'restin' evenin' … waren't it?"

With the door slammed shut behind Ezra, Gaylee glowered at Father, the tip of her nose close upon his face. "There is no good that can come from this, Dell! My God, Son! Dispatch that creature out into the storm and do it now! Pray, why must you allow for even the smallest show of kindness when you know as well as I that he is a spy for Nash?"

Father drew Gaylee into his arms. "There, there, Mother," he purred reassuringly. "That poor fellow's no spy. And even if he were, what harm can he possibly do us now?"

What harm can do? That crafty cretin? As allus, Uncle Dell's acting all up'n blinded by his natural-born Christian kindness. He allus saw the best in people — one a them tarnal traits, as if you needs reminding, that has a way of coming back an biting you on the arse. Not that any of this matters no more, but thank ye, my dear departed friend, I now realize what happened at our humble end of the road that night! We had some silver pieces gone missing. Ma an Da thought they had put all our valuables in the trunk but when we was finally settled back in the house we noticed how we was down a candlestick or two. It ware a mystery! Mother blamed the larceny on Broom, but Father said, nay. It's far more likely, says he, that in all the rukus we dropt them down the well or threw them out with the slops. When you're expecting to see your house torched and you finds nothing more'n a few bits of silver gone missing, yer happy enough to leave well enough alone. We soon forgot about our losses. Who needs silver candlesticks anyway? All that polishing!

Whatever became of Weed I wonder? That tacky-fingered old snake never made it a Missippi to get him one of Montfort Brown's two hundred acre tracks, that much we know for certain because nobody got em. Can't remember ever seeing him hereabouts, leastwise not after he showed up with that tarnal wig. As far as I know he simply up an disappeared, or maybe he died, or jest sunk back into the ooze where he belong. – JB

Escape to Norfield

It was an hour before dawn on Monday when I saw my chance to grab the fowling piece and creep from the house. My plan was to join William and Jabe and in due course, the Militia. The improving weather meant traveling the eight miles to Aunt Sarah and Uncle Jabez's farm in Norfield would be easy enough. We had received word the day before that the Redcoats had left Danbury early in the morning via the Ridgefield Road. Based on that heading, their route back to the ships would take them through Wilton Parish and only a mile or so away from the Lockwood's door on Godfrey Road. I figured that would be the best place to start looking for them.

Instead of heading up Compo Road where prying eyes might see me, I stepped off our porch and snuck down to the river where there was enough salt grass to give me some cover. From Jessup's dock on the edge of the marsh I made my way back up to solid ground where I could easily wade across Dead Man's Brook and then steal through the back yards in the village. The sun still hadn't yet poked through the trees when I came to the Country Road Bridge. There wasn't a soul to be seen in the diffused grey light allowing me to safely cross and head north. Reaching a rise left me with an unencumbered view back down the river. In the gap between the hills, I could see Bald Mountain profiled in the distance. The sun had just risen, turning the handful of gnarled candlewood pines that dotted its rounded top into tiny slashes of gold. The weather had indeed broken. There were wisps of fog lying flat in the hollows, all covered by a pale blue dome of sky bringing with it the promise of drying roads and a reasonably easy trek to Lockwood's farm. The only thing slowing me down was a need to remain ever vigilant against the possibility of running into patrolling Redcoats. The byways ahead of their advance were sure to be reconnoitered, and while their scouts might allow an unarmed woman anticipating an interesting family occurrence to pass through their lines without incident, a boy out on the road with a fowling piece and a bag of powder wouldn't be so gently treated.

The countryside through which the road to Norfield cleaved was as dark and heavily wooded as it remains today. To my left, the West Branch was tumbling fast and hard, the swampy bogs along its banks were brimmed and oiled with skunk cabbages, but the road, as I had hoped, was reasonably dry. The understory beneath the towering oaks and chestnuts was greening with the coming of spring. As I strode at a brisk pace up the deeply rutted road, all my senses were keyed to the possibility of approaching horsemen. My heart was pounding, yet I knew there was no time to even think about pausing to rest. I must keep going, and so I picked up my pace, looking back over my shoulder frequently to make sure I wasn't being followed, and at every new turn I came upon, I took stock of the terrain, making note of where the densest thickets could be found should the need arise to suddenly disappear into one.

I wasn't a mile from Godfrey Road when the sound of horses sent me scurrying up an embankment and diving into a briar patch. They were coming at a canter, down the hill in my direction. From my hiding place amongst the thorns and behind a downed tree I was unable to determine who the riders were. There were three, maybe four in all, and after they trailed away, I broke through the brambles and slid back down to the road. From the look of the hoof prints there were at least three riders. I felt certain they hadn't seen me, but no sooner had I turned to continue on my way when a horseman, who must have doubled back, came soaring down the embankment to block my path. He reined to a sudden stop, with his big bay horse straining against the bit, snorting and showing its teeth. Foamy sheets of sweat were streaking down the stallion's neck and shoulders, lunging and stamping so near to my face I couldn't see the man pulling upon the reins.

"Why, if it isn't our gallant Pigeon Spy!" boomed a familiar voice, and I found myself looking yet again up the barrel of a Light Dragoon's carbine. I jumped back and saw that the soldier glaring at me from beneath the leather helmet with its chestnut colored plume was none other than Lieutenant Digby Soames.

He motioned his carbine towards the fowler I was holding at my side. "I'll have that," he said calmly, giving me no choice but to surrender up my firearm. "It's a fine piece," he offered while carefully examining the ornate lock and butt plates. "English made I see," and with that he gripped the end of the barrel in both of his hands and violently dashed it up against the nearest tree, splitting the stock nearly in two and instantly rendering my father's prized fowler useless. "And, now 'tis English un-made," he said with a wry smile and courteous nod, and handed the ruined firearm back to me.

"What are we to do with you?" he asked while taking up his carbine again, gazing at me from over its sights. He took a breath and turned his head in the direction the other cavalrymen had ridden. "By all rights I should take you prisoner."

He thought for another moment while I remained standing below him. I was fully expecting him to drag me off to the British van, when without another word he extended a hand and pulled me onto the back of his horse. The humiliation of being so easily bagged caused me great distress. My captor could have at least shown me enough respect to bind my hands together, but he obviously felt confident that the sight of his sword and carbine would keep me from leaping to the ground and making a dash for the trees. Resigned to disgrace, I settled glumly behind the kit attached to his saddle. "There's no time to spare," he explained from over his shoulder while spurring hard towards Godfrey Road.

To my great surprise, we rode straight to the Lockwood's farm, which was teeming with activity. A pair of rag tags stood by the gate at the front of the house, with another pair of equally dissolute looking characters further up the road towards Georgetown. A number of horses, saddled and ready to ride, were tied to the hitching post. My Uncle Jabez was engaged in conversation with a tall, neatly dressed man out in the yard at the side of the house. There was something about this man I didn't like. His distinctive maroon waistcoat and his shock of unkempt ginger hair looked both dangerous and familiar to me, although I couldn't at first think precisely why. The entire scene had an unsettling affect upon me; as if I had just awakened from one of those dreams immediately forgotten save for the queasy turning it leaves in your stomach. Just as I was about to get a better look at the ginger-haired man's face, a group of five or six other men carrying muskets and knapsacks emerged from the barn and crowded around them. Most unsettling of all was that nobody in the yard seemed the least bit alarmed about a British cavalryman suddenly arriving at the gate.

"What brings you back so soon?" my uncle asked upon our approach, which I thought a strange query. Who were these men, I wondered, and what the devil were they all doing here? When Uncle Jabez saw it was me on the back of the Lieutenant's mount he chortled and said something to the effect that he had half expected to see me appear. He looked over the shoulder of the ginger haired man and nodded towards the barn, a sign to Soames to take me there, and while we were trotting away the man in the maroon coat turned, allowing me to get my first clear view of his face. He was the unpleasant fellow we had met two years ago at the home of Thatcher Sears, the man Cesar told us to be ever wary of, the man he called John French.

My dear Haynes, how is it possible that you didn't meediately recognize that nasty feller? Good Lord, man, he was one of The Committee's most carefully watched Tories! Uncle Joe called him one of the damndest enemies of liberty that ever was. They tried getting the goods on him for donkey's years! He was a man you surely should'a known even if you never did run into him at the Sears place. He was the rascal what made a fortune in rum an tea an God-knows-what-other tin pots an pinching shears he could get his hands on. And to think he ran this gainful ring a his'n right neath the nose of everbody, including our very own Home Guards! Yes by jingo, old Frenchy was one of our good Uncle Joe's fiercest competitors or closest collaborators, takes yer pick.

Maybe it was because I lived closer to the ferry than you did. Maybe that's why I knew the carroty-pated man was John French even before you said who he was. I was allus crabbing or fishing down by the landing. I saw what went on. Yea, I can still see him waiting on the dock in his fancypants maroon waistcoat looking business-like, an can still hear the passengers twittering off'n the side, askin the ferryman to inspect them

85

crates on that dandy's dolly. I think he owned a general store of some sorts in Norwalk, but everybody knew that were just a ruse for the aldermen. Personally, I rather liked the man. I was allus happy to help him hoist his bundles from the dolly onto a wagon or visa versa. He'd give me handfuls of rock candy. Extra heavy loads, and he'd even pay a few bits!

Everone in Compo knew John French. Yer father surely did. You mightn't likes to hear it, but Uncle Del was at the ferry doing business with that devil fairly regular. Why was it, do you think, Gaylee allus had plenty a tea to brew? Do you really think yer father would allow a squabble with some siffliss-headed Sovereign on the other side of the Atlantic ocean get in the way of that old hellcat's breakfast and afternoon quaffs of tea? Where the devil did you think he got the stuff? You think India Lap-sang grew on trees?

I tell you what. I learned a thing or two about business from Mr. French – was just old enough to begin thinking bout setting up a few lines of trade of me own. I sometimes wonder what would a happened had the war lasted a few more years. Yes sir-ee, nothing greases the wheels of commerce better'n a good hot war! -- JB

"What of William and Jabe and our cows?" I urgently inquired of my uncle.

"Your cows are safely penned below," he replied without looking up. "Aunt Sara will tend to you anon."

The Lockwood's barn was large and imposing – just what you'd expect of a prosperous Connecticut farmer. It had three ample bay doors – all barred shut on this morning – and was built into the hill giving it a cellar for livestock that opened to the pens at the back. Above one of the side bays there was a gable extending from the main roof with a shuttered window topped by a hoisting post. Soames walked his horse over to the center bay. A sour-faced man with a musket was leaning against the wall next to the cutout for the cold weather door. It too was barred shut. The whole barn looked as tightly sealed as a rum barrel. Soames ordered me to dismount and tossed me down the broken fowler along with Father's gun bag emptied of its powder and ball. "He'll be no trouble," he said to the man at the door before steering his horse back to the road.

As soon as Soames cleared off, the man with the musket put his boot to my backside and shoved me through the narrow hatch, sending me sprawling to the middle of the threshing floor. I heard the door slamming behind me, rattling in its hinges and engulfing the interior of the barn in darkness. The only available light came from some owl holes cut high into the walls above the rafters. I remember getting slowly to my feet, dusting off my britches while blinking my eyes towards the shafts of light. From some distant corner a pigeon cooed, and I thought I heard a voice calling my name. "William?" I inquired of the gloom. There was no response, save for the rustling wings of the pigeon that had taken flight. As my eyes were beginning to adjust to the dark, the door behind me opened, flooding the barn with daylight. Who's there? I wondered, but before I could even turn around, I took a vicious blow to the back of my skull. Sickening pain went shooting all the way down to my feet, and I was out cold.

Uncle Jabez's Barn

When I regained consciousness, the silhouette of my cousin Jabe's head was all I was able to see. With so little light, it took my brain a few moments to piece together where we were, but after blinking through the pain and fog, I remembered I was in my Aunt and Uncle's barn. What had struck the back of my head so hard? Why were we in the barn, and not sitting by the fire in the kitchen? Who were all those men in the yard and out on the road? I sat up slowly and leaned back against the wall. There was a ringing in my ears and my aching head felt as big as a milk bucket.

"Where is Will?" I slurred.

"I pray not in irons," Jabe said, and moved a little closer, turning my chin sideways in order to inspect the back of my head. "You've got a bump bigger'n a turnip," he observed, "but I suspect you'll live."

Looking about, I could see we were seated inside an empty storage stall. Save for the owl holes above the rafters, all the doors and windows were shuttered closed, making our confines dark and shadowy. There was a wall on the other side of the threshing floor where you'd expect to find another storage bay. In the middle of this wall stood a door that was padlocked shut. Beyond the familiar sounds of the livestock that I could now detect stirring faintly in the cellar below, the barn was eerily quiet at a time of day when it should have been bustling with activity. The stillness weighed in the air like a presence; the unnaturalness of it deepened my anxieties.

"Where is Will?" I asked again.

"Escaped. Two nights ago. Aunt Sarah came with our supper and when the door opened behind her, he took a chance the old sour-puss's musket wouldn't fire and made a dash for it."

"Escaped?" I cried. Perhaps I misheard. "What do you mean, escaped?"

"We were made prisoners," Jabe sighed, hugging his knees to his chest, "and now Cousin, you are a captive too."

"Captives? In our own aunt and uncle's barn?"

Nothing was making any sense. My thoughts began careening at a sickening pitch. The pounding at the back of my head was fierce and disorientating. It seemed as if my confusion and fear and pain had pinned me helplessly against the wall. I felt a wave of nausea and I nearly swooned once again, until a surge of anger allowed me to regain my composure. I got to my feet and boldly ran from the storage bay to the cold weather door. Pushing down on the latch and shouldering with all my strength against the planks did nothing. The door wouldn't budge.

Jabe's voice from behind the dividing wall sounded matter-of-fact. "It's barred from the outside. You can shoulder ever last one of 'em if you have a mind too, but all the doors is barred."

"What about the windows?"

"Barred."

"The hay chutes!" I cried, running back to the storage bay. "We could slide to the cellar!"

Jabe pulled a stick of straw from his mouth and regarded it thoughtfully. "Be my guest, but your brother and I already tried that one, and got good and roughed up for our troubles, not to mention splinters in our arses from the slide. Go on, put your ear to the floor and listen. Hear that growling alongside the cluckings of the chickens and the geese? That's them bastards snoring! There's a whole passel of rum-soaked Cowboys down in that cellar, coming and going at all hours of the day and night, taking turns at sentry. They may be sleeping off their toddies now, but you'll soon know what they're about."

I was incredulous, still not grasping our situation. "Who are we to be so heavily guarded?"

"Well, it ain't just the two of us they're keeping their eyes on. It's what's behind them padlocked doors that counts. They'd a-flicked a pair of scalp nits like us to the fire faster than you can say George Washington if it weren't for Aunt Sarah and Uncle Jez! These fellows ain't your regular-minded Tories. They ain't up to any good, and we're just messing up their affairs. I tell you what Cousin … you won't find a more murderous gang of libertines than what's down in that cellar, or a more fearsome bunch than what goes up and down them stairs behind that padlocked door! No by jingo," he sighed while laying back on a bale of hay for a pillow, "Uncle Jez is Toried through and through, and I reckon he's putting his business where his mouth is. Aunt Sarah is good and Toried too, but bless her heart, she arrives with breakfast, lunch and supper, sweet as can be. Her biscuits and gravy go down a treat. Your brother can be all high and patriot-minded if he wants – and you can get yourself another turnip growing on the back of your skull if you so desire – but this-here Minute-man's content to sit this-here total jamble of a war o-u-t out!"

"Come Jabe!" I cried. "You are making no sense. Tell me what is going on!"

With hands behind his head, and the blade of straw dangling jauntily from the corner of his mouth, Jabe proceeded to fill in as many of the blanks as he could from the bits and pieces of conversations he managed to glean from the other side of the floor and walls during the three days of what he termed his "barn arrest." He started with a piece of good news. Since Jabe had heard no mention of William's capture, he assumed he was able to escape through the yard, and was now somewhere in Bethel where the Militiamen were meant to assemble under General Silliman. Meanwhile, with continued steady rain, Saturday was uneventful as best Jabe could surmise, but on the following morning he had heard rolls of musket fire in the distance and believed "a right smart engagement" must have taken place, and not too far away. Not long after hearing that gunfire, a large number of men began converging down in the cellar and up in the loft. They were "chirping happier than crickets" Jabe said, and had spent the better part of that day and into the evening downing their grogs while merrily toasting one another for having routed the Patriots.

We didn't know it then, but there had indeed been a battle on that Sunday, just a few miles from the Lockwood's farm, in Ridgefield. After the British had taken their toll on the military stores at Danbury, they left town via the Ridgebury Road. They had expected to be welcomed by swarms of Tories – friendly locals that would provide them with plenty of extra horses and wagons to carry off their spoils, but when only a small handful of Loyalists materialized, the British were left with no choice but to burn all of the pork, beef, flour, tents and shoes they had piled into the streets and get back to their ships at Compo as fast as possible. They got as far as the town of Ridgefield where the Americans, now under the command of General Benedict Arnold who had appeared on the scene from his home in New Haven, were waiting for them behind a barricade. The Redcoats were able to outflank the Minute-men and sent them running, but took casualties in the process, sleeping that night on their arms on the green in Newtown in order to lick their wounds while remaining combat-ready. The British had scattered the Americans for the time being, but found themselves in territory far more hostile than they had ever anticipated. They fully expected Arnold to regroup his forces overnight, and worried that he'd have another plan in mind to cut off their retreat. Given the gravity of their situation, they broke camp and formed into their column well before dawn. They were running low on ammunition, still over fifteen miles from the safety of their ships at Compo, and found themselves on Monday morning in a desperate race to the Sound.

At about the same time the British were breaking camp in Newtown, Jabe was awakened in the barn by a loud argument out in the yard. The ruckus occurred just hours before my arrival, and as far as he could make out, our normally soft-spoken Uncle Jabez was taking on the entire British high command single handedly. "I tell you what," he contended, "there's a feisty side to Uncle Jez that he keeps hidden beneath a bushel. You should a-heard him. He was in a right high dudgeon – something about the Redcoats being a day late and dollar short – and he waren't the least bit shy about letting them tarnal Lobsterbacks know how he expected them to keep to their side of some sort of bargain they had made – some deal involving provisions and loyal men-in-arms – while the Redcoats were shouting back that he could protest all he wanted, but that all bets were off.

God only knows exactly what they was hollerin' about out there," Jabe despaired. "I can only tell you this. Uncle Jez is up to something that ain't no good, and now he's madder 'n tarnation, and mightily scared. And them Redcoats are madder 'n tarnation too, and just as scared. As best as I can tell, there ain't nothin' what's gone as planned, and now there's going to be hell to pay!"

After giving me a moment to allow all of that to sink in, Jabe continued with his account. "Don't be lulled," he cautioned, "by all the quiet at present. Put to rest any thoughts of sliding down one of them hay chutes and slipping through the yard and out into the woods. Sure, they'll be some what's down there sleeping with the cows and lambs that's so pickled you could walk right over them, but they'll be others down there too, and they'll be sure to have their wits about them. And don't forget there might be even more of them sons a bitches wandering about in the yard. They're as thick as mustard they are, and them Cowboys would just as soon see us skinned alive as keep us under guard in here! For three whole days they did nothing but chirp and sing about getting out and shooting Patriots, and now there's a stink of panic in the air. They've turned as snarly as a bunch of cornered coons. It wouldn't take but the slightest misstep to set them off. Why do you think that old sourpuss out there beamed you with the butt of his musket just for walking through the door too slow?"

In Jabe's estimation, it weren't just the Cowboys we needed to worry about. We also needed to be wary of Uncle Jez and Aunt Sarah. They weren't merely Tory sympathizers with one misguided son enlisted with the Provincials, as we had believed; they were active collaborators themselves, and if Jabe was even halfway correct in his assessments, waist deep in treason. The loft was stuffed with all sorts of contraband – mostly bags of corn and wheat flour as best as he could figure – meant to be loaded onto wagons for the Redcoats to secure as they made their way back to the ships at Compo.

This was something almost impossible for me to accept. The Uncle Jabez I knew was a peaceable farmer – a man of high morals, a church deacon who routinely attended to the poor. For several years, when her own children were small, Aunt Sarah ran a Dame school from their house. Even before William's and my recent visit with them, I had thought of them both as being kindly people. They were the last people I'd ever imagine engaged in nefarious activities that could get them sent to New-Gate or dangling at the end of a hangman's noose. And yet, as Jabe was slowly forcing me to see, they could not have been merely spur-of-the-moment opportunists, nor, as I still wanted to believe, unwitting participants forced by circumstances to yield to the will of an invading army. No indeed, their enterprise was extensive, and as the four-wheeled chaise they purchased following the war would ultimately attest, it was quite a profitable business indeed.

Jabe and I had been huddled in the barn for about an hour when Aunt Sarah came trundling through the door with two pails of bean porridge. She was bonnet-less and out of breath, her face as grave as a sailor's wife. As she handed us our gruel she gently felt for the bump at the back of my head. "I'm so sorry, Haynes," she said quietly, squeezing my hands in hers as I remember her doing so often over the years. She paused for a moment, staring down at her feet. I thought perhaps she had been crying. "It never should have come to this," she said, and then, suddenly, she was gone. A man reached in to slam the door behind her, leaving Jabe and me standing in the storage bay staring at one another as the sound of the iron bar, falling hard against the bracket, went echoing through the rafters.

"I still don't understand why it is we're being held against our will!" I shouted. "If Aunt Sarah and Uncle Jez truly are up to something untoward or treasonous, why in heaven's name would they want us here to witness it? And how is it they could have possibly known when you and William arrived on Friday with the cattle that you were intending to join with the Minute-men instead of returning for home?"

Jabe placed his hand on my shoulder. "'Twas the letter," he explained. "The one your father had written, sealed, and ready to deliver even a-fore we left Compo. We was sitting at Aunt Sarah's table tucking into our Injun Pudding when William hands the envelope over, and when she was done reading she leaves the kitchen all of a hurry, and when she comes back she has Uncle Jez along with three of the stoutest farmhands you ever saw. We look up from our bowls, and she says how's she's awful sorry but that she's been asked by your tarnal Da to keep us would-be Minute-men safely in their care and out of harm's way until the current crisis is over and passed. It's for your own good, says she, and then she turns to Uncle Jez and points to the letter she's still holding in her hand. Look, she says to him, tie them to a barn post if that's what it takes, and the next thing you know we're stuffed inside this tarnal place banging at the doors and windows in the pitch darkness until we've gone and beaten our fists to bloody cinders."

Learning that my aunt and uncle were participants in the infamous London Trade, and in cahoots with the frightful Cowboys, were hard pieces of information to absorb, but the discovery that my father had managed to maintain his rigid control over us – and in such a scheming, underhanded way – was more than I could bear. I felt a rage rising in me matched only by the rage I'm sure William felt when he too found himself ensnared in Father's trap, held captive in a barn while the enemy went rampaging through the countryside. There was no way I was going to sit on a hay bale with Jabe and miss out on my chance to turn back the Redcoats. I determined then and there to escape from that barn. I didn't consider for a moment the odds stacked against me, and began a careful inspection of the hay chutes. There were three of them, cut into the floor at the back of each of the three storage bays.

"Use the middle'n if you must," Jabe said with a sigh of resignation. "There's a pile of old moldy hay below that'n. It'll shorten your jump and jest might quiet your landing."

"Thank you," I whispered while peering down the chute. "When I get to the ground hand me down the musket. I have no lead, nor any powder, and it won't fire anyway, but they don't know that."

"All right then, you damned fool," Jabe relented. "I can see you're just as bull-headed as your brother. So look here, if the stars align and you jest so happen to get lucky enough to steal through that devil's drawing room, and if you somehow make it across the yard with your head still attached to your shoulders, and iffen' you find yourself safely in the woods, head south, and stay clear of the roads if you can manage it. If there are any Patriots out and about, I reckon they'll be somewhere's down near Compo."

The short wooden ramp of the hay chute was pitched far too steeply for a person to step upon, so I sat at the top with the edges of my shoes wedged firmly against the sideboards, and managed to scuttle my way down the splintery boards as careful as a mouse. When I got to the end of the chute, I jumped to the ground without rousing any of the Cowboys. There weren't but a handful of them, sleeping like angels in the hay against the far wall. The geese and chickens fluttered some when I landed, but the cows and the sheep barely stirred. Most of the livestock was out in the yard where the sun was shining so brilliantly it blinded me. After blinking away the glare, I looked immediately overhead and saw that Jabe was already dangling down the broken fowler, which I grabbed and started tiptoeing towards the yard.

I knelt behind a pork barrel in the corner of the open doorway where I could get a look around. There was nobody standing guard that I could see, but there were voices coming from the front of the barn. Two Reds were eating hay from a trough off to the side, with other cows and sheep standing about in assorted clumps. The line of heavy woods lay about a hundred feet beyond the pen. The animals would provide some cover, so I figured getting to the fence undetected was at least an even bet – and it appeared easy enough to vault. Once on the other side, the dash to the trees would take me down a gentle slope. It would go fast, but I sorely wished that the stretch of open ground were a lot shorter!

The voices coming from around the corner hadn't moved any closer, so I reckoned it was as good a time as any to make my move. Bending low, I skulked to the nearest clump of cows. "There," I whispered to the first set of ears I could find, and began slowly feeling my way between their flanks. After a few steps the cows began snorting and quickly separated away from me. Luckily, there was another cluster of cows but a few steps ahead. Just as I reached this next safe haven though, and was taking a deep breath to steady my heartbeat, I heard the voices coming closer. "There," I whispered again, hoping to calm the beasts, and to keep them pressed around me. The men's voices came drawing closer still. It seemed as if they were standing at the corner of the barn, putting them only a few rods away. Terrified that they'd spot my feet, I did my best to keep my steps aligned with one muddy fetlock after another until I ran out of cows to hide behind, leaving me with no other option but to bolt for the fence.

"Oy!" a man shouted as I went leaping over the rail and into the open field. I ran for the trees with all the speed I could muster – with the whole lot of them shouting now – expecting to hear a gunshot ring out at any moment. With just a few feet of open field to go I zigged and zagged, hoping to foil some unseen marksman's aim, but instead of being struck by a musket ball, I felt a sudden crack to my ribcage that sent me tumbling face-first to the ground. A split second later, they were upon me, pummeling my back with the butts of their muskets. I had lost all my wind from the blow to my ribs, reducing my cries of pain to a pathetic string of hollow wheezes.

"Roll over you stinking coward!" one of the ruffians growled. Getting to my knees, I turned to face my assailants, still gasping for air. There were five or six of them, all wielding their muskets like clubs above their shoulders. Standing among them was the sour-faced guard who had only an hour ago knocked me senseless to the threshing floor.

"Well, well," the guardsman taunted while snatching Father's gun from the ground, "if it ain't Patriot Boy on a lark-about with Papa's fowler! Thought you'd bag a brace of Redcoats with this busted birder, did you?" Keeping his eyes trained on me, he handed over the broken gun to the fellow standing next to him, and the men began passing it around to one another, each taking a turn pretending to prime and fire it, laughing sneeringly at its split stock. "What're ye to do now?" the guardsman asked menacingly. "Uncle's up road with the Dragoons, and Aunty's locked away in her bedroom, down with a case of the vapours or so they says. It's just we cocks left in the yard."

With that they began closing in again. One of them kicked me in the same ribs that had just been cracked, crumpling me sideways and triggering another paroxysm of painful wheezes. From out of the corner of my eye I saw another one of them bending over, hugging his own ribcage and mimicking the whistling sounds coming from my lungs to the loud guffaws of his compatriots. Just then the sour faced guardsman kneed me in the center of my chest, whipsawing me back upright. I reeled to the side but managed to remain balanced on my knees. "Look sharply when we're talking to you!" he snarled, and struck me in the eye with the butt of his musket, sending a pinwheel of blood down the front of my smock. Before I could even cry out in pain, I was covered in a maelstrom of violent blows. There was no escaping the fists and boots that came raining down on my head and eyes from all directions.

"Let him be!" roared a man's voice from a distance, and the horrible pummeling petered to an end. I managed to rise to my hands and knees, and from between the tangle of legs surrounding me I could see the boots of a man striding towards us down the field from the barn. As the boots moved closer, my assailants stood aside, creating an alleyway for the man to step into. I spit out a thick gob of blood and looked up, and there, against a narrow patch of brilliant blue sky, appeared the familiar thatch of iron hair and the chiseled face of my father.

Running High But Clear

They didn't even bother to ask who he was or what he was doing there assuming, I supposed, by the cut of his clothes and his gentlemanly bearing that he was a man of authority. In any event, they stood aside, allowing Father to put his hand beneath my shoulder and help me to my feet. With my head pounding and my ears ringing for the second time that morning, Father gazed into my face, assessing the damage. Blood began to flow down over one of my eyes, which I did my best to blink away. With his forearms resting gently on either side of my neck he opened his mouth, stretching it wide in order to get me to do the same.

"Well, at least you've kept your teeth," he observed after a while, and took out a handkerchief from his pocket and pressed it onto the deep gashes around my eye. "Hold that there," he continued and turned his head to stare down the crowd of men around us. There were a few restive rumblings, but they backed away, revealing the broken fowler lying on the ground. I watched as Father's mind came to terms with this additional piece of information, and braced myself for a blast of his anger. When he looked back up at me though, his expression had not altered; he was unruffled. Not wanting to reveal any weakness to my attackers, I too kept my composure, putting on a brave face. The last thing I wanted was to give these hooligans the pleasure of knowing how much pain they had inflicted, but when the corners of Father's mouth turned up with the hint of smile, I lost all pretense of manly pride. I was unable to control myself any longer and broke down with a gasping sob, burying my shattered face into his shoulder.

The next I remember, we were sitting by the kitchen fire. By then, my eye was swollen shut; Aunt Sarah was patting the cuts and abrasions on my face with cool compresses, and Father was cutting a bandage to tie around my head. In addition to these head wounds, there was the matter of the ribs on my left side that were now stabbing me with nearly every breath. Jabe was there too, freed from the barn and looking over Aunt Sarah's shoulder while thoughtfully consuming a large chunk of corn bread. In that light, with my back to the window, and in spite of the chaos still unfolding around us, what struck me – and what I was noting for the first time in my life – was just how much my aunt looked like my father. Her thick head of hair was a bit greyer than her younger brother's, and her features were softer, but her piercing brown eyes were unmistakably Bennett eyes, and so very familiar to me. Tears were streaming down her face, and from the look of her, she had been crying all morning. I listened as she told Father how Uncle Jabez had pressed upon his "business associates" – her phrase – to step up and increase their schedule of deliveries, and that their loft was now bursting at the seams with barrels of dried pease and beans, apples and peaches. The transaction was meant to be simple and discrete, but it soon spun out of control. Somehow word of the planned rendezvous had gotten out, and their farm soon became a gathering point for all manner of Tory opportunists. Some were looking to escape with Tryon while others were merely hoping to use the presence of his troops to settle a score with their Patriot neighbors and join in what they anticipated were going to be great spoils of war.

I also heard her tell how the British Quartermaster had informed Uncle Jabez within that very hour that the column was marching down the Ridgefield Road, running out of time. Their commanders feared the Americans would regroup and outrace them to the Country Road Bridge, which, given the recent heavy rain, was the only place to safely cross the Saugatuck River and return to their shipping. With so little time to spare, the British couldn't afford to be saddled with the provisions stuffed in Uncle Jabez's loft, even if he had been able to supply them with adequate means of transport.

The situation had turned desperate for them both: bad for the British because they were in danger of being trapped by the Americans – perhaps even forced to surrender – and bad for my aunt and uncle who suddenly found themselves in danger of being caught with their hands in the cookie jar. They had clearly gotten themselves in over their heads.

"We won't be able to conceal all of those barrels from prying eyes forever," Aunt Sarah lamented. "All these comings and goings have placed us in grave danger. Our efforts to do what is right have fallen apart ... Oh Dell, we hold no sway over these awful miscreants," she whispered while tenderly attending to my cuts. "Just look at what they have done to your boy!"

"Yes," Father said. "He's safe now. What word of your Jabe?"

"God only knows," she fretted, pausing briefly in her ministrations to my face. "There was a battle yesterday, with casualties we have been told. We can but pray he is not among them."

Until just moments ago, I was thoroughly defeated, wishing I had never sneaked from the house and that none of this had ever happened. As Father and I were walking through the pack of Cowboys and into the house, all I wanted was to go home, to sit by the fire with Mother and Gaylee and play jackstraws with my brothers and sisters. But as I sat listening to Aunt Sarah, and hearing it straight from her that she and Uncle Jez were giving aid to the enemy, and realizing without a shadow of doubt that Father obviously had prior knowledge concerning all of it, my patriotic passions went rising yet again. I found myself hardly able to even look at Father, and felt as determined as ever to defy him and join with the Minutemen, my throbbing eye and aching ribs be damned.

From his tour of duty during the last war, Father had a good idea for how long it would take the battalions of British Regulars to break their camp in Ridgefield and march to the bridge in Saugatuck. He asked Aunt Sarah if he could borrow one of their horses. If we moved quickly, we'd get to the bridge before midday and might beat them to the crossing. He'd return in a few days himself to bring back our cows, but if we left now, there was at least a small chance he'd be able to find William before the trouble began, and bring him home too.

Jabe and I were given saddles for a pair of Aunt Sarah's horses; Father was on Timothy. Bouncing on the back of the cantering horse along the rutted Newtown Turnpike with a couple of broken ribs was not pleasant. It took all my strength just to hang on. Father had seen Militiamen arriving from all parts of the colony the day before. He believed that with General Benedict Arnold now in command, this odd assortment of Americans could be organized into a respectable fighting force. If anyone could get Minute-men ready to do battle, it would be the hero of Quebec, a man possessed of nearly limitless ambition, famous for his fighting spirit. It didn't take a trained military strategist to know that the logical place for the American rebels to make a stand would be on the high ground just west of the bridge. From such a strong position, it would only take a few hundred men to prevent the Redcoats from crossing. If there was to be another battle it would be on Old Hill, and that was where we headed.

When we neared the juncture with the road from Ridgefield, we heard drums through the trees and slowed our horses to a walk. We could see that the road ahead was clear. The Redcoats were somewhere high on the ridge to our right. They were beyond our view, but we could hear them well. Father said nothing, but I know he was thinking about spurring the horses and making a dash for it.

"What the deuce?" came the sudden cry of a familiar voice, and out from the woods sauntered three mounted Redcoats, including the ever-present Lieutenant Soames! He stopped his horse on the opposite side of the West Branch, leaning forward on his saddle, slowly shaking his head and whistling through his teeth. "Is that who I think it is beneath those bloody bandages?"

"While I live and breathe, if it ain't Deliverance!" another familiar voice shouted, and out popped Uncle Jabez, followed by John French in his maroon coat. The lot of them quickly splashed across the shallow stream and joined us on the road.

"We're off to scout the high tide ford," Uncle Jez announced in an excited voice. "And what, pray tell, are you doing here?"

Father explained our situation and asked after the junior Jabez. "By all accounts he's performing his duties with honor," Uncle Jez replied with pride, and then proceeded to apprise us of the dilemma facing the Redcoats. The main column was nearby, halted on top of Chestnut Hill and able to see a large force of rebels – nearly two thousand they reckoned – assembled just where Father had surmised they'd be, two miles to their front on the other side of Poplar Plains and atop of Old Hill. The Americans had at least two field pieces with them, and with their commanding position, filing along the narrow road to the bridge would position the Redcoats on the wrong side of a turkey shoot. Having badly miscalculated both the time it would take to complete the invasion and the amount of resistance they would encounter, the Redcoats were out of rations and running low on ammunition. It was a forgone conclusion that Tryon would never agree to surrender, so the field commanders were at that very moment making preparations to take the hill by storm. The outcome of such an assault would be a dead certainty. Well-trained soldiers would drive the rebels from their position, with bayonets if necessary, but there were sure to be heavy casualties – on both sides.

"You should have heard Erskine and Agnew," Uncle Jez effused, "the two in charge. Here their army lies at the brink of disaster and there they are, squabbling like an old married couple. I tell you, the Governor looked ready to throttle them both!"

Soames interrupted. "Come man, we must go!"

"I've told them already," Uncle Jez plowed on, showing scant regard to the young Dragoon in charge, "the guides with the Provincials know how much rain we've had. The Saugatuck won't be crossable until tomorrow, but if Erskine wants to check the fording place once again, I'm happy to take these fellows to see for themselves."

They were about to ride away when father jumped from Timothy and dashed to block their path. He grabbed hold of Soames' stallion by the bit. "There's no need to waste any more of your valuable time," he declared. "I waded across at the ford myself, just over an hour ago. The river is still running high, but it has cleared. A man on foot will see his feet. Pray, go and tell your commanders. There is a rising tide, but if you move quickly the army can make good its escape at the ford!"

"Why should I trust what you say?" asked Soames.

"Because," Father replied, his voice firm but carefully measured, "I believe my son William is on that hill that stands before your army. He's but a boy, and I could not bear to see him, or other boys just like him, injured or killed. Please, Lieutenant, cross at the ford! For mercy's sake, run to your ships and leave us here in peace!"

Soames stared down at Father, his mind working. He then looked over at me, still slumped on my horse. His eyes crinkled into a smile. "Promise me one thing Pigeon Spy," he said with a quick tap of a finger to his plumed helmet, almost like a salute. "Make this the last time we meet!"

He then turned to Father. "All right, good sir, I believe you. He turned next to Mr. French. "If I let Mr. Lockwood go, will you be able to pilot us to the ford?"

"I know the way like the back of my hand," the ginger haired man replied.

He pointed now to my uncle. "You! Get back to your poor wife!"

He next ordered the three of us to stay safely to the rear. Lt. Soames and his squadron of Dragoons including John French, spurred their horses and headed up the slope towards Chestnut Hill. We listened as the hooves went clattering over the mossy stones, and the first and the last Redcoat I would ever meet my entire life was gone.

The Battle of Old Hill

We took the advice of the Lieutenant and backtracked a few rods up the pike and made our way to the northern brow of Chestnut Hill. We dismounted and scrambled onto an outcrop of rocks where we could look across the gently undulating patchwork of Poplar Plains and clearly see Old Hill rising in the distance. From our vantage point, the Patriot's defensive line looked like a garland of grey-colored holly crowning a dome of open farmland. Only by looking closely could you tell that the garland was alive with movement, bristling in place, with an occasional glint coming from a musket barrel or perhaps a brass button as it caught the midday sun just so. The sky was a brilliant blue, with a stiff freshening breeze making for the kind of spring day in Connecticut you wish could be preserved like a ship in a bottle. The fruit groves planted on the hillsides made pockets of pink snow, encircled by the greening pastures, all framed by the ridgeline that was rusted red with the emerging buds of the hardwood trees. So incongruous it was to see such peaceful countryside whilst knowing that two armies were set upon it, bristling for battle.

Immediately below us, the road where the Redcoats had recently passed was littered with haversacks and empty cartridge boxes. The air swirling in their wake smelled of freshly chiseled granite. We couldn't see any of the troops at first, but their drums and fifes echoed up from a hollow just over the brow. Following the movement of the music led us to fear the commanders had decided against making a retreat over the ford, and were instead going forward with their frontal attack. Sure enough, a column of Redcoats soon came into view, marching straight as a dagger towards the exact center of the American lines, their fifes and drums blaring, their regimental colors unfurled horizontally in the wind. They marched four abreast, over the green folds of pastureland, slowed occasionally by having to cross a stone wall or sidestep around a farmer's pond, but steadily proceeding ever closer to the base of the hill. I tried to imagine where William might be positioned in the American lines. There was no question in my mind that he would have gotten his hands on a musket, and felt equally certain, knowing how fiercely determined my brother could be, that he would have squeezed himself to the front rank, and was now watching the column approach from somewhere near the center of Old Hill. I stole a quick glance at Father, who stood motionless, his face drained of color.

When the column neared the trees growing along the banks of a brook, it disappeared like a snake down a rabbit hole. After a while, all that remained of the enemy was the muffled sound of its drums. The Redcoats were out of view for so many agonizing minutes we almost dared to believe that they had disappeared for good. Jabe scrambled from rock to rock trying in vain to find a place that would allow him to see where they had gone. "They've up and vanished," he concluded with a nervous laugh, and then in his next breath he cried "Look!" as a lone color bearer spat out from the trees, a good fifty rods to the right of the spot where the column had vanished. A moment later, another flag appeared, this one fifty rods to the other side, and before we knew it, a dozen flags and banners had materialized in the open ground just beyond the woods, followed in the next breath by slashes of scarlet seeping from the treetops. In a dazzling act of black magic, the Regulars had gone into the ravine as a pointed dagger, and had come out as a long deadly scythe. They slowly advanced over the uneven ground; their shouldered bayonets fired by the sun, creating the illusion of a lighted fuse traveling along the ground as it swept up the hillside. Father judged that their lines stretched nearly half a mile, and it looked as if they would be able to easily engulf the Americans waiting on the hilltop before them.

The British were about to cross the walls and fences that marked Partrick Lane when two yellow flashes and a cloud of smoke billowed from the side of Old Hill. Although it took several seconds for the sound to reach us, we knew right away that the Americans had fired their heavy field pieces. A section of the right side of the British line crumbled, with soldiers falling into confusion while mounted officers went darting all about them. To our surprise, the entire British line seemed to melt away, reversing direction and leaving behind several bodies – scraps of scarlet littering the hillside. From the top of Old Hill the garland appeared to bristle and glint all over again. Seconds later we heard a sound that began as a low rumble, and grew to a sustained roar. What a magnificent, blood-stirring sound it was! The three of us clasped arms, as the jubilant huzzahs of a thousand Patriot voices flooded over us, drifting across the wind.

William and I spent many an afternoon watching Uncle Joseph's company of Home Guards drilling on the green in Taylortown, and oh, how we'd laugh! There was Uncle Joseph, nose reddened from drink and dressed in his hunting shirt, thumbing frantically through his Norfolk Military Manual trying to get three dozen farmers, drovers and general layabouts to act like soldiers. It hardly ever mattered which orders he barked: "Shoulder firelocks!" … "To the left face!" … "To the right wheel!" … his hapless recruits would stumble all over the green, and invariably work themselves into a hopeless tangle. How different it now looked when professional soldiers are put through their paces! When the Regulars first ran from the hill and congregated just above the row of trees below us, they too looked to be in a hopeless tangle, and on a vast scale, but the skillful officers soon had them back in their lines, and with colors flying and drummers drumming, the scarlet scythe was once again sweeping up the hill.

After stepping over their dead, the Redcoats on this second assault made it to the other side of Partrick Road before the American cannons opened fire, and as before, the canisters felled a few handfuls of soldiers. This time, however, the holes in their lines were quickly filled and the Regulars continued edging up the hill. A minute or two later, when the left of their line was about even with Lee's tobacco barn, we saw bright flashes, and in the next instant Old Hill was completely obscured in smoke. This time, dozens upon dozens of Redcoats fell to the ground along the length of their line. It looked to be an absolute slaughter, and by the time the rattle and roar of the American muskets reached us, the surviving Redcoats were already scurrying back towards the brook, their frantic retreat once again punctuated by a rolling thunderclap of American cheers.

In spite of Father telling us not to be so quick to declare victory, Jabe and I were beside ourselves with joy! He threw his hat into the air, and when he remembered that my battered ribcage and bandaged eye prevented me from doing the same, he snatched the hat from my head and gave it an equally hearty hurl. Jabe went skipping about the rocks, happier than a fiddling Negro. The Patriots atop of Old Hill had shown the British army that the bark of determined Minute-men had real bite! My count of the British dead was approaching one hundred when, just as Father had cautioned, the officers accomplished what any reasonable person would think was impossible: they had their men back in formation and were readying them for a third march up the hill. How, I wondered, could their commanders be so cavalier? After seeing so many of their men fall to the American guns, how could they order so many hundreds more to their sure death, and most baffling of all, what could make a soldier brave enough, or foolhardy enough, to obey such an ill-conceived order?

Over Partrick Road the scythe drew forward once again, over the crumpled bodies of the fallen, over the walls and fences and into the open ground beyond the road, resolute and surging, edging ever closer to the killing field. The line had moved some few feet further up the hill than on its previous attempts when it inexplicably paused. No American musket or field piece had yet been fired. The British drums grew silent. Other than the soundless fluttering of their flags and banners, the entire line of Redcoats stood stone still. For several eerie minutes the battle seemed to have reached a standoff. Then, at some unseen signal, the drummers and fifers stationed at their different points behind the lines began playing in unison, louder than you could possibly believe at that distance. At the sound of these drum beats, the edge of the attacking scythe appeared to fold open and I realized that the Redcoats in the front row had done what opposing soldiers the world over feared most of all: they had lowered their bayonets, followed by a deep-throated "Haugh!" as loud as a cannon shot.

The Americans opened fire, and Old Hill was once again engulfed in a cloud of white smoke. This volley however, must have been aimed high – or so I initially concluded – for I did not see a single Redcoat fall, nor did any of them break ranks and run. They didn't charge up the hill either, as I fully expected them to do, but instead, in one smooth motion, the attackers turned on their heels, and the soldiers began marching in a quick-step back down the field and towards the line of trees. They passed over the bodies of the fallen, and then, in what looked to be yet another act of British black magic, the little pieces of scarlet lint strewn about the fields – the bodies of the soldiers we all believed just moments ago had met their Maker – began to rise, seemingly from the dead. All those hundreds of fallen Redcoats were now picking up their firearms and trotting along behind the orderly lines of their retreating comrades.

"A feint!" Father cried, as Jabe and I stood dumbfounded. "This entire battle," he effused, taking the two of us under each of his arms and squeezing us to his chest, "has been nothing more than a charade. A wonderful, blessed charade!"

As the British lines disappeared into the trees, the garland of American militiamen on the distant hilltop looked for a moment to be stuck in place. Motionless the Americans remained, until like a drop of lamp oil spilled into a pail of water, they began to break apart in all directions. A few clumps of soldiers drifted off towards the Country Road Bridge, some ran straight to the rear and disappeared from our view, still others raced down the hill in pursuit of the retreating Redcoats who were now racing furiously towards the fording place.

There were about a hundred Minute-men who showed enough courage to run in our direction, chasing after the enemy down the hill. When they reached the road, they took cover behind the walls and hedges and fired their muskets. The rattle of their arms was met by a wide plume of smoke emanating from the woods below us, followed by the single roar of musketry. None of the Patriots looked to be harmed by this returning fire, but they remained pinned to the road until all the smoke had cleared. First one intrepid soul, and then another two or three, and finally all one hundred of them were darting down the grassy hillside and disappearing into the woods in pursuit of the enemy.

We could no longer see any of the combatants. The only signs of battle were the random popping of musket fire, punctuated every few minutes by the roar of a disciplined volley, all of it sliding eastwards through the trees in the direction of the ford. After about an hour the battle sounds subsided, and we thought perhaps it was safe to continue on our way home, when the loud report of a cannon echoed up the ridge, giving us pause. It sounded close, and in spite of Jabe and my pleas to get back on our horses and follow at a safe distance behind the action, Father ordered us to remain exactly where we were for a while longer.

It was getting on to midafternoon when a sound like the rumble of thunder drew our eyes back towards Old Hill where a puff of white smoke could be seen rising above the trees. The plume was now several miles away, rising well beyond the crest of the hill. In just moments, that first rumble turned into a sustained roar while the puff of smoke billowed into a storm cloud, white and churning towards the sky. The battle had begun again in earnest; it seemed to be raging somewhere on or near Compo Road, and uncomfortably close to our farm and house.

This was enough to convince Father that it was time for us to get moving. Now instead of having only William to worry about, he feared for our family still in Compo, and ordered us to get back on the horses. We rode down the ridge. Not knowing precisely where the battle lines were drawn, Father thought it best to cross at the ford instead of the bridge, so we headed due east. When we got to the cart path that led down to the crossing, signs of the army were everywhere. The path itself, softened by the recent rain, looked as if a flood had rushed through. Everything was matted and littered with all sorts of debris left behind by the Redcoats wishing to hasten their escape – haversacks, canteens, cartouches and powder horns, hats and blankets. A wagon with a broken axle was abandoned midstream, and what looked to be a pile of women's skirts was clinging to the underbrush on the opposite bank.

The path leading up the steep hill from the east bank of the river was also rutted and gouged, making it a tough climb and very difficult for me with my sore ribs and one good eye to stay in the saddle, so I dismounted and walked. All day the wind had been building, and as I neared the top of the hill, a sudden gust buffeted my face, bringing with it the unmistakable boom of a cannon shot. As I sit here at my desk years later, I know that nearest cannons from either army were miles away at that particular moment, but at the time, due perhaps to my weakened state of mind, the loud report from the distant fieldpiece sounded so close upon me, I fully expected to be blasted off the hill by a wad of canister. I jumped backwards to take what little cover was afforded by the rocks whereupon I noticed that the ground around me was splattered with blood. At first, I thought it was my own blood that was spilled there, but after a quick inspection of hat, heart and limbs, I felt satisfied I had not been hit, and thought only about getting off the open trail and into the woods. Looking anxiously around me, I saw that there were also smatterings of blood spreading on the ground away from the rocks, leading towards the safety of the underbrush. In my growing panic, I raced hard after these splatters, which took me back down the cart path at an angle, eventually crossing it by a cluster of serviceberry trees. How odd, I remember thinking, not only was there blood on the ground, it was also splattered high above me, on the newly opened blossoms of the trees. From the periphery of my mind, I sensed that Father had by then gotten down from his horse. He was shouting to me from across the wind, imploring me to stay where I was, but I could think of nothing beyond getting to safety and crashed through the underbrush where I espied a boy about my age on the other side of a small clearing resting against the trunk of an ancient chestnut tree with what looked like a musket lying across his lap.

If only I had listened to Father, and stayed with Jabe and the horses. Had I kept my composure and done as told, I might not have gotten that better look, nor would I have erupted in such a shameful fury. Worse than striking Father with a rock balled in my fist, were the terrible words I leveled against him. Awful words I was too proud to ever take back. Had I merely obeyed, none of it would have ever happened. I never would have seen those fingers reaching gently towards the bed of pine needles. So calm they looked, as if poised to pick some violets, or to pinch a Lady's Slipper. Had I only listened, I would have missed the grisly sight. I would have simply gone home and William and Cesar would have spun their yarns, and Nate, Esther, and Mary would have oohed and aahed and I would have been spared a thousand dawns of waking nightmares.

You had yer tarnal blue devils Haynes my friend, that much I'll allow. I allus were awful sorry for that, but we sure drownd a few a them sorrows a yern over the years now, didn't we? Lookin back though, an even you have to admit it waren't all just tragical what come from them battles that day. Take our cousin Trow Crossman fer example. He made a gainful enterprise from it, an nearly all his life! He was on that hill with all them other brothers of the blade, watchin them Redcoat feints, an was fine bout soldierin so long as he was tucked behind a barrycade, but when Genral Arnold tried to get them fellers to attack across the bridge, there waren't none of em that would go, an not especially our Trow. Run headlong into them tarnal cannons? What kind a nick ninny would do such a fool thing as that? Well, Arnold waren't no turncoat coward (ha!) so he commences to bully them boys, shoutin and carryin on, ridin through the ranks on his horse, callin em names an such, an there's our Trow – cant ye jest picture him, with that unoccupied bookish expreshion he sometimes gets, standin there thinkin, you kin holler all ye like Mister, but I ain't goin nowhere's, jest before he gets whacked on the noggin by the back of Arnold's sword! Nocked him cold (which was a convenience, leastwise to a soldier done with fightin) an opened a gash that became the scar that brout him fame an fortune. I tell you what, London ain't got nothing on us! They got their Traitor's Gate all right, but we got our very own Trow's Brow! For a dram of rum, he'd pull back his hair an show you that ugly purple scar put there by our countries most celebrated Traitor. Give him two drams an he'll let you touch it! He waren't no soldier old Trow, but he sure had himself a nose for business! -- JB

Runaway Rachel

September 9th, 1827:

My eldest grandchild, Rachel, went missing from her home the day before
yesterday. She is but thirteen years old, and to make matters even more
worrisome for her distraught parents, on the morning when they realized
she was not safely tucked in her bed, a violent hurricane with driving winds
strong enough to tear away rooftops and topple trees, came roaring up
from the tropics. Just by happenstance, this fearsome tempest coincided
with a gathering storm of a far different nature. Certain young
acquaintances of Rachel's, along with a few other unsavory characters in
town, have been taunting her of late, making vulgar insinuations about a
certain friend she has chosen to associate with, and generally making her life
miserable. As I half expected, Rachel's parents are holding me to account
for this unfortunate turn of events. They contend that I created the
maelstrom that has been directed towards Rachel, and were it not for me,
and my involvement with the Anti-Slavery Society, Rachel never would
have been so awfully harassed and thus, never would have run away. There
is a certain truth to this assessment, and I stand culpable, but none of that
was important, I advised my daughter and son-in-law, while urging them to
think clearly about the matter at hand, and not to go off on hysterical
tangents. They actually feared that the poor child might have been
kidnapped by one of the hooligans, which was of course, ridiculous! Yes,
the taunts that Rachel has been experiencing are indeed ugly, and many of
the people who stand in opposition to the just treatment of Negroes harbor

strong resentments towards our cause, and a small handful of that number may even be considered dangerous. All of that may be true, but these are not the lawless days of 1777, and nobody is about to kidnap the poor girl simply because she had befriended a Mulatto, and was the granddaughter of an abolitionist. I mean, honestly now!

I, on the other hand, never panicked, and had a strong inkling where Rachel had gone. I reckoned I'd find her hunkered down in the hidden hollow on the other side of the ridgeline, and so, while her parents went frantically searching through their neighbor's barns, the various riverside quays and the stage depot, I headed into the woods and my secret spot; a most propitious hiding place – the very same shadowy niche, in fact, where Broom herded the livestock on the night the Redcoats were on their march to Danbury. A place I often went to collect my thoughts, to gather liverwort and other woodland medicinals. Sure enough, I found my granddaughter nestled in a shallow ditch behind the familiar ledge of rocks, covered in evergreen bows, just as I had once showed her how to do.

She burst into tears when I pulled away her evergreen roof, and fell into my arms. I found her to be thoroughly soaked and a bit chilled, but otherwise in fine kettle. "Dear, dear Rachel," I whispered into her ear, holding her tight until her tears were spent. She asked me why it should be that some people could be so unkind, and told me that even her own parents were displeased with her new friend, that they did not understand her. I confessed to feeling much the same way when I was her age, and I told her that I too found myself almost constantly at odds with my parents. I told her also that in spite of what she may be taught in church, or what her grammar school matron may assert, it was important that she seek her own path, and if that meant doing battle with the world from time to time, then so be it. I told her that the way people treated one another when I was a boy – during both the war against England and the more vicious warfare waged against our own neighbors – was in many ways very similar to the way people treat one another today. While sparing her of details, I told her about my lifetime of recurring nightmares, and how, after an accumulation of unbearable events, I once ran away too, and not for the reason of getting away from people, so much as for a strong desire to become unseen by them; to go deep into the woods in order to blend in with the wildness of nature and to sit and think. "Yes, that's it" Rachel said pressing her head against my chest, "yes." And I told her about a man I met on my travels who helped me to understand that in spite of my inherent contrariness, I was not a Goer, but a Stayer at heart.

Rachel gazed up at me with a quizzical look upon her face. I tried to explain further. "The world, you see, is largely comprised of two groups of people, Goers and Stayers. Both are dreamers, but the Stayers are fixers too, and I believe that you, dear Rachel are a Stayer."

"What does that mean, Henny?" she asked, looking perplexed and a bit sad.

"It means, dear child, that it is time for you to come home."

Brain Fever

In this dream I'm struggling up a steep hill. The wind is blowing, building to a gale, draining all the living color from the landscape, the greens and yellows and the reds. As I near the crest of the hill, it takes all my strength to keep from being blown away. My fingers dig into the ground. Father comes into view above me. He is tethered to the rocks with a rope tied around his waist, and is shouting something, and I shout back, but am choked by the suffocating blasts of wind. Nothing coming from our mouths can be heard above the roar. He's clutching the English fowler in one hand while reaching towards me with the other, his fingers splayed. I reach out my hand towards his, inching closer and closer, but the wind prevents us from grabbing hold. With one last lunge, our fingertips touch just as the wind sends me swirling, and as I careen helplessly backwards, I see that he's thrown the fowler after me like a lifeline. It spins against pewter clouds, pin wheeling rockets of bright red blood.

Was it brain fever, madness, or merely some sort of prolonged bout of the vapors? Difficult to say. I just know that like Rachel, I was overcome with a desire to run away, and it now seems as if an entire period of my life went missing. It is hard to recall what year it was exactly, although it was sometime before Evacuation Day in 1783. That much I know. I had been Mr. Gilbert's apprentice for a year or more, learning to be a sail maker, and I know too that I had already met Kezzie, because Mother had given me the very same brass thimble Father had given her, and because it was Kezzie who was waiting for me when I returned.

My general plan was to walk to Canada, which to my convoluted young brain seemed more sensible than stealing off to the Brooklyn docks to arrange passage to Nova Scotia, along with thousands of other uprooted citizens. Cesar and I had talked about such a scheme because the British were manumitting any Negro servants who crossed into their lines. The plan was to have Phyllis and the twins steal away with us after one of our apple scion sojourns. With traveling papers easy enough for me to forge, we were going to secure a whaling boat to take us across the Sound to Huntington. That of course, never happened, and without Cesar and his family as prospective traveling companions, a voyage to Nova Scotia on a British ship didn't sit well with me. I wasn't a Loyalist, and didn't relish the thought of trying to explain my political views, scrambled as they were, to some sanctimonious British naval officer. I was but eighteen or nineteen years old and not yet made a freeman, a young man with diminished prospects, a lost soul plagued by nightmares. Better, I reasoned, to take to the more familiar woods, where for nearly a year, I slept in corncribs and in caves, trapped rabbits and stole cabbages, hardened spears over campfires, painted my face with red ochre and chokecherry juice, and glared maniacally at the workaday world from behind the dark cloak of our New England woodlands.

I departed in the early spring when there were still pockets of snow on the ground. It was before the 25th of April – a date that was turning into an unofficial holiday in our village, and marked by toasts to the Gallant Seventeen. We had been living in what Gaylee called a "poor man's farmhouse" (four rooms, a sleeping loft and an outdoor kitchen) down by the ferry for what felt like an eternity. My older siblings and I had all been farmed out in one form or another. The palms of both my hands were blistered and raw from pressing iron needles through thick canvas, but that was nothing compared to the pain of seeing Uncle Joseph and Aunt Sarah promenading up and down Compo Road in their gilded riding chair. That injustice was more than I could bear. All of it was, and so I made myself a bedroll for traveling. I packed a haversack with an overcoat and leggings, a hatchet, pocketknife, a brass pocket compass, a tinderbox from the smokehouse, three days' worth of biscuits and dried pork, and hid them all in the barn. On the night of my departure I tiptoed to the dresser and retrieved the thimble I kept hidden in the bottom drawer. After one last look around, I slunk from the loft, got my gear from the barn, and headed north.

My first stop was Devil's Den in Norfield where I intended to spy on the Lockwood's for a day or two, thinking that was all the time I'd need to find answers to the few remaining questions I had about them. Instead, I lingered for over a fortnight in the impenetrable tangle of woods behind their farm; waylaid, as it were, unable to turn away. I lived mostly on Indian cucumbers – switching to peppery pigweed when it got warmer – and when I was successful at sieving minnows from the brooks that gurgled through tree roots and over smoothed stones, I ate them too, in one quick swallow, raw. From my various hiding places, I was able to observe the comings and goings of my Aunt and Uncle's secret enterprise. On some evenings a wagon, sometimes two or three in succession, would trundle up to the barn. Shadowy figures would unload foodstuffs. Occasionally they'd struggle with crates filled with what sounded like pots and pans or ironware. I recognized the twisted shape of the sour-faced man, the very one who had drubbed me with his musket years before. He was the one who drew on the rope to the pulley in the middle of the night, its rhythmic toll a lonely squeak as the great bundles were slowly hoisted to the second story window of the barn.

During the light of day, the farm hived as normal. It was yeoman industry at its finest and as pretty as a picture. And then, every few days or so, after the delivery wagons had come and gone, a different wagon would arrive, this one larger than the others, its bed covered in canvas. Uncle Jabez would walk down from the house to greet this wagon personally. I'd follow the glow of his lantern, first flickering through the cracks of the barn siding as he and the driver made their way up the back stairs, and next knifing through the outlines of the shuttered window as they settled into the loft. I glowered from my lair, conjuring a picture in my mind of my uncle taking a ledger from its locked drawer, pouring himself and the driver their glass of Madeira, and calmly squaring the accounts.

I watched these comings and goings as the spring air warmed, bedding down each night only after I was sure there'd be no wagons to observe. I had three or four places where I could get my sleep that I'd go to on a kind of circuit depending upon the weather. On nights that were warm and fair, I had a soft mossy pallet between two downed trees in an opening with a full view of the sky. On nights with a cold wind, I'd sleep on a bed of pines wedged between two sharp heaves of granite. When it rained, I'd repair to a rudimentary lean-to that I built in the middle of a dense cover of young hemlocks. I spent my days watching the spring rolling up slowly from the Sound, greening as it went, and dedicated my nights to spying, coiled like a spring. I took pleasure sneaking into the barn before dawn, feeling my way along the wall, and leaving a calling card on the door to the loft. My signature was sometimes as simple as a single Jack-in-the-pulpit stem or a clump of moss. On my last night I left my injudicious aunt and uncle a string of braided saw grass, spooled as nicely as you please around the shanks of the padlock. They weren't ever caught aiding the enemy, but they at least knew they were being watched.

How invincible I felt during those weeks in Norfield! How transcended! I fancied myself an Algonquin Medicine Man, mixing potions and casting spells. But my aim was to get to Canada, and it eventually became time to continue on my way. From the Lockwood's farm I tramped along the ridgelines until I reached the Housatonic River. I headed upstream, arriving in a few days at the base of Coltsfoot Mountain near the little hamlet of Cornwall. The countryside there was as rugged and sparsely populated as I imagine it must be yet today. Living off the land in that corner of the world, at that time of year, was an entirely different kettle of fish than surviving in the gentle, well-tamed hills of southern Connecticut. Only the most rough-hewn souls would dare to scratch a living in such a forbidding place. There were but a handful of forlorn farms lurking in the hollows or edging up the hillsides. It was unbearably hot and humid that summer, and the only way to get relief from the fetid air with its swarms of black flies, was to wade out into the center of the river and hunker down in a pocket of quiet water behind a boulder. I've since been told that even when the weather is fair and dry, the Housatonic always runs the color of milky dark tea, with sucker holes deep enough to drown all but the most attentive wader. Due to the damnable flies, I became very familiar with the multiple runs and pockets of this dangerous waterway, spending long hours waist deep in its murky currents, shivering until well past nightfall because the only thing more blood thirsty than the daily clouds of black flies along its shores were the ravenous mosquitos that came out from its eddies at dusk.

If it were only the insects that plagued me, I would have been fine. But there was also the cut to my elbow, and a general weakness brought on I suppose from so many weeks of living on mostly roots and berries. I never knew exactly how the injury to my arm came about. I wouldn't have realized I had hurt myself at all had I not noticed the tear and the bloodstain on my shirtsleeve on the day I stepped into the shadow of Coltsfoot Mountain. Perhaps I fell, or caught my elbow on a nail or a splinter shunting in and out of Aunt Sarah's barn. In any event, it was a small wound that never healed. After a few weeks, it was merely red and uncomfortable, but in the days after that, it festered and started to ooze. Eventually, it got so swollen I could no longer bend my arm. It throbbed incessantly, and if I even so much as brushed it past an ostrich fern, the sudden burst of pain was enough to make me scream.

Gathering food became more difficult and was soon impossible. I must have gone for days without a single bite to eat. I had grown feverish and decided it was time to find a farm and throw myself at the mercy of whoever might let me in. But first, I needed to rest. I lacked the strength to take another step. The last thing I remember was lying down in a patch of grass in the shade of trees alongside a stretch of the river that ran fast, tumbling over and around large boulders. Evening was about to fall. I was too weary to even think about swatting away the feasting insects, and lay staring into the sky, paling to grey and alive with spinning mayflies, praying for a healing breeze and surrounded in layers of sound coming from the river.

What a beautiful noise it was to surrender to! There were the barely perceptible bass notes I could feel more than actually hear as unseen rocks on the very bottom of the riverbed continuously fussed and settled. Then there were the booming sounds coming from the main currents whacking against the boulders and reaching my ears at various pitches all at once, and finally the bubbling swirls, closer to the bank, tailing off into endless scatterings of ascending notes that ran their different scales until all I could hear were tiny pin pricks of sound; little silver drips miraculously breaking through the roar and coming at me from God only knew where as I drifted peacefully into oblivion.

When I awoke, the first thing I saw were beaver pelts spread across dark walls. A variety of pickaxes and hammers were littered about on a well-swept dirt floor. In the distance, I heard what sounded like an entire colony of owls, barking and hooting and wailing to one another. I was lying on a pallet of pine bows and wondered where the devil am I? I was disoriented and frightened, and would have tried to get up and run were it not for the smell of meat cooking on an open fire along with the sound of fat sizzling onto hot coals. Hunger pangs, and a pure animal instinct to live, kept me anchored dead in place. I wanted to ram all the food I possibly could inside me, but the effort it took to merely lean my body towards the captivating sounds and smells coming from the fire sent my head spinning.

"Hold steady there, Captain," came a voice from the dark. "Ye need to walk afore learning how to run all over again."

Crouching next to me was a man of indeterminate age. He had shoulder length white hair that was tied with strips of leather into a multitude of queues, quite neatly arranged, but springing from his skull in all directions. His long, hoary beard was similarly festooned. Belying his white hair that suggested a man as old as Methuselah, was his complexion, which was ruddy and hale with nary a wrinkle. His eyes were weepy and red-rimmed, but glinting with intelligence. He was dressed all in leather; his shirt and trousers neatly sewn but covered in retreating tides of old sweat stains. We were inside a cave that he had turned into a serviceable domicile – quite cozy, and about as large as a few stacks of hay with an open door. He was squatting on his haunches stirring a yellowish gruel with his fingers in a small wooden bowl, and in spite of his distinctly animal appearance, he smelled vaguely of peppermint.

"This poultice is drawin' owt the poison," he said, while dabbing some of it onto my elbow. I could see that the swelling had gone down and the wound had turned a darker, less fiery shade of red. "Goldy-seal," he explained. "Good for fest'rin' sores and just about anything … ulcers, rashes, boils, fevers … It'll even make you shit if'n that's thy complaint."

My jovial host introduced himself as Asa, and described how he had found me burning up with fever and lying unconscious by the river. He showed me the crude travois he used to drag me up the mountain, and said I'd been unconscious for two days, fearing until he saw me sit up and squawk, that my heart might give out before my fever broke. He didn't offer me slices of the possum he was turning on a spit and served me instead a clear broth made from its juices seasoned with herbs and tulip tree bark. As he squatted next to me pulling strips of meat from the greasy carcass with his fingers and stuffing them into his mouth, I closed my eyes and sipped down the broth, doing my best to pretend that the animal my broth was made from – that creature grinning at me on the spit – was one of Father's prized piglets, and not the rodent it actually was.

"You've been a-blay-th'rin' some," Asa chuckled, taking my empty bowl. He scrubbed it out with a dirty finger and sat down on a bench fashioned from fieldstones. "Goldy-seal can pull the blay-ther owt from thy arm, but only thou," he said, pointing to my chest and then to my face, "can pull it owt thy head." I lay back on my bower and looked over at the strange man who had saved my life. The last winks of the fire went flickering across his face, casting eerie shadows on the pelts behind him. He nodded courteously and smiled, busying himself with his hodgepodge of vials and tinctures, humming a nameless tune. The owls in the distance continued to call. Closer by, some fox kits yapped, then quickly calmed. I blinked away the wood smoke, rolled over and fell asleep.

I kept company with Asa all summer, not moving on until the first of the trees started to turn. I needed that time to regain my strength, and to learn all I could from this odd yet highly resourceful man who was living so freely off the land. He was originally from Wales, which was mining country with terrain, he said, similar to the Litchfield Hills, leading him to believe that somewhere in these mysterious mist-covered mountains, great quantities of iron ore could be found – perhaps copper as well, even gold. He was determined to discover these minerals, and had spent a long time – most of his life as best I could tell – in search of them, wandering with his axes and hammers in a circuit that took him northwards through the Berkshires and into the New Hampshire Grants, but always back to the slopes of Coltsfoot Mountain where he believed he had the best chance of striking a valuable vein. It wasn't just the money he was after. I became convinced of that. What I believe he wanted most of all was to prove to all the other prospectors and speculators – and perhaps most especially, to the upstart miners in nearby Salisbury, that he had the better nose for ore.

To sustain himself, Asa relied upon what could be snared, stabbed or dug from the forest floor. There were always plenty of critters to throw on his fire – squirrels, partridges, raccoons, rabbits and possums, caught in the ingeniously simple deadfall traps and sapling snares that he had scattered in different places about the hills. White perch and rock bass were deftly speared from clear, blackwater ponds. He gathered edible greens and roots, berries and mushrooms, and baked a variety of flatbreads seasoned with wild onions and garlic mustard. His baking oven looked like little more than a random pile of stones, but it worked like Billy-o; as well as any Dutch oven ever made. Maintaining a steady supply of ingredients for his dough was a simple matter of venturing down to the farms and trading beaver and raccoon pelts for sacks of wheat and corn flour. He carved wooden animals – mostly owls, because the hills around Cornwall were seemingly bewitched by them – that he'd give to the farmer's children as presents, never expecting anything in return for these little talismans, but always happy to accept a jug of cider or beer should they be offered.

In addition to pointing out the wide array of wild edibles that could be gathered – dozens more than I ever imagined existed – he taught me how to bait and set animal traps and snares. Most important of all, he schooled me in the art of starting a fire without the convenience of a char cloth. He told me that fire was an everyday battle, and one I'd have to win if I were to have any chance of making it all the way to Canada. The New Hampshire Grants was rough country, with few roads, treacherous mountain-passes and weather that could take a turn for the worse in the wink of an eye. With reasonable luck, he figured I could make it to Montreal in less than a month, but if I wanted to arrive alive, I'd need to be able to start a campfire in any weather. Cedar and birch bark shavings for the tinderbox required frequent replenishing. Deadwood snapped from the undersides of trees for the kindling and logs must be gathered every day. To hone my survival skills, Asa left the responsibility of starting our nightly fire completely up to me, an investment of time and effort that would prove to pay dividends.

What a boon companion Asa was! Although he'd be gone for the better part of each day, searching the hills for minerals and checking his traps and snares, he'd return each evening with an amalgam of treasures to sort and categorize: iron pyrite, garnets, gleaming bits of plumbago, magnetite and anthracite coal, plus a rabbit or a pheasant to dress for the spit. How strange I must have seemed to this simple man of nature, so black I was, and full of moods. Looking back, I'm sure he believed my running to Canada was a harebrained notion. He never said as much directly, but I know it's how he felt. "Why Canada?" he once asked. "Why not Mexico or China? Civilization is civilization. If ye truly wanted to run from the war and all the rest of it, why not head for the Dry Tortugas? Now that would be getting away!"

In spite of his friendly and outgoing nature, Asa listened far more than he ever spoke. There was something about him that made me open up, and I told him everything, or all I could remember. I told him about my Father and the treason he committed. I told him about the wounded soldiers in our house and the incriminating powdered wig one of them left behind. I told him about Uncle Joseph and Aunt Sarah taking possession of our home. I told him about the fires and Cesar. I even told him about the blue fingered boy I stumbled upon in the woods.

I also told him about Kessie, the girl from across the river who'd come to our house in the afternoons, hired on as an extra pair of hands for Mother once Gaylee moved to Taylortown. I told him about the evening Mother took me aside and pressed the thimble into my palm. She had a look of complete exasperation. "Give it to her," she implored, "for pity's sake!" I told him how even after we had moved into the little house, and I was apprenticing with Mr. Gilbert, and Kessie's contract had been taken over by my aunt and uncle, our paths would often cross at the end of the day – down at the ferry, on the Compo side. I made it my business to jostle myself to the bow of Meeker's ferryboat where I could scan the opposite bank and look for her dress, periwinkle blue, so easy to pick out from the scatter of people waiting on the landing. After a few poles, we'd be close enough for me to make out her chestnut colored hair, the way she wore it, pulled over one shoulder. Next to come into view would be her smile, and along with it the tiny flicker of a thought that I never had the courage to fully believe: oh my, she's as happy to see me, as I am to see her!

I can picture her now on that last afternoon, young and pretty. She is sitting beside me on the riverbank next to the launch, her bag of sewing resting in her lap, the sun playing across her features as she gathers up an errant wisp of wind-blown hair, and returns it to its rightful place behind her ear. As always, I was wishing our time together were longer, and that we were not sitting in such a public place. I had something urgent I wanted to say, but didn't know where to begin. There was a silence that she filled with a conspiratorial whisper – probably some amusing comment about the passengers crowding up and down the launch, guessing who among them were smugglers or spies. It was a game we often played, an effort to make light of the never-ending war, and all the privations and dislocations that came with it. I was about to guide the conversation to the subject pressing most upon my mind, when from out of the corner of my eye, I noticed of all things, a mussel shell drying in the salt grass and I went and retrieved it.

"Look," I told her holding it up for her to see, "blue is a color so rarely found in nature."

One Eyed Meeker wasn't old yet, just mean, and he shouted angrily to us from his scow, letting us know he was about to push off. Kessie got to her feet and began to run to the launch. I shouted for to her to stop, and clambered up the bank. She paused, allowing me a moment to tell her whatever it was that was so important. From over her shoulder, One Eyed Meeker was grousing and carrying on as he always did. Some of the passengers were impatiently grumbling too, but I still had time. I wanted to confess my feelings to her, to tell her that the only thing that could keep me home would be the hope that she loved me too, but as she stood there staring up at me with those piercing eyes – the exact shade of midnight blue as the mussel shell I still held in my hand – I found myself suddenly struck dumb. Totally cork-brained! I lost all courage, and was only able to feebly repeat the inanity I had pompously proclaimed only moments earlier: "Blue is a color you hardly ever see in nature."

I let her run to the ferry and I watched it push away from the landing. The sun was sinking towards the trees on the opposite shore, silhouetting the scow and all its passengers, but I could see it was Kessie with the sewing basket under her arm making her way through the crowd to get to the rail at the stern. I heard her exclaim ere she got too far from the shore, "Don't be daft, Haynes Bennett! Look to the sky, as much a part of nature as anything I know! See how blue it is!"

That was the last I saw or heard from her for nearly a year. I told Asa about all of it. I told him even about what haunted me the most: those images I couldn't erase from my memory. The sight of Cesar running hatless beneath the burning rafters, and the look on the boy's face as he sat against the rock with his arm resting in his lap – and all of these terrible scenes coming to pass simply because my pacifist of a father, that careful man of reason, could no more choose sides than leave things well enough alone.

"Thou ain't made for the wand'rin' life," Asa declared out of the blue one night after we had finished eating and the fire had died down. "I be one of the Goers, and thou art a Stayer, an' like I always says, it takes all kinds to make an angel's stew."

When I asked what he meant, all I got in response was the steady buzz of his snoring. Outside our cave, the night sky blazed. Two horned owls, one nearby and the other somewhere down by the river, were calling to one another. The nightly din of crickets and cicadas seemed slower than in the weeks before, a sure sign that autumn was approaching. As I too drifted off to sleep, it suddenly occurred to me that I hadn't been tormented by one of my terrible nightmares since the day I awoke in Asa's cave. The war felt centuries removed. If not God, then it was His creation that I had to thank for such a miraculous improvement to my spirits. I understood also that Asa was part of the cure. My heart swelled with feelings I couldn't put into words, and I resolved to thank him in the morning, even if I couldn't say exactly what it was I wished to thank him for. I wanted to share with him my cheering thoughts, but when I awoke, the fire was cold, and not only were all his axes and picks missing, so too was his haversack. Asa was gone. He was off to another corner of his universe, and I thought no better sign could have been received that it was time for me to head straight for the next leg of my journey too.

The Road Back Home

I followed the Housatonic northwards through the Berkshires and was rewarded by a stretch of glorious weather, with warm days and cool nights. Sticking mostly to the ridgeline that paralleled the river kept me away from the farms and farmers and all their earthly entanglements. The trails were dry, and with the jungle of summer dying down, well thinned for easy traveling. I practically bounced along beneath the trees. Breaks in the canopy brought beautiful views, glimpses of America's primal past, before we cleared the forests and scorched what lay below. The brilliant sunshine firing upon the golden chestnuts, red oaks, and orange maples was enough to steal your breath. The air was more fresh and clear than I ever knew it could possibly be. So church-steeple clear that one evening when I was building my fire on a dome of open granite high above the river, I could see westwards all the way to the Catskills. To the north, the Green Mountains saw-bladed against the far horizon, and I swear, looking back to the south, I could see Long Island Sound – it must have been over a hundred miles in the distance – laying like a silver ribbon of glass beneath a sky of quartz.

Not far from this outlook, the Housy made a sharp turn to the east. I thought it best to continue following along her banks, knowing that she must turn again to the north and cleave towards Canada. The communities in this part of Massachusetts, although sparsely populated compared to

Fairfield, bustled smartly with a number of mills churning on the river and its tributaries. It was here that I happened to cross paths with a small family of Quakers: a father, mother and daughter, although the two women looked so close in age it was difficult for me to tell them apart. Referring to one another as "Brother" and "Sister" merely added to the confusion. They had come all the way from Framingham and were taking the road to Niskayuna, a community newly settled near Albany. I say they were Quakers because they were dressed as such. Their speech was like Quakers too, full of "Thee's" and "Thou's," but they presented themselves to me as dissenters of that religion, aiming, they avowed, to join a woman named Mother Ann, the spiritual provocateur of what are now commonly referred to as Shaking Quakers.

These odd pilgrims had with them an old pack mule that they led by a rope. The two bulging sacks slung over the poor, half-starved animal's back held what I assumed were all their material possessions. After introductions, we agreed to dine together and found an appropriate spot far from the road to make our camp for the night. They seemed friendly enough, and we chatted amicably throughout supper. They proselytized little about the tenets of their faith, only to say, like other Quakers I have known, that they relied heavily upon revelation from the Holy Spirit, and that they believed all of mankind were creatures of God, even the fallen among us. What struck me most about them however, was how innocent and blithe they seemed, like children licking icing from a spoon.

After supper, the three of them stood in the clearing and began singing psalms, many I didn't recognize. I sat back, hands clasped contentedly behind my head anticipating some pleasant entertainment around the campfire, but to my disappointment the music that escaped from their throats soon became anything but entertaining. Their voices grew inharmonious and grating – a serenade by their mule would have been easier on the ears – and what a strange hymnody it was! The first psalms they sang were slow, almost dirge-like. After a while, as the tempo quickened, they began stamping their feet and raising their forearms up to their chests.

"Come Brother," the man pleaded, his arms pumping to his chest in an almost mechanical way, beckoning me to join with them. "Come share the gifts of the spirit!"

Thinking it impolite to decline, and, as the lonesome traveler that I was, I did as requested and stood beside him. The man and I took our places facing the two women who never paused in their singing, their eyes now closed, their faces fixed in rapture. What we were engaged in was a primitive sort of Country Dance, with the men and women stepping forwards and back from one another, with the dying campfire in between. With such repetitive verses and simple steps and arm movements, it was easy to follow along, and I was soon in the rhythm of things, and rather enjoying myself. There was something alluring about surrendering to their discordant sounds. How tempting, I remember thinking, to simply fall into the loving arms of our Creator!

Things may have ended differently had not the pace of the singing and dancing increased so precipitously. I soon found myself sweating like a horse, and had become so exhausted the man had to catch me ere I stumbled headlong into the glowing embers of the fire. Such a fall would have burned me badly, and the lunacy of all of that frantic behavior suddenly twigged. It wasn't God's grace that I saw reflected in the faces of these Quakers, but something far more akin to glassy-eyed mindlessness. I stepped away and took refuge in my bedroll, practically diving into it. So enrapt the dancers were, not one of them took the slightest notice of my hasty retreat. Peeking from beneath the blankets, I watched as they continued to thrash about the fire. When they started singing in total gibberish I got worried, but when they fell to the ground and began twitching like skewered rabbits, rolling about on one another in a manner that was decidedly untoward, I reckoned I had seen enough and that it was high time to skedaddle.

I packed up my belongings and gave the last of some apples I had recently filched to the sorry old mule, and left the three of them howling in a writhing heap on the ground. Let them have their gift of the Holy Spirit, or whatever it was that made them lose their minds! I was off again to Canada, following the course of the river under a clear night sky, grateful to be rid of those Shakers, and so ably guided by one of my dearest and most constant friends, the good old Man in the Moon!

In a few days, the Housy dwindled to a series of marshes forcing me to bushwhack northwards through a long stretch of trackless hills. In another few days of rugged trekking, I arrived at the banks of a medium-sized river flowing to the west towards the Hudson, or perhaps Lake Champlain. Knowing that it too would eventually turn to the north and the Canadian frontier, I decided to follow this sparkling river to its source. By then, all the leaves had fallen from the trees and the nights were turning cold. Not wanting to be caught out in the wild in the dead of winter, I felt an urgency to step up my pace. Late one afternoon, I came to a part of the stream where the opposite bank looked more amenable to travel, and so I stepped into the icy waters, thinking I was at as good a place as any to cross over.

The river at this point was so narrow I practically could have heaved my haversack to the far bank. There were no slippery boulders with which to contend, the bottom was lined with small stones and gravel, and the stream looked to be no more than waist deep out in its middle. I had every reason to expect a quick and easy trip to the other side, but was sorely mistaken. Having never before waded into such a crystal clear river meant I was completely unaware of how strongly it could magnify objects lying on its bottom, and thus, when I strode onto what appeared to be a gravely ledge of knee-deep water, I immediately found myself in over my waist and sliding down a steep bank of silt. The speed and strength of the main current was also something I badly misjudged. I was soon bouncing on my toes just to keep my chin above the surface, while at the same time, being rapidly swept downstream.

I sputtered and flailed in this near-drowned condition for a hundred rods or so, until I came to a bend where the current pressed me up against a bank of stones in shallow enough water to regain my footing. My clothes, bedroll and haversack were so sodden and weighed down, it took every bit of strength I had left to climb from the river and onto the sandy bank. It was near dark with clear skies bringing with them the promise of a hard frost, and had my tinderbox not kept its seal, it may well have been my last night on earth. To my additional good fortune, some beavers had built a lodge along the bank just a few yards from where I washed ashore, giving me ready access to enough dried timber for a nightlong fire. With the blaze going strong, I stripped naked, hung up my clothes and blankets, and covered myself in a great pile of dried leaves and every other piece of riverside detritus that could help keep me warm and sheltered through the night. Buried deep inside my ragged mound – which to an outside observer must have looked like a poor cousin to the neat and tidy lodge built by the industrious beavers a little further down the bank – I gave thanks to Asa for teaching me all he did about starting fires. I shivered throughout the long night, nearly frozen solid by dawn, and waited until the morning's sun rose high enough in the sky to finish drying my clothes.

I headed upstream. By midday, I arrived at a more propitious spot to make my crossing and was about to do just that when I noticed I was also standing in a place with an unencumbered view of the mountains looming to the north. They looked menacing, rising in jagged lumps and gauzed with snow. With little in my stomach and only a faint chance of snaring a rabbit or stumbling upon an orchard or unguarded root cellar any time soon, with my clothes still damp, and my joints still thick from the previous night's cold, and with no clear idea of how to wend my way through this maze of formidable mountains, I fell to my knees in despair. I crawled to the riverbank for a drink and as I was lowering my hand, I saw my face reflected on the water. The person staring up at me was an utterly unrecognizable creature, with a scraggly beard and wild tufts of hair bursting out from beneath a tattered woolen cap.

Staring into the eyes of this strange being made me realize that I was completely and infinitely lost. There was no way I could find my way through those mountains, nor reach Montreal once I got to the other side of them. What on earth had I been thinking? Why, in the first place, had I embarked upon such a fool's journey? How could running away from home – in a kind of frenzy not much more rational than a Shaking Quaker's campfire dance – help to bring an end to the war, or improve my lot in life? I was a young man, tarred by the sins of my father and forced to give up my place at Yale, and while I wasn't ever going to become a doctor, I had a trade, and with it a path forward. Yes, I had seen the horrors of war and suffered great losses, but so had many others, including Kessie.

As Asa proclaimed, civilization is civilization, and I determined then and there to rejoin the only one I had ever known. I took my drink of water, got to my feet and turned for home. I got back to Coltsfoot Mountain and the familiar cave a week or so later, just as a snowstorm was blowing in. Bands of wet driving snow clung to the trees and slathered heavily across the ground, making it impossible for the time being to travel any further. Thankfully there was an abundance of flour and chestnuts in Asa's stores, and after a few days of hearty sustenance and warming fires, my strength and spirits were revived. Alternating days of additional snow and accumulating sleet kept me trapped in the cave for over a fortnight. When the cruel weather finally relented, I took a chance it would hold long enough to see me through to the coast, and filled my bag with hard tack and bid farewell to Asa's world. I sat on the stone bench and took one last look around at the homely domicile he had created – the fire pit and rudimentary oven near the cave's opening, the animal skins lining the walls, and the shelves laden with his dozens of crocks and vials. I left him with an ample stack of dry firewood and gave the floor a good sweep. I gathered up my meager belongings, and before stepping out into the sunshine, I took my compass from my haversack and placed it on his pallet for the old Goer to find.

I followed the river south, avoiding farms and other travelers on the roads as best I could, and arrived at the outskirts of Danbury in two days. From there, I walked straight through the night, making it to the Norfield crossroads just as the eastern sky was beginning to pale, and from over the brow of the hill I was able to discern the distant waters of the Sound, a welcome sight indeed! It had turned bitterly cold, and I was tempted to seek warmth in the meetinghouse, but in spite of the cold and with legs as weary as oaken logs, I knew there was no time to tarry. When I got to the edges of Sipperly Hill near the fording place, the sky behind the trees had turned to pink, and when I slunk slowly past the old homestead on Compo Road, I was cheered to find that the windows were still dark. I had made it in time, I thought to myself, and headed straight to the ferry.

Meeker's scow was on the opposite bank, and while sitting on the launch waiting for it to cross, I perceived a certain cast of light in a way I had never quite seen before – that precise scattering of sunlight which is quite distinctive to the corner of the world where I was born and yet live. I saw it that morning brightening the rooftops of the warehouses in Norwalk, and have seen it many times since in the crisscrossing shadows of the undulating farm fields, and in the changing colors of the marsh grasses that crowd the tidal creeks. It is the same constancy of light that coppers the wings of migrating geese in the evening sky over the Mill Pond, and that glints and shadows the pebbles strewn across the sandbar at the beach at dawn. It is the same cast of light I see this very moment, a golden patch upon my kitchen floor that is readying to march across the room before making its steady ascent up the contours of my bookcase. It is the same light that fell upon my face as a boy dashing through clearings of ferns, and the same that fell upon the backs of my ancestors as they raked hay in their fields, or hammered shingles onto the roofs of their newly built houses. It was cold that morning waiting for the ferry to cross, and time could not move fast enough for me. I had been wandering about the edges of the world for so long, but when the sun finally broke over the trees on Bennett's Rocks and lit upon the chimneys of the warehouses on the far side of the river, I saw that certain cast of light, and knew I had made it home.

Meeker began to pole across at last, and in a few moments I saw the bright blue dress I had been waiting for. Meeker tied to the launch and the passengers began filing off. Kessie walked up the ramp with her bag of sewing under her arm and turned straight to me as calmly as if we had only been parted for a day. She put the sewing kit down at my feet and fell into my arms. I don't remember what it was we said just then, or much else about it, but I do remember taking her hand and pressing Mother's thimble into it.

She hugged me hard again and reminded me how my Aunt Sarah turned into an insufferable despot whenever she came to work even a little bit late, and so she needed to go. Before she got too far down the road, she turned around and smiled.

"Of course I'll marry you, Haynes Bennett," she called, lifting the thimble into the air. "But first you'll need to shave!"

Oh, what a rare beauty Kessie was! Eyes bluer than the ocean, hair the color of new spun gold. I tell you what, when she was first hired out by yer Ma and was stuck up in yer attic, the lads were like bees to honey to her, and that's a fact. And I don't mind a-telling ye (as if you didn't know!) I was out there with them boys that summer, tying rags to the ends of your Da's ladder to keep it quiet against the clapboards, hoping to coax that honey of a girl to step down and join our jolly band. Boneheaded bumpkins such as us didn't have a chance with her and knew it from the start, except maybe our crafty Cousin Trow. He was able to pass himself off as the sort of fellow he reckoned a book reader like Kessie might go for. As you know better'n anyone, her favorite book from your Da's library was the Shakespeare, an in particular his book of sonnets. When we tippy-toed through the yard like we did on most nights that summer and saw the candlelight shinin out the attic window, we huddled neath her garret like a pack lovesick puppies with a picture in our minds of her sitting with the candle shinin on her hair an with that little book of poems resting in her lap.

You and William was never in on any of these tomcatting ventures of ourn seeing how you wouldn't dare make the slip past yer Ma and Da. But war or no, we was out 'n about practically ever night with a whole bunch of the usual lads an the one or two lasses we managed to convince from time to time. Lucky for us it was so tarnal hot up there beneath them rafters — hot enough to roast a pheasant Kessie always used to say — and so breathless uncomfortable, she wasn't going to get no sleep anyways, and so after some weeks of throwing pebbles at her window an whispering for her to please, please come down, she finally agreed to climb down the ladder an join us. No doubt the heat worked in our favor an truth be told, that was probably the only reason we was ever able to talk her down, although I remember hoping against hope — as did all we fellers — that it were me she burned to see, that it were me, an only me, she could not resist!

I remember once when we was all piled into the springhouse. That ware a favored spot on our nightly circuits an as good a place as any to drink our grog and escape them tarnal summer doldrums. We had a candle or two lit and Kessie had her book of poems opened in her hands with the light casting upon her lovely face and a-glinting in her eyes, and there was that rascal Trow laying at her feet quoting her line for line about how his love were like a summer flower an how true minds doth a marriage make an all the rest of it. He made quite the strong impression I must allow — who'd a guessed he could have ever memorized all them poems? Well anyways, he got carried away on this particular night and when he could not quell his passions any longer he gets to his feet and declares in front of all of us as to how he loves her more than poems could ever say, and she tells him hard, an in no uncertain terms, how her heart was already taken and for goodness sakes to sit down and mind himself. We asked her who it was she had her heart so strongly set upon but she wouldn't say, although it was a commonly held belief that the lucky lad was none other than your brother William. But that didn't stop Trow who doffs his hat and gets down on one knee and piteously entreats: if I cannot win your heart then allow me to at least own a snippet of your hair! He begs and begs for his token keepsake and she looks at him with a peculiar look an finally relents, saying all right, I suppose what's the harm in that? so I went an fetched the shearers that Ma had hanging on the wall for cutting twine and sausage links and such, an I hands them to her and she pulls her hair around to her breast and as she snipped off the end of her braid, we all stood about her and sighed a collective sigh. I swear, it took our breaths away!

That warn't the worst of my love sickness, nor the end of Trow's case amour. The end for Trow came later that summer; it must have been the middle of September. We was down at the beach, trolling ankle deep across the sandbar where the flukes come to spawn, each of us letting out a squeal ever time we chanced to step upon one of them slippery critters nestled just below the sand – what great sport that was! Everything was going fine until I hears a commotion up ahead. I couldn't see what exactly happened, I just know that Kessie cries out loud, an in one swift motion she yanked that devil Trow's shirt over his head, as deft a maneuver as you ever saw, that trapped his arms in front of his face an made him stumble with a terrific splash headlong into the water, an before he could get to his feet Kessie was long gone! I've never seen a body run so fast, with her skirts pulled up, splashing barefoot through the shallows, scatterin sparks of phosphorus in all directions. Out across the bed of seaweed she sailed with all them wicked stones and broken shells to plague her. Such a vicious terrain would have cut a mere mortal's feet to shreds, but not our Kessie, she never broke stride! What pluck that girl had, an what a bewitching sight she was to see, with her skirts an hair a-flying in the moonlight. I don't believe I've ever loved a girl more fiercely than I did Kessie at that moment, an not for years until I met my Hannah an the spell was finally broke.

Pray, Haynes, how did such a tiny little feller like you pull off such a catch? You, who was meant to become a doctor an winds up a lowly sail maker's apprentice instead! Imagine my surprise – everbody's surprise – when it's four years later an you come creeping back from your escape to Canada or whatever the deuce that was, and we all finds out that it were you what Kessie fancied all along and not your tall and handsome older brother! But like I allus used to say, watch out for ol Haynes. No matter what you throws at him, there, by jingo, is a feller who boxes above his weight! -- JB

Night Stirrings

October 16th, 1827:

Last night when I blew out the candle, I thought I saw a pine torch out on
the road. My heart stopped and then flailed against its riggings. I dashed to
the window, and peered into the darkness. To my relief all looked fine –
what I had espied must have been nothing more than the moonlight
reflecting on a barn window, or perhaps striking upon a broken bottle lying
in the grass by the wood shed. The old tensions are building yet again. All
the menacing signs are in evidence. Our dear, excitable Jesse isn't the only
one to hear the mutterings down at Disbrow's. I've heard them there too.
I've even heard them during the fellowship hour at church, drifting to
within earshot from the far corners of the room. It's no secret that we
members of the Anti-Slavery Society are seeking investors and endeavoring
to nurture support for our dream to establish a school for Negro girls. The
resulting backlashes, those rumblings that can so easily turn into the threats,
of turning on a penny into actual acts of violence, are like echoes of the
waves of certain troubles I have long known. They are the familiar growls
from the unsavory characters among us – the Ezra Weeds of the world –
who are ruled not by reason but by anger and fear. They are the louts from
the taverns ceaselessly spoiling for a fight, men unable to formulate a
coherent thought of their own, but cunning enough to turn chaos to their
advantage, and always at the ready to undertake the distasteful biddings of

others. The damnable Mr. Weed is long gone, but men like him will always be around, and men like Elijah Abel will always be there to top-up their flagons and fill their heads with nonsense. They are the ruffians who called themselves Skinners or Cowboys during the war. They are the ones who burned down our barn, and they are the very same people with the same reptilian passions that ransacked my loft in the dead of night. They did not torch it – only God knows why – but they tarred and feathered Dagger Barnes at dawn, and dragged him to the Green.

I first met Dagger when he was but one of the many itinerant riggers I used to hire whenever sails were ready to be hoisted. He was a big man, over six feet tall, a coffee-colored Mulatto with a huge cascade of black nappy hair, barely contained by his crimson watch cap. He hailed originally from somewhere near Groton, and had been freed when he turned twenty-one, I always assumed, by a Mr. Barnes. He looked to be about the same age as my own grown children, but it was difficult to tell for certain. No man I ever knew could slush line or fit out a ship any more smartly than could Dagger Barnes. He was as steady of foot and as calm of mind walking out on a spar as you or I might be standing on the decks below. This, and his reliable work habits – a quality further assured by his strict aversion to strong spirits – made him one of the most sought after of all the riggers. Sail makers from Stamford to New London competed for his time and talents, which was why the very first major decision I made after taking full ownership of the loft on Cove Street was to make Dagger a permanent employee, and to place him in charge of the riggers who came and went. And what a sound business decision that proved to be! Kessie always said I may not have a nose for profits, but I know how to read a man's character, and I saw the reservoir of virtue in Dagger from the moment I laid eyes upon him. Not only was he the most capable and hardworking foreman in my loft, he soon became the man I'd turn to most often for a second opinion on a wide variety of those little nagging questions that can make such a big difference in the quality of a finished sail – how much bag or belly a certain tops'l might require, or how low to place the clew on a jib. I don't believe I'd have attained the level of respect I was able to attain with ship owners, had I not benefitted from that well-seasoned seaman's eye, and the loyal counsel of Dagger Barnes for all those many years.

It is no wonder the mob singled out Dagger. I had seen how people regarded him while he walked freely on the street, or sat with me for a meal in one of the taverns dotting the waterfront in those years. He was such a striking man, quiet, yet radiating with self-assurance, a proud fellow who looked others straight in the eye. There was so much that one could admire about him, with but one minor flaw in his character that I could see: vanity. Dagger was at all times keenly aware of his appearance, and the strong impression he invariably made upon others. He never ventured out of the shipyard in his workman's smock. He was always well turned out in public. And in spite of his wild mane (a key aspect of his carefully managed persona) and the blotches of pitch permanently marking his face and hands, there was a distinct air of both potency and respectability about him. This, I believe, is what rankled. The mere sight of a neatly dressed dark-skinned man striding so confidently out in public was enough to get the roustabouts going, and the knowledge that such a swarthy alien could have a dozen or so journeymen working under his supervision – most of whom were white – catapulted them over the ramparts. They wanted to send me and the entire town a message before other business owners followed my practice of not only employing Free Negroes, but of putting them in charge. Of this there can be no doubt. Dagger Barnes represented so much of what they loathed about a restless world that was changing all around them. The fact that he was quartered with his wife and family in a room above an unassuming, and I must admit, rather run-down looking sail maker's loft filled to the ceilings with turpentine and tar, made him and my modest enterprise irresistible targets.

I was awakened at sunrise by one of Dagger's sons who had covered the three miles through town and over the Country Road Bridge on a dead run. To save precious minutes, we roused One Eye and returned to Norwalk by ferry. It was a cold winter morning, forcing us to break through thick shelves of ice on both riverbanks. I worried that such conditions might easily impede the efforts of a bucket brigade should it come to that, and was sickened by the thought that the biting wind and frigid temperatures would most definitely make the terrible ordeal Dagger was likely facing all the more unbearable.

When we got to the loft, everything was eerily quiet. There was not a soul to be found. Even the neighboring stores and warehouses – usually showing signs of activity at that hour – looked deserted. Every last window in the place was broken, and the big room had been thoroughly ransacked. Cordage and canvases were unrolled and strewn everywhere. The walls and floors looked as if they'd been painted with pitch and where glittered by shards of broken glass. "What of the night watchman?" I asked the boy. "And where, by God, was the constable?" He told me the night watchman was dead drunk per usual, nor had he seen the constable – only the sound of his rattle attested to his presence, heard in the distance above the shouts of the crowd. It must have been total chaos, I thought, so very frightening, and after tearing through each of the rooms upstairs to make certain there was no one left behind and in need of our attention, we ran up East Avenue towards the square.

There was a large crowd assembled, which looked to be starting to break up. We broke through, and there was Dagger – or a pitiable creature I presumed to be Dagger – propped upon an upturned barrel of pine tar on the back of somebody's mule-drawn wagon, covered from head to toe in chicken feathers. A cadre of angry men were reeling around him, prodding him with long poles. Dagger was doing his best to fend them off, although he was clearly exhausted and at the point of collapse. The feathers clinging to his shock of African-like hair made his head appear preposterously large, giving his tormentors something extra to laugh about. They aimed their poles at his torso and as each blow landed, his head would jerk, sending a cloud of feathers billowing into the air. "Dandelion! Dandelion!" they laughed and cried. The boy started to run to the aid of his father, but I restrained him. "We must find the constable!" I shouted into the poor lad's ear whilst scanning the sea faces around me, and there he was, in the shadows behind the throng, standing in a desultory pose on the steps of the courthouse, musket in hand. I charged over and demanded that he put an end to this awful viciousness. Although I am quite sure he recognized who I was, he acted as though he couldn't hear my pleas from above the ruckus. It was only after I persisted in my demands that he bothered to look at me directly, whereupon he let out a puff of air from his lips and observed with a sigh, "Well, I s'pose they're about worn out by now." He sidled his way through the crowd, grabbing hold of one of their poles and turned to face the tormentors, who quieted at the sight of his badge and musket. "Fun's over, you toss pots," he cried to the cluster of half-opened maws that circled around him. "Go home an' sleep it off … Go on, git!"

Once the crowd dispersed, the boy and I helped Dagger down from the wagon and slowly walked him back down East Avenue, our arms held firmly about his waist, taking the weight of his battered body between us, gagging from the pungent stench of the pine tar. As we were walking down the hill towards Cove Street, his wife raced up to meet us, her young children trailing behind her skirts like a brood of chicks. "Dagger! Eldridge!" she cried, and took her husband tenderly by the hand, pausing for a moment to stand back and regard the sight of him. "At least the bastards kept your trousers on," she observed calmly. "I'll take it from here, Mr. Bennett," she said, informing me that they'd be boarding with Mrs. Betts for the time being. With a gracious air, she turned to escort her husband the rest of the way down the street. After a few steps, Dagger wheeled around to face me. He hadn't said a single word up until that moment, but he took a breath now, and squared his shoulders. "We're gonna clean up that damn loft," came a voice from behind the feathers. "You'll see, Mr. Bennett. We'll be back in business a-fore those cracked sonsabitches sobers up!"

It's hard to believe that was ten years ago. Seems like yesterday, and already they are back. So far, we've only seen some pieces of siding ripped from Jesse's barn, and had a rock thrown through our window. Please, let that be the end of it, I thought to myself as I crept into the bedroom. My mind began to race as I groped in the dark for my sleeping cap, staying as quiet as I could lest I awaken Kessie. There were no unusual sounds coming from outside, no shadows dancing up the walls, only the reassuring buzz of my wife's steady breathing as I settled beneath the blankets. I hadn't had a nightmare in years, and to keep another one at bay, I nodded off to visions of apple trees, their emerging blossoms pinking distant hillsides.

Rachel's Bind

October 20th, 1827:

Rachel is sitting by my side this morning, something that has become a regular ritual of ours since about the time I took up this diary and began reflecting upon my youthful past. She is just budding into womanhood. How delightful it is, and surprising to believe, that a girl of her tender age might enjoy my company as much as I enjoy hers. I love how she joins me in the kitchen to share the light of my lamp, and to pour over my books of poetry. Our afternoons and evenings together – especially now that the leaves are turning – remind me of my weeks spent in Asa's cave, with me tending to the fire and turning the spit, and with him huddled in the shadows, sorting through his herbs and mineral ores. As it was with Asa, she and I are each well occupied and therefore speak little to one another, but in those brief moments taken to sharpen the point of my quill, or to rub the lamp smoke from my eyes, I take great pleasure in silently observing her at my elbow. She has the raven hair, the dark intelligent eyes, and the even facial features of the Bennetts, and I should think the boys in town find her pretty. Indeed, if I am not mistaken, there are at least a few lads from the neighborhood that I see on occasion out in the yard who look far too old to be playing blind man's bluff with my younger grandchildren. I strongly suspect that their true aim is to fabricate a chance encounter with the bewitching young girl sitting beside her old Henny on the other side of the window.

Rachel feigns little notice of these older fellows who jump and play out in the yard. There is however, one boy who ventures by more often than the others, a boy, whenever he leaps into view, who brings a touch of red to Rachel's cheeks. He is none other than the son of the aforementioned Dagger Barnes. His name is Eldridge, a tall fellow who happens to be very light skinned – a complexion even fairer than his father's – and someone who could easily pass for white, which is, of course, scant consolation for Rachel's parents! I have seen Rachel and Eldridge talking together after church, and running hand in hand at the river's edge. In their innocence, they have done nothing to hide their growing friendship. We all wonder what Eldridge's ultimate intentions with Rachel might be, and although it seems unlikely to me that he might actually become her suitor one day, there are those in town who think differently. His persistent interest in Rachel has already caused an ugly stir, and I suppose, to prevent even more furor, I should speak with my daughter Mary and her husband Thomas. As aghast as they are sure to be once they learn that the Mulatto boy is still appearing at my window, my advice to them will be to step away, and allow nature to run its course. I have long been of the opinion that once a romance has been sparked between two young people – especially when there is African blood upon the char cloth – there is very little anyone else can do to extinguish such a passion, before it is ready to fade in it's own good time.

When I look at Eldridge today, and in spite of the fact that he is so young with only the faintest hint of peach fuzz above his lip, I can't help but to be reminded of the escapades of Happy's Broom years ago. Short of employing shackles, there was simply nothing Uncle Moses could do to keep that man from running off! Thankfully, he never stayed away long. He always came back to the farm, never failing to complete his work. Uncle Moses seemed prepared to overlook these nocturnal wanderings of his amorous servant. Were it not for the complaints of various neighbors, whose servant girls were the objects of Broom's desires, I am quite certain Uncle Moses would have happily turned a blind eye to all of it. "There's no fighting such a fierce force of nature," he would often lament, throwing up his arms.

There was one episode in particular – I believe it must have been before the war – when Broom was discovered to have been running off to Judge Sturges's on a nightly basis. This went on for months. During some weeks, it seemed as if Broom was making the trip back and forth between their two farms seven times in as many nights, and he was quite bold about it. I even remember him openly boasting to Jesse and me about how he could cover the five-mile trek – mostly off the roads and through the woods – in under an hour! All this began when the Judge came into the possession of a servant girl named Nancy – a beguiling wench she was, inherited from his brother (or some other close relative) who had passed away. Broom becoming enamored with this beautiful girl was nothing out of the ordinary, and his nightly escapades on this occasion created very little consternation for anyone – for anyone that is, with the exception of our Cesar. From his perspective, Broom's behavior brought with it an unthinkable level of risk. I do not believe that even Father – who had years earlier promised to free Cesar once he had accumulated enough money from his joiner's earnings to buy Phyllis and their girls from the Judge – fully understood the ramifications, or even gave the matter more than just a passing thought. This left it up to Cesar himself to try and keep Broom in his bunk. And thus, when an opportunity presented itself, he concocted an elaborate plan, a plan that required assistance from Jesse and me as it so happened, even if we were far too young and naïve at the time to have a clue what we were doing, or what was at stake.

As a grown man who has dedicated a great deal of time and effort to the cause of abolition, I can now understand what Cesar was up against. He anticipated right from the beginning that with no use for two grown Negresses, the Judge would want to sell one of them as soon as he could get around to it. In those years, a young, unspoiled servant girl such as Nancy was likely to fetch a higher price than would an older house servant such as Phyllis. This, of course, gave Cesar reason to feel at least somewhat assured. If all went as expected, the Judge would sell Nancy, and everything would turn out fine for Cesar and his family. The only possible fly in this jar of ointment would be if the unspoiled girl, as she stood on the auction block, were to have been unable to disguise the fact that she had, as Jesse later phrased it, "swallowed a melon seed." This would have lowered her value considerably, at which point there would have been no telling what the Judge might have decided to do. Perhaps his kind and virtuous heart

142

would have prevailed. On the other hand, we all knew that the Judge was a practical man who clearly enjoyed his worldly comforts, and so his decision of which wench to sell might easily have come down to a cold calculation of dollars and cents. That was the potential outcome that Cesar so greatly feared, and given the ferocity of Broom's present state of rut, the poor man was utterly beside himself with worry for weeks.

Cesar saw his chance to take matters in his own hands one Sunday. When he saw that Broom hadn't showed up for church, he knew exactly at which altar his knees were bending towards that morning. The moment we got home, he went to Father, and under some pretext or another, convinced him to write out a pass. He then took me aside, asking me to go into the house and secret out paper, quill and ink. Jesse had come home with us that day, and was, as always, eager for intrigue and adventure. While I went looking for the writing implements, Jesse made himself useful by distracting Mother and Father with his fiddle playing. Cesar was out hitching the team, and in no time the three of us were sitting on the buckboard, making tracks for the Sturges's estate. When we arrived at the gate on Mill Plain Road, Cesar was ready for bold, decisive action. He told us there was no time to lose, and ordered us go to the door and ask to see the Judge, while he went round back to the one of the outbuildings. We were to inform the master of the house that Cesar had come to make a few minor alterations to the gazebo he was in the process of building out by the fishpond, and to ask him to be so kind as to retrieve the design sketches from his study. "Stalls him," Cesar said. When we asked why, he replied "Juss do it," and when we asked him how, he gave us that look of his you never wanted to argue against and hissed, "Figger sumptin!"

Thankfully for us, both the Judge and his wife were away for the day, which left it to their daughter Priscilla to greet us at the door. She was a girl about our age who, in spite of her aristocratic airs, proved friendly enough. When we made our intentions known she happily obliged, leading us into the study where she found the drawings we were after on her father's desk. Sensing that not enough time had elapsed for Cesar to get done whatever it was he wanted to get done, Jesse cleared his throat as we were making our way back to the front door. With hat in hand, he asked our elegant hostess for some lemonade. "We are sorely parched," he proclaimed in his most charming voice, and to our great relief, Priscilla obliged yet again, and summoned Phyllis to make us all refreshments. We returned to the study were we were joined by the young twins, Promise and Gift. We sat in a circle – the first time, by the by, that either Jesse or I ever sat in an upholstered chair – forming a most agreeable party. While we sipped our lemonade, the two adorable girls stood dutifully beside their mistress who was taking obvious delight in braiding their hair. This tender scene, which fully occupied the attentions of our hostess, proved fortuitous, as it prevented her from seeing what Jesse and I espied, just at that moment, through the double windows over her shoulder. There was Cesar, chasing Broom across the lawn, prodding him with a pitchfork as the poor fellow, indecently clad, and with a look of great distress etched upon his face, went hopping along on one foot, whilst desperately attempting to steer his other foot into the unoccupied leg of his britches before while hastily making our excuses to leave.

By the time we got out into the yard, Cesar was already seated on the buckboard with reigns in hand and with what looked to be a bundle of lumber wrapped in canvas lying in the bed of the wagon. The twins, who hadn't up until then realized that their father was on the premises, squealed with delight when they saw him, leaping as gracefully as two black panther kits onto his lap.

"Dare, dare, liddle lambs" he whispered, planting kisses on their foreheads before shooing them back down to the ground. "Tells yer Ma dat Ize be back anon. Reg'ler time.

"The sketches!" Priscilla suddenly remembered. "Wait here while I fetch them for you."

"Doan fuss none, Miss," Cesar replied. "Ize done ready fix't wha' neet fixin'," and with a courteous tip of his hat, we were off.

Once we had traveled a ways up the road and were safely out of sight, Cesar pulled the wagon to a stop. "You decent yet?" he inquired of the bundle behind his shoulder, and out popped Broom, who had somehow managed by then to look presentable, with his shirt and britches in their proper order and buttoned.

"You tarnal black billy goat!" cried Jesse in a show of righteous anger. "I'm a-going to lash you myself one'st we get home!"

Cesar told Jesse to hush while reaching for the quill and paper. "We cant's be out'ins braw daylight wid dis damn rascal," he said turning to me. "Makes de bess pass ye knows ta makes, an signs it Moze Bennett."

When I finished writing out the document with my uncle's signature forged upon it, Cesar looked at it approvingly and folded it into his shirt pocket. He then took hold of the pitchfork and turned to confront Broom. Cesar was on his feet now. His eyes narrowed into two black pinpoints, with the tribal markings on his cheeks looking more fearsome than I had ever before seen them. "Iffin Ize evvva kitch ye tom-cattin' a'gin, it won't juss be yer backside dat'll feels dis foke! Ize swears Broom," he continued in deathly earnest, "I'll kill ye!"

Broom shook with terror and fell prostate onto the bed of the wagon, saying how sorry he was for all the worry he had caused, and swore to the "Blessed Baby Jesus" that he'd never see Nancy again. A more convincing display of Christian repentance would have been impossible to imagine! I believed at the time that the affair had come to a close, and Broom did remain true to his word for a while, but here's the rub: he was only able to keep to his bunk for about a week! The amorous young Negro was simply unable to resist Nancy's charms for long, and in spite of – and perhaps in part because of – the presence of Cesar's threat, he carried on with her as fervently as ever, right up to the day she was sold.

So I wonder, what can Mary and Thomas possibly say or do at this point that will keep the apparent desires of Eldridge in check? These two children may indeed be young, but it is plain to see that the warmth of feeling growing between them is a force of nature if ever there was one. The more impediments that Mary and Thomas – or anyone else for that matter – put before them, the fiercer this force is likely to become. Let me say it again – my counsel for those two, should they ever think to seek it, is to remain calm, to wait patiently for their lovely, idealistic, and strong-willed daughter to come to her senses. I am quite sure she will eventually tire of this otherwise worthy, yet entirely unsuitable Eldridge Barnes.

Cesar's Stand

The next time I ever saw Cesar armed with a pitchfork was when we arrived home from the ford on that bright April afternoon in 1777. Cesar was standing by the front door, with his three-pronged weapon aimed down the road. So much had transpired in so short a period of time. When we stepped into the yard, it didn't seem possible that I had slipped through that very same doorway only twelve hours earlier. So much had changed by then. In the morning, I was simply following the creed of our fellow red-ribbon'd Patriot lads, chasing after William as I had vowed to do, hoping to find Redcoats, and to be wrapped in glory slaying them. By that afternoon, I found myself beaten, disillusioned and ashamed. Even now, a lifetime later, I find it difficult to gather it all in. There's simply a limit to what the mind can absorb and remember. But this much I know for sure: the sight of Cesar standing sentinel at our front door that afternoon was like an elixir for my aching ribs and feverish brain, as soothing as a draft of laudanum and honey. He had on his best tri-cornered hat and emerald green Sunday coat, and although he was clearly agitated, shifting his weight from foot to foot, I knew instantly he had matters well in hand.

To our relief, the house and barns showed no sign of serious damage. The grounds were piled with litter, and Mother's freshly tilled and staked kitchen garden had been trampled flat, but that was all. As we were making our way through the orchard, Cesar had his back to us, swelling his shoulders like a tomcat, training his pitchfork towards a few Militiamen that had come into view just then, sidling up the road. They approached with their muskets limping at their sides, the sound of gunfire sputtering in the distance behind them. Exactly what Cesar thought he might accomplish with his three tines against their muskets I couldn't say, but he stood his ground, with an attitude of body that warned, "don't dare cross me." We got down from our horses and watched the Minute-men as they passed silently on the road, which was when Cesar caught sight of us.

"Lawd amighty" he called, "if you ainna sight fwa sory eyes!" He bounded over from the door, all the while keeping his weapon trained on the men who were well past us by then. "Gwoine!" he shouted to their backs with a jab of his pitchfork.

"Where is everybody?" Father asked anxiously.

"In de sella wares dey belongs!"

Father asked Jabe to rub down the horses and handed Cesar his ruined fowler. "Take this," he said. "Hold it fast under your arm and aim it at the road. Even cracked in two, it'll make a more noteworthy impression than that useless pitchfork." With Cesar left standing guard on the porch, we ran into the house and found Mother, Gaylee and my younger brothers and sisters down in the cellar huddled on an assortment of apple crates drawn in a tight circle on the dirt floor. They all rose to speak at once when we clattered down the stairs, but soon deferred to Gaylee who told of what had happened that morning. Long before the battle began, they knew the Redcoats were coming, and thought about fleeing, but with so much chaos and danger out on the roads, they decided there was no safer place to be than in their own cellar. Grandfather William had wandered off (a regularly occurring symptom of his derangement) and hadn't been seen since breakfast. No telling where he had gotten himself to; they could but pray it was someplace away from the fighting. That left only Cesar to watch over them, to keep them and our property safe and secure. Mother stuffed the candlesticks and our Bassett pewter in a box, and hid it in the brook that runs behind the rocks. Gaylee distracted the children with games of jackstraws and cat's cradle on the kitchen table, while Cesar ran about the barnyard shunting the draft horses into their stalls, securing the rest of the livestock in their pens in the barn.

When Mother had finished hiding our valuables, she ordered Cesar to the top of Bald Mountain where he could see into the village and keep everybody apprised of developments. Militia had been pouring into Saugatuck all night, and by mid-morning he reported that the entire square was choked with armed men. The ragtag assortment of combatants milled about the Liberty Pole until uniformed officers on horseback herded them and a few field pieces across the bridge. Cesar could see that the Americans had taken a position on top of Old Hill facing north. At first, their line was short and thin, but with every passing hour their ranks were swelled by the steady arrival of additional soldiers. Some came up the roads from Norwalk and points west, while others came down the roads from points east, until there were so many Minute-men on the crest of Old Hill, and in such a commanding position overlooking the Saugatuck's only bridge, Cesar was able to ascertain exactly what we ourselves had concluded from our vantage point on Chestnut Hill. The Redcoats were trapped. Getting across the narrow bridge and back to their ships at Compo looked nigh impossible. He thought the British might move their transports up the coast to Norwalk as a way to avoid the bridge completely, and thus, for a few fleeting moments, he and Gaylee and Mother were comforted with the hope that there wouldn't be a battle coming their way after all. But Cesar saw no sails moving westward behind the Shores, and when he came back with the news that a thread of crimson could be seen forming on the distant hills towards Ridgefield, Gaylee and Mother knew there'd soon be a pitched battle, and that it would spill over to their side of the river, putting them directly in the middle of the fray.

As Gaylee was telling us this, Cesar remained standing at a spot where he could keep a wary eye on the road, while at the same time, overhear the conversation in the cellar. "Tells dem 'bout dat Gawd damt Ezra Weed!" he shouted down the stairs. Gaylee chinned back a reply. "Mind your language!" she scolded, and continued with her account. "Yes," she concurred, "Ezra and some others had been seen skulking around the neighborhood at dawn, gunnysacks in hand." They could be seen looking down wells, splashing into brooks and knocking apart stonewalls – scouring all the likely hiding places for valuables. Thank goodness Cesar was there to shame and chase them away from the yard – "charging like a stallion from the barn," Gaylee told us, "armed with his pitchfork. Scattering those awful scoundrels just as the guns from Old Hill commenced their fire."

"— Daz right!" Cesar shouted from the porch. "De whole house begans ta shake!"

We turned again to Gaylee. "The awful rolls of gunfire faded in due time," she said, "only to give way to the sound of wagons pounding down the road, with the cracking of whips heard over the frantic cries of the drovers. There were soldiers crowding around the well – shouting just out in the yard, elbowing for a drink. No sooner had the wagons trundled away, than waves of fresh gunfire began sounding from the direction of the bridge. "Like rolls of thunder," Gaylee cried, "coming through the village and growing louder all the time." At one point, they thought the Redcoats had fired a volley directly beside the house. Wisps of smoke began seeping below the door and billowed down the stairs, filling their nearly pitch black hiding place with the acrid smell of sulfur. The children began to wail, all of them were choking from the smoke, and while they felt an instinct to run, they could do nothing more than huddle closer together, and when they thought it couldn't get any worse, the loudest report of all suddenly rocked the entire house – closer still, but from the direction of the beach – followed by the sound of musket balls striking the barn.

" – Lawd amighty!" Cesar shouted from the porch, pacing now like he did when he was excited. "Oona heard such a tebble nise! Bang it went, den bat-bat-ba-aa-aa-aa-at!"

It was then that Mother jumped to her feet and raised a hand to interrupt the story Gaylee and Cesar were telling, her thoughts shifting from the horrors of the recent past to the urgencies of the present. "Where's William?" she abruptly inquired of Father, running towards him, reaching for his arms. "Is he not with you?"

"Nay, I fear he is with the troops at the beach," Father answered, and before she could get hold of his extended hand, we felt as much as heard an enormous percussive boom – and then a second one – coming from the Sound. Father, Mother and I ran up the cellar stairs and out onto the porch where Cesar stood with eyes as big as pewter plates. I had never seen my mother more distraught. She elbowed past me, chasing after Father, her face distorted and red as she began to pummel him on his back with her fists.

"You promised to bring them BOTH home!" she spat through tears. Father turned to face her, endeavoring to grab her wrists and stop the blows that were landing now about his face and neck, but she persisted, bringing up welts on top of the mark I had just put below his eye, flailing like a mad woman until her fury was spent.

"He is but a boy!" she sobbed at last, and buried her face deep into his shoulder.

William's Return

When William came walking up the road after the battle on Compo Hill, he had Grandfather with him, collected from where he found him leaning against our unfinished stone fence at the foot of Bald Mountain. Mother pushed away from Father and ran to embrace her son. William held a musket at his side. His face was blackened with smoke and grime, but I could tell by the way Mother inspected him before gathering him once again in her arms, that he was not injured.

The two of them remained standing next to the well in the shadows of the lowering sun. Gaylee went to Grandfather and slowly led him back to the porch, where the rest of the family was now gathered. Cesar took a moment to re-secure the bandage across my eye and then tenderly placed an arm around my shoulder. The children each found a place on the porch steps where they sat chin in hands, dazed. There was no further gunfire and none of us spoke for the longest time. Mother was holding William tightly in her arms, while out on the road random collections of downtrodden Militiamen continued to pass silently by.

"Cowards! You had them outnumbered!" Grandfather blurted, and Gaylee told him to hush while pulling him into the house. "You had them outnumbered!" he shouted again, this time loud enough for the soldiers out on the road to hear, but none acknowledged him.

When Gaylee had Grandfather tucked into the house, Father

moved to bring William and Mother inside too. The children scooted over to make them a path up the porch steps and watched silently as William slumped over as if out of breath, leaning onto the railing.

"He's right," he said, turning to Father. "We did have them outnumbered. We were in our lines, ready to charge. Colonel Lamb climbed atop the stonewall that runs at the head of Gray's Creek, shouting "seize the prize!" and even after they fired their cannons, with grapeshot falling hot around us, we found the courage to cross over the wall. I went over the wall with them Father, I truly did, but when the marines assembled and came roaring towards us down the hill, with the sun flashing on the steel of their bayonets, the whole mass of men just in front of me turned heel and ran. And Father," he continued with tears forming rivulets through the grime on his cheeks, "I ran too! As fast and as far as my legs would carry me! I ran and ran and ran!"

"Let me have that," was all Father commented while taking the gun that William still clutched tightly in his hand. He sniffed at the end of the barrel. "This musket has never been fired," he quietly announced, and walked towards the barn where there was an opening to the sky between trees. After checking that it was primed, he cocked the hammer and fired into the air. It made a terrible explosion, throwing him to the ground with a violent recall. He looked over at William who stood agape. Mother stood next to him with her hands over her ears. The soldiers still filing past out on the road hardly broke stride as the sound of the blast went echoing around them. They didn't even bother to look up. "You had at least two balls wadded in there!" Father exclaimed.

That night after supper, Cesar and whatever Irishman we had bonded at the time, moved out of the servant's quarters so that William and I could sleep on their bunks, away from the others in the loft. We had both run towards the enemy. We had both held visions of Redcoats falling and of flags being taken, but when the day was over and the smoke had cleared, neither one of us had fired a single shot. Our soldierly intentions not withstanding, when Cesar blew out the candle and crept from the room, we rolled over in our bunks, falling into that dead sort of sleep only hardened soldiers know.

Early Assurances

The smoke from the battles on Old and Compo Hills had barely cleared when we knew we were in grave danger. "De boo hags" were coming, as Cesar would say, and I was hoping that Jesse, in his usual cheery manner, would find a way to distract me from my worries. Whisperings around town were getting louder by the day. The mere fact that Father had chosen to remain in the house on the first night of the raid was enough to raise suspicions and, as we had feared, his subsequent activities had not gone entirely unnoticed. In spite of the rain and the gloom, our oxcart had indeed been seen out on the road on Friday night, and when Father's coat that he had used to cover the body of the boy at the ford showed up at Disbrow's, he made no attempt to deny that it was his, and boldly entered the tavern in order to claim it. As of that point in time, however, nobody had come right out and demanded an explanation about the oxcart, or asked what business Father had been attending to at the ford, or why a self-proclaimed non-combatant such as he would even be remotely close to the battlefield at all. I suppose this short period of grace was due to the standing he had in the community. He was, after all, a man who had served his country well in the last war, and was known to be an upstanding citizen, an honorable man of his word. He was indeed honest, and painfully so, which was precisely why Mother and Gaylee – and all of us – were so worried that if anyone were to ever pose an incriminatory question, he wouldn't be able to stop himself from baring his chest and telling the entire story. As he was leaving

Disbrow's with his coat in hand, there came some rumblings from the nearby tables. It wasn't clear what anyone had said, nor were the comments presented in a manner that required a response, and yet to my great distress, Father paused by the door. My heart was in my throat. Mother's face went ashen. "Come along, Dell," she whispered urgently. Father ignored her, turning instead to address the upturned faces. "I was at the ford, you damnable fools, in search of my son William," he declared, which was of course the truth in its narrowest sense. The wags sat grinning over their flagons, exchanging glances, and before Father had a chance to say another word, Mother took hold of his arm and herded him out the door.

I remember when Jesse first asked me about the rumors he was hearing, wondering what Father was planning to do about them. It was a week or so after the raid, and I told Jesse everything, probably saying far more than I should have revealed, even though I had every reason to believe Jesse had already learned the worst of it from his brother. We were at the Tipping Rock, the secret place where we so often spent time freely talking about whatever was on our minds. Jessie was standing atop the little boulder, pushing with his legs to make it seesaw back and forth. He was always one to see the silver linings, and I desperately wanted to hear him say that everything was going to turn out fine for us. I told him how Uncle Joseph had come to our house after the raid – that first time, before the wig was found in our kitchen. At that point, while there were indeed all sorts of rumors circulating, Father was not in any real danger. He felt he had nothing to hide, and when Uncle Joseph pressed upon him to come out with the entire truth, Father went against the wishes of Mother and Gaylee and didn't withhold a single detail. He told about the soldiers on our porch, and about the surgeon cutting the ball from Captain Lyman's leg. He told about the comfort Mother had provided to young Betts and to the other wounded Provincial as they were being conveyed to the beach in our oxcart. He told about Aunt Sarah and Uncle Jabez and the provisions that they had stored in their barn, and how their plan to turn these valuables over to the Regulars had gone awry. He told about our ride back to Compo, and of his hope of finding William before the battle on Old Hill started. Worse still, he told Uncle Joseph about how he had assured Lieutenant Soames that in spite of the heavy rains, the river could be crossed at the ford, and freely confessed how he had pleaded with the Dragoon to pass this intelligence along to his commanders, giving the Redcoats their chance to escape from the trap General Arnold had set for them.

Jesse absorbed all of this whilst steadily rocking back and forth atop our secret stone. He didn't appear overly concerned by anything I was telling him, which brightened my mood, but when I told him what Uncle Joseph had proposed on that first visit, his rocking motion slowed, and his demeanor darkened. Uncle Joseph assured us that he could protect Father from the Committee, but only if he agreed to stick to the barest truths of his story. Father, he advised, must emphasize that the soldiers that requisitioned his oxcart did so at gunpoint. Nobody had seen the Redcoats enter our house, so there was no reason to mention anything about Captain Lyman or the young Betts. Cesar was the only person seen in the cart as he drove it back from the beach, so there was also no reason for Father to reveal that he or Mother had attended to that errand at all. Most importantly, he mustn't breathe a word about the business in Norfield, or about his actions at the ford. He only needed to stand by the simple truth he had already made public: that he had forded the river and came upon the boy, simply because he was looking for William and me.

I bared all of this to Jesse, and he seemed unperturbed, which made me feel better, but when I told him next how Uncle Joseph had placed his hands upon Father's shoulders and uttered the words, "Trust me, Brother, your secrets are ever safe with me" Jesse stopped his rocking altogether. After a long silence, I spun upon my seat on the ground in order to get a view of his face. I saw that he was poised dead still, with his hands resting at his sides, gazing down at me with an expression upon his face I had never before seen. He seemed ready to speak and I searched his eyes, hoping to find in them the familiar and reassuring twinkling, but he turned away instead, and spoke quietly to the trees. "Nova Scotia, I hear tell, is not nearly so tarnal frozen nor as awful desolate as many claim."

Haynes, Haynes, Haynes! There ware indeed nary the dimmest twinkle in them eyes a mine that day. "Trust me" Uncle Joseph says. Trust him? The minute you told me that one, I knowed your goose was as good as cooked, wig or no wig, coat or no coat. How a feller as smart as you waren't able to add two an two and make four is beyond me! Yer Da told the truth and never wavered, but that rascal Uncle Joe only ever told the truth what suits. Everbody knowed he ware marching his Home Guards round

155

an round from here to Black Rock, allus keepin us a good pigs holler away from any mischief on them nights when there ware a wagon from Norfield parked at the river's edge, ready to lade. We knowed all about it, figgerin it ware a harmless enough enterprise an something worthy a turnin a blind eye to, but once it twigged on me that Uncle Joseph not only had something to gain from yer Da's Toryisms, that he now had something big to lose iffen yer Da ever got called into court an forced to testify, I knowed right then an there that you was as good as done. I couldn't yet see exactly how that crupted Captain would manage it or when, but I know'd somethin were a-comin if he ever got his chance, and when it came, I know'd it were a-going to be somethin sorely, sorely bad!

Dust ups and Disputes

My nightmares didn't begin right away. There were too many other disturbances to distract my mind in the months following the Danbury Raid. For one thing, William made his first attempt at joining Uncle Joseph's company of Home Guards. He was under age but that wasn't the issue. The requirements for becoming a soldier were much more strictly geared to a lad's physical stature than to his actual date of birth – and William was a big strong strapping fellow in the summer of 1777, I'd say fully grown. His name was thus duly entered into the book of muster, Company Six of the Fourth Regiment, and he was presumed ready to report for duty until Mother learned of it. To her, of course, the chronological age of her eldest son was the ONLY thing that mattered. As soon as she caught wind of what William had gone and done behind her back, she marched into Disbrow's and told the recruiting sergeant to strike his name from the rolls. This led to a conflagration within the family of epic proportions that stretched over a period of days. It sparked fully into the open when Mother and Aunt Sarah were with Cesar at the dock as he was unloading firewood. The flames quickly spread. They were shouting so loud, we could hear them all the way up at the barn, compelling Father to go and investigate. Mother was contending children shouldn't be the ones to settle disputes between intemperate and foolish old men. As you might expect, Aunt Sarah took offense at that, saying her husband was no fool, and that there can be no intemperance when the cause is righteous. Before long, Uncle Joseph was down there too, with Gaylee out from the kitchen –

without her bonnet, looking quite the harridan – and began pumping hard on the bellows for good measure. Around and around they all went until after a while you couldn't tell who was arguing for what. Uncle Joseph used the opportunity to remind Father one more time about the Oath he still hadn't signed and about the shame that his indecisiveness was bringing upon the family (not to mention all the dead chickens and manure thrown down our well) while Father parried by declaring that Oaths of Fidelity were not worth the paper they're written on.

"You stubborn fool!" Uncle Joseph roared. "Allowing young William to serve will help clear away the clouds of suspicion that yet hang about you. Don't you see? What can be wrong about a willing and able fellow defending his country from Tory and foreign raiders?" To which Father countered that lawless incursions such as these were better left to constables and the courts, and not to the armed rabble he called his Home Guards. "And it wasn't just a dead chicken!" Gaylee oared in for good measure, shaking her fist at Father. Griswald, the tanner, was secretly poisoning our well with arsenic. She was sure of it. If anyone needed proof, all they'd have to do was look at the water she's been passing of late, which she boldly proclaimed was black as tea.

What's with you bookish Bennett's? You may be educated an all fancy pants but damn if you waren't too tarnally thick skulled to know when to keep your bone boxes shut! We waren't the only chickens within earshot of Jessup's wharf in them days, not by a long shot! There were plenty of nosy neighbors looking for any excuse to trim our sails. I remember this particular argument. Twas a real snorter! You could hear them hellcats caterwalling from Country Lane all the way to Bennett's Rocks! We mere mortal Bennett's never felt 'twas necessary to let the whole world know where we stand on the price of pease an porrage or whatever else there is to fuss about. We minds our own knitting. An I tell you what, when that old harridan started chasing Uncle Del from the barn to the docks an back again announcin to the whole world that her piss had gone black, an that Griswald was the one who done it to her, well, that simply waren't good. No wonder the bolts a leather we paid good money for was stiff an cracked! – JB

Mother was the one left standing tallest when the shouting finally died away. It took a few weeks, but she won her case by ultimately bringing the other women over to her side. After all, Aunt Sarah and Gaylee were mothers too, and once their natural instincts were appealed to, nothing else mattered. So William's name was struck from the roll, as Mother had demanded, but the coals of that family argument remained just below the ashes for years. Some say they glow red still.

The next thing was, right around this same time, Grandfather William died. We all knew his days were numbered, but his passing came as a shock nonetheless. The whole family rode up to Norfield a few weeks later to settle his estate. I remember standing in Uncle Daniel's hall, peering over the shoulders of my cousins and seeing the old coot, Grandfather's executor, as he sat behind his big mahogany desk in the library. He was stooped and palsied, squinting through spectacles so smeared it was a wonder he could see at all. Gaylee and the rest of them were assembled for the reading of the will, arrayed in chairs around Uncle Daniel's desk like herring gulls circling in the wake of a fishing boat. We children were scooted from the room and put our ears to the door as soon as the servant pulled it closed, shushing one another to silence, anticipating that an entertaining argument might soon come spilling through the keyhole.

We could hear Uncle Daniel mumbling, but couldn't make out what he was saying before he fell into a paroxysm of wheezy coughs. When he regained his breath, he paused for another second longer and cleared his throat, gulping down a gallon of catarrh, which must have revived him, for what he said next came through the keyhole clearly cadenced, with emphasis of voice on the final five words of a long, lawyerly sentence: "… to share and share alike."

With that, the seagulls began squawking all at once. Our ears were still pinned to the door when Aunt Sarah came bursting through it, spilling us to the floor. We were piled upon the Oriental carpet and watched as a hand reached over our heads, groping for the doorknob. The door was clicked back shut, and as soon as we had gotten to our feet and were neatly reassembled around the keyhole, Uncle Joseph came bursting through with a face even blacker than his wife's, knocking us to the floor all over again.

Hoo-eee! I wisht I culd a been there! Shares an shares alike. Uncle Joe musta shot the cat all over the desk when he heard that'n! There he was, Captain of the Guards an not getting any richer, leastwise not in any ways he could show for it legal, an on top of that he was fighting mightily with the Committee (or so he claims!) to keep your Da from losing everthing, living in the big house with all them plans for apples and cherries and pears and all the rest, an he was now put in the line to receive merely an equal share of what was gonna be left! Your Da could a paid Gaylee a thousand pounds for that farm an he an your Ma could a been stuck wiping drool from Granpa William's chin til Kingdome come, an Uncle Joe STILL would a figgered the price weren't fair, an that he needed to be better compensated. Uncle Joe, an Stephen, an Tad, got their rightful piece a the Long Lot all them years ago. All WE we ever got were hardly more'n a few pewter plates an candlesticks, which we accepted with no complaints thank ye very much! Pray, what's with you uppish Bennets with all the money? I spose for some folks there aint EVER enough to go round! – JB

There was more fomenting yet to come. The old patriarch had hardly settled into his eternal resting place before Gaylee and Mr. Morehouse, a recent widower, became betrothed. His son, an outspoken Tory, had recently escaped to Long Island with his family, vacating his town home on Old Hill, and Mr. Morehouse and his seventy-year-old bride were more than happy to serve as caretakers. All would have been fine had they only waited a while longer to tie the knot – at least until Grandfather's headstone was up! Gaylee was no doubt relieved to be living on the other side of the river, but the last thing we Bennetts back in Compo needed right about then, was something else for the neighbors to titter about. And my God, how they tittered!

The Last Apple Run

Finally, there was that year's apple run, so galling at the time, and so very heartbreaking now that I think back upon it. Our first stop was at Judge Sturges's farm. Cesar had come with us as he always did to give him a chance to spend a day and night with his wife and girls, while Father and I continued on our circuit collecting scions. He had already saved enough money to buy Phyllis by this time, and soon would have had enough to buy his daughters as well. Cesar was ebullient. Seeing those little urchins run from the garden and jump onto the wagon was a welcome splash of joy for all of is in what had become a never-ending sea of wartime troubles. How they both giggled so, digging wildly into their father's coat pockets in search of the little toys and keepsakes he liked to carve for them. How happy it made Cesar to hear their squeals of delight when they found their treasures. How full of love Phyllis appeared as she stood beside the wagon saying, "scoot now," to the girls so that Cesar could jump down and embrace her. Father and I paused to watch them walk together back through the gate, where Phyllis veered into the kitchen garden, and Cesar continued on to the barn with his bag of tools, to start on whatever work the Judge had planned for him.

I knew immediately that this was going to be a different kind of apple run. Instead of inviting us into the house for some refreshment, as he customarily would do, the Judge merely called from an upstairs window, asking that we go on ahead to the orchard on our own. He sounded cold and preoccupied – I'm sure Father thought so too, but we did as requested, and went alone to select the cuttings we were after. The Judge also chose not to look in on us and when we had collected all our shoots and it was time to leave, calling again from the same upstairs window, not even showing his face. He told us that returning by noon the next day would be fine by him, and that Cesar will be ready, and then he bid us to be on our way.

At our next stop, a farm in Black Rock and always one of our best sources for new cider varieties, we got an even chillier reception. The servant who greeted us at the barn informed us that his master was away, although I had my doubts. He told us that because of some hard frosts that spring, their apple trees were showing signs of weakness and should not be stressed any further with our cuttings. From there it was on to another one of our regular stops, at a farm near Ash Creek, where the farmer himself told us outright, and in no uncertain terms, that he didn't wish to share any of his apple scions with the likes of Tories such as us.

Father took all of this stoically. His only show of pique was to slap Timothy hard with the reins, declaring emphatically that we were done with apple cutting for the day. We would have turned back and collected Cesar that afternoon and been home in Compo by evening had Father not previously promised to pick him up the next day, so we spent the night in town, at the Sun Tavern. When we arrived, there was nobody that we recognized sitting at the tables or staying for the night, which was fine by us. We had seen enough of people, and took to bed early, grateful to be tucked into a room upstairs all to ourselves, one of the best in the inn, overlooking the green.

"If I'm not mistaken," Father remarked peering through the curtains, "it was in this very room that my great grandfather spent the night when he testified against that witch." I walked over beside him and looked through the window. The sun was resting on the horizon, leaving us enough light to admire the lovely perennial beds fronting the fine homes that bordered the green. Eighty years ago, during the witch trial, there wouldn't have been as many houses; the town would have looked newly cut from the forest. But on this golden evening, the chestnut trees planted around the square stood as wide and as high as mountains. From through the tangle of their limbs we could see a few people below our window, making for their homes. Barn swallows went swooping low over the green. A young couple went walking arm in arm from the gazebo. A towheaded boy came into view, struggling to herd a few uncooperative geese past a pond choked with weeds. "That's where the superstitious fools gave that poor woman her water test," Father noted, and I kept quiet, not wishing to engage in idle chatter. "We better slip out of town before dawn," he chuckled, "in case this latest bunch of fools demands to see if we sink or float!" I continued to keep my attentions focused on the green, an act of defiance, which had the desired effect of silencing him. From out of the corner of my eye I discerned that he was gazing at me as he often used to do, and more intently than I could bear. I turned to confront him. "Why must you always stare at me like that!" I cried. This took him up short, and I fully expected a sharp reprimand for my impertinence, but to add to my annoyance, he merely smiled, while gently tussling his hand through my hair. I recoiled from his touch, and sauntered over to the bed, signaling that I was done with him for the night.

The next morning, we did manage to find a farmer willing to deal with us. But he was the only one, and so we got to the Sturges's much earlier than planned. Even still, Cesar was already waiting for us at the gate. When he climbed up into the riding board with us, he let out a sigh and tossed his bag of tools into the wagon bed where it landed with a clunk.

Cesar whistled through his teeth while settling onto the seat. "Lawdy, oona gwoine an paw-sinted da well, Massa Dell," he chided, as we trundled away from the Judge's gate. His neck craned to see Phyllis and the girls who had emerged through the grape arbor to bid their farewells. They stood illuminated in a shaft of sunlight with the dust from the wagon swirling through it. Cesar and I struggled to get one last look, and in my mind, the three of them remain standing there to this very day, motionless in the dappled sunshine, their eyes softened by a tender sadness, until we rounded the corner and were gone.

More Stirrings

March 14th, 1828:

The winter's towering snowdrifts look finally to be vanquished by the coming of spring. There are only a few pockets of dirty slush and ice remaining in the shaded corners around the yard. It's been months since my last entry due to a bout with a debilitating fever. The ague lingered painfully in my joints – and especially in my shoulders and hands – making it impossible to sit or hold a quill for any length of time. With the recent thaw however, life appears to be slowly returning to normal, including for Jesse, who has come home from Disbrow's fully in his cups. He obviously indulged in one of those three-hour lunches he takes from time to time. Between the breaths of his blathering drunkenness, he warned us that certain fellows of our mutual acquaintance have gotten wind of my plans to convene yet another meeting of the Anti-Slavery Society in his barn. Kessie and I managed to plant the old fiddler in his favorite rocker where he is at present blissfully sawing logs, but the news he conveys is troubling indeed. In his estimation, the threats against me were of no mild character, and this time, the louts truly meant to see them through. I'm not quite sure what to make of this. On the one hand, these are many of the same miscreants who tarred and feathered Dagger Barnes, and tried their best to burn down my loft a decade ago. I was told later, by the night watchman, that a number of them actually stumbled up the street that night with combustibles at the ready, but were too inebriated to even get their torches lit, which makes me wonder: If they were too higgledy-piggledy to burn down a wooden building chock-a-block with turpentine and tar back then, why should any of us worry overly much today about their true intentions or wherewithal to set fire to Jesse's barn? In any event, our good cousin has put Kessie and me on notice. He's done with worrying about those who take exception to my work with the abolitionists, or as he puts it, my work to free and educate those "tarnal Chimney Tops." If those "idiot toss-pots" down at Disbrow's go so far as to break but one more of his windows, or should they rip away but one more piece of his barn siding, Kessie and I will need to find a new situation, even though Jesse says it would break his heart to see us go, and I believe him.

I have been battling these same bottom-dwellers all my life. I grow weary to think how long the battle has lasted. It is astonishing how many people – including, I might add, highly educated and otherwise virtuous Christians – are of the firm belief that our African brothers and sisters are hardly more than beasts of burden, put on earth by God to serve our needs. Alas, even my dear friend Jesse leans towards this unenlightened point of view. I often wonder how the two of us, having shared so many of the same experiences growing up, could see this question so differently. To me, given all that I have witnessed first hand, there is only one conclusion to draw about the Negro race, a conclusion I find nearly impossible to believe others can't draw as well. You have to ask, how could a man as accomplished, and as wise, and as compassionate as Cesar be seen as anything less than fully human? Consider also the troubles visited upon Dagger Barnes, a man of unassailable virtue, who rose up from slavery to become a respected member of our community. How could there be anyone who feels it is their right, their duty, to prowl the streets in the dead of night to pull a man such as him from his bed, so that they may derive some sort of sick satisfaction from covering him with tar and feathers? Even more unfathomable, how is it that these brutish men could have hauled their victim into the town square in broad daylight, directly under the nose of a duly elected constable, and mercilessly prod him with their pikes? How in this day and age, and in a country founded on such noble ideals, could they have so openly committed such dreadful crimes and not be arrested?

I think also of this man's son, Eldridge. What a remarkable young fellow he is! He was at my side that morning, an impressionable boy, forced to bear witness to the degradations suffered upon his father, and condoned by the authorities meant to protect us all. I thought perhaps that this experience might sour the lad, might make him, as he came of age, spoil for revenge against the ignorant powers-that-be, but he didn't choose that path. He chose instead to say his catechisms, to dedicate himself to his lessons, and to make the most of himself. I took notice of Eldridge's moral character and admirable ambition, and encouraged him to follow in the footsteps of his father. I offered him an apprenticeship in my loft, and when he declined my offer to climb the riggings, expressing a desire of instead becoming a carpenter, I arranged his apprenticeship with Mr. Platt. I hear the boy is doing exceptionally well, in spite of having to contend with some awful trials of his own. Alas, the ability of the beast to sniff out even the faintest scent of black blood can never be underestimated. Eldridge has had to fight with the other boys in Platt's employ, nasty fellows, who regularly take sport in pilfering his tool bag, or ambushing him at the end of the day as he walks back to his room above the workshop. Once these young brutes discovered who – and what – Eldridge was, there was no holding them back. They took up the mantle, handed down to them by their parents, of thwarting any and all advancements made by boys such as him. We've had laws in this state for twenty years now that insure the gradual manumission of all remaining slaves – free Negroes and Mulattos may even one day deserve the right to vote – and while these boys tormenting Eldridge may not be conversant with all the legal details, they certainly sense the changing tides. In their minds, people of African descent living in Connecticut may be free, but they will always be inferior, they must always have less, they must always be kept down.

Whenever I consider problems such as these, I am reminded of the day when I was first stirred to the call of abolition. It was on an oppressively hot Sunday in July long, long ago. I was twelve years old, sweltering in my Sunday clothes and attempting by sheer force of will to make the shaft of sunlight hasten its journey across the meetinghouse floor to signal the midday hour and our release from the pews. When the morning service seemed ready to conclude, I was aghast to see the Reverend Ripley climbing yet again to his pulpit. He told us he had a special announcement we would all be most anxious to hear, and proceeded to read aloud the Declaration of Independence, a fresh printing of which he had only earlier that same day received. He spread out his arms in his usual imposing fashion, looming like a raptor above a multitude of fluttering silk and paper fans that had turned the entire sanctuary into a single entity, a kind of strange, multi-winged creature. It was so breathlessly hot. All I wanted at that moment was to escape, to get outside to enjoy a meal in a shady spot overlooking the sea, but as soon as the Reverend took up the broadside and started to read, all qualms about my clammy cravat were forgotten. I remember hearing those now famous words for the very first time: "All men are created equal with the unalienable right to life, liberty and the pursuit of happiness." How noble! How stirring! I remember also an overwhelming feeling of righteous indignation as the Reverend spit forth each of the many injuries set upon us by the tyrannical King George. When he was finished, and had put the paper down, I got to my feet and added to the spontaneous applause that erupted – the first and only time in my entire life that I ever witnessed such a raucous display of emotion during a church service. In spite of being too young to fully appreciate such high sentiments, I felt as ready as anyone to pledge my life, fortune and sacred honor for the sake of our new nation!

In that moment, two faces appeared before me in close succession, faces that became forever seared into my brain, images that set a course for the rest of my life. The first image came when I looked down to the far end of the pew, anxious to know how Father was reacting to the stunning news we had just received. He had come to his feet along with the rest of the congregation, but he was not applauding. All I saw was a blank expression, that all-too-familiar face of his that gives no indication of what he might be thinking or feeling, a face so incongruous to the wild excitement circling around him that I knew others would take notice of it. I knew also, given the fresh gust of wind that the delegates in Philadelphia had just blown into the sails of the rebellion, that an expression such as his, portended trouble for him, and for the rest of us.

The second memorable face was seared into my brain an instant later. With the thunderous ovation still echoing off the walls of the meetinghouse, I looked beyond Father and up to the gallery where Cesar and the various other Negro servants sat in their places. None of the people in that corner of the balcony were standing. None were applauding. They each sat silently on their bench, completely motionless save for the continued fluttering of the fans beneath the row of black faces, faces that appeared to meld into a single, like-minded countenance. All men are created equal? What cruel hypocrisy! In the silence of that collective 'dropped jaw' glaring down from the balcony, those Negroes were proclaiming loud and clear that there can be no virtue, nor any justice, in a nation that speaks so eloquently of inalienable human rights, while at the same time holds other human beings in bondage.

Two faces seared into my memory on the day when independence was declared. One, dispassionate and unreadable that left me with a stomach-turning sense of dread, the other darkened with unmistakable loathing that left me with a steady and determined sense of resolve.

So, yes Jesse, I will talk to the committee. But first, I'll come over to the house and rouse you from your rocking chair. I'll knead out the kink you're sure to have in your neck, and for the sake of your peace of mind, I promise to arrange with the committee members to find a change of venue. We will no longer conduct any of our meetings in your barn. But know this: If young Eldridge Barnes can stand up to the bullies, I can too. Yes, I will do everything in my power to keep the hellions from your door, but you'll simply have to accept the fact that no matter what they're grousing about down at Disbrow's, I will continue, with one determined step after another, to fight for those tarnal Chimney Tops!

Seeds of Our Downfall

I believe we could have outlasted the shunning from our neighbors. Had Father only been able to hang on a little longer, bygones would have been bygones, the suspicions would have subsided. We could have kept our farm, and Father would have found partners willing to trade their scions for his apples grown in the big new orchard he had planned. While it was unrelenting, the spirit-breaking pressure exerted by unforgiving neighbors wasn't what precipitated our downfall. Not even the Committee played a hand in it, at least not directly. No, in the end, it was Ezra Weed, and a greasy powdered wig, that did us in.

We should have known Ezra couldn't be trusted anywhere near our house with none of us home to watch him. We were tiptoeing down a razor's edge once the Redcoats marched past our door, and Ezra was just the sort of rogue to seize the blade, to happily draw our blood with it, so long as he might have something to gain. When he blew into our kitchen that night, it had been just hours since we had wiped away the gory mess. More time was needed to fully consider what had just occurred, to make sure all was in order. Father should have listened to Gaylee, respected her instincts, and made the scoundrel find shelter from the rain elsewhere. By God, he should have shot the bastard dead!

The next morning, Father made the opposite mistake. He should have overridden Gaylee's wishes and trusted his own better judgment. He wanted us to skip church that morning, arguing that we stay at home in order to keep an eye on our own affairs, and avoid a roomful of meddlesome parishioners. To Gaylee though, there was never a good reason to miss church. "God is our one true judge!" she declared, leaving us with no other option but to gather our Prayer Books and pile into the wagon. The only concession Father got from her was an agreement to arrive late enough to miss the morning fellowship. We may have dodged troublesome questions that would have inevitably come during that social hour, but there was nothing we could have done to avoid the sea of, shall we say, unwelcoming stares that greeted us as we walked through the doors, and followed us all the way to our pew.

The sanctuary that morning was only partially filled. Most of the New Lights in our parish were riding fast upon the wings of war, and thus, a good number of our able-bodied men were off with the Militia. Other families were no doubt huddled in their hiding places, or traveling to the homes of relatives living a safe distance away. As we walked down the center aisle, people were not seen quietly preparing themselves for worship, as they normally would be doing. They were downright buzzing in their pews, their vexations and anxieties palpable. I felt as if the entire congregation wanted to rise up with queries about what we must have seen or heard on the night of the landing. With shots fired so close to our front door, there surely were reports for us to relay! I'm sure they also wondered why Father wasn't in the field with his brothers, and why for that matter, we were attending church at all, given that our house and farm were located so near to the British fleet still laying at anchor off Cedar Point. It wasn't hard to read their thoughts: Why would any family residing directly in the path of a wanton enemy saunter into church as if it were just another Sunday in April? No right-minded family would be so reckless, unless, of course, assurances had been received from nefarious sources, that their livestock would not be stolen, and their house would be spared the torch!

The Reverend Ripley thundered from the pulpit in his usual fashion that day, reminding us how the sons of Reuben bravely went forth to battle, and how in spite of being greatly outnumbered by well-armed enemies, they proved victorious. "The able-bodied men of that biblical tribe put their trust in God, as the good men of Fairfield must do now!" he roared. "For our cause is righteous, and God will always be on the side of those who love liberty and fight for their freedom!" Although Mr. Ripley never shook his fists directly towards Father as he spat these lines, he might well have. All eyes were on us yet again, and while Father sat expressionless, I squirmed on the pine boards with the heat rising in my face. The Reverend's words rang like cannon shots: "Fifty thousand enemy camels! Two hundred and fifty thousand enemy sheep! One hundred thousand enemy soldiers! All felled by the valiant sons of Israel!" His sermon may have bounced off Father, but it swelled my warrior soul, stiffening my resolve to steal away that night with Father's fowler, and when the Reverend dramatically tore away his churchly vestments to reveal a military chaplain's uniform, I was ready to jump out of the pew and blast away at King George himself!

Meanwhile, how could we have known, as we sat inside that house of worship, that back home, temporal screws were turning against us? The last order Mother gave Ezra as we were leaving for church was to replenish the kitchen firewood. Who could have guessed that such a mundane request would have such dire consequences? Naturally, Gaylee blamed it on Providence. Father blamed himself for listening to her. I take my share of the blame for neglecting to pick up the wig when I retrieved the Captain's hat from the mantelpiece. How could I have been so careless? If only Gaylee or Mother had swept up the very last bits around the hearth as they had done a thousand times on a thousand other occasions. If only one of them had merely thought to peer behind the stack of firewood. If only the ball from Nate and Ester's game of Jacks had rolled behind the logs as it so often used to do. These are all questions that my surviving brothers and sisters and I continue to ask one another, and find impossible to answer. We feel sick about it.

Finding Father's coat on the body of the boy killed at the ford was never seriously questioned, not then, nor in all the years since. After all, there were many non-combatants following on the heels of the battle tending to the dead and the wounded on that afternoon. Any one of them could have used their own coat or shawl to cover a body until it could be properly interred. But the greasy ball of powder and hair that Ezra found crumpled behind the stack of firewood in our kitchen was a far different matter. It was the one piece of physical evidence that a determined prosecutor could have used to seal his case against Father, to make the serious charge of treason stick, and it had now come back to haunt us: Captain Lyman's wig.

This is how, on his second visit to our house in those early days after the invasion, Uncle Joseph explained the situation to my father. I overheard the entire conversation while hidden in the stairwell to the loft. Uncle Joseph had just days before assured us that in spite of all the rumors that were circulating, there was no hard evidence against us, he could keep the Committee assuaged. But, the recent discovery of Captain Lyman's wig in our house changed everything. Ezra Weed had waited a week before turning it over to his master, Captain Nash, who thought it best to discuss the situation with Uncle Joseph before turning the evidence over to the Committee. There was no question about the wig's origin. It was curled and clubbed in the exact style of a British officer's campaign wig, and made of human hair. It was commonly known that neither Father nor Grandfather William were in the custom of wearing a wig, much less one of such fine quality, making the presence of it in our kitchen on the Sunday after the landing virtually impossible to explain away. Uncle Joseph told Father how it took a great deal of persistence on his part, and some very clever horse-trading, in order to convince Nash not to pursue his patriotic duty, and prosecute the case. Yet, thanks to his influence as a respected Captain of the Home Guards (as Uncle Joseph immodestly phrased it) neither Weed, nor the wig, could do Father or our family any harm. Both had been dispatched – the wig to Nash's woodstove, and Weed to the Western Reserve. There was nothing more to worry about. All of Father's secrets, Uncle Joseph purred, would be safe with him. So as long as Father now did his part, the entire matter could be forgiven, and more importantly, forgotten.

All Father needed to do to make the whole affair disappear for good and all, was reimburse Uncle Joseph for paying off Ezra Weed's debt of indenture to Mr. Nash, and to sign his Oath of Fidelity. I heard Father's footsteps going down the cellar stairs where he kept his safe box, and heard him trudge back up, walking slowly across the kitchen floor to the table in front of the hearth. In my mind's eye I could see Mother and Gaylee sitting at the table – expectancy brightening their faces as Father approached. My heart quickened, daring to hope against hope that my stubborn father was ready, at last, to sign that infernal scrap of paper.

"Here's your hundred pounds," I heard him sneer, "but swearing an oath to you, or Elijah Abel, or anybody else on that damned Committee will not keep my family safe! I shall not sign. And, now dear brother, I humbly ask that you take your leave." And as those dreadful words hung in the air, I sat in the darkened stairwell, squeezing my knees to my chest, struggling to understand the ways of a world turned upside down, stunned and confused, seething with anger.

An Uneasy Calm

In spite of Father refusing yet again to sign his Oath, we went for two full years without suffering any ruinous reprisals. Yes, many continued to give us the cold shoulder at church and on the docks, we had our share of downed fences and stolen wagon wheels, and one morning Father had to cut down an effigy from our chestnut tree with a sign pinned to it that read "Traitor," which was definitely alarming, but there was no more mention of Ezra Weed, or the wig, and we managed to keep the farm afloat. The major campaigns of the war had moved south for the time being, but the so-called "Whaleboat War" – that shadowy conflict fought mainly between privateers, smugglers and other banditti out on Long Island Sound – was steadily escalating. The taunts, tar and featherings, and well poisonings between neighbors had devolved into out-and-out felonies, tit for tat kidnappings, even murder. Many of our nights were filled with terror, with Cowboys sweeping in from Westchester, and Tories washing up from New York to rustle livestock and burn barns in retaliation for similar crimes ("acts of war" or so they claimed) that had been committed by marauding Skinners and Patriots upon their homes and farms. The strain was felt by all, and especially by fence sitters and suspected Tories like my father. After Danbury, he was much more circumspect about expressing any views that might be misconstrued by the Committee, or that might give some drunken Sons of Liberty an excuse to slip a noose around his neck. As more and more men were imprisoned or stripped of their property for committing acts deemed inimical to the patriotic cause, there were more and more violent reprisals. Remaining neutral in such a climate was becoming nigh impossible. Father coped by keeping his nose buried in his orchard plans, and seemed as self-composed as ever, save for a nervous habit he developed of clicking his teeth on the stem of his pipe whilst sitting by the fire with his books in the evenings. From her chair on the opposite side of the hearth, Mother would look up from her needlework. "Dell!" she'd snap when she could stand the clicking sounds no longer, and he'd look over, blink both eyes shut for a moment, and then quell his jaws.

With Gaylee gone from the house, Mother had increased domestic duties laid on top of a growing pile of worries (this must have been the year we hired Kessie), most principally her worry about William. Once he turned sixteen, there was nothing she could do to prevent him from joining Uncle Joseph's Home Guards. Her only consolation was that he wasn't off with the Continentals, starving in some military camp. Jesse's brother, Jabe, had joined the Company too, and in Jesse's and my estimation, our older brothers had it far better than we did. They at least were spending their nights in useful occupation, out on patrol doing what they could to keep our shores safe. We, on the other hand, were left to lie in our beds, stunned like frightened rabbits beneath the linens, cocking our ears towards musket fire muttering in the distance, anxiously sniffing the night air for signs of smoke.

I coped during these months, I realize now, by singing aloud with my dear friend Jesse. Our lifelong tradition of music making began some years earlier, when Jesse's Uncle Gideon passed away, leaving his mother to settle the estate. They tell me that when the trunk containing Gideon's personal effects was opened, they discovered a violin, and that when this treasure was taken from its case, Jesse's eyes lit up like lanterns. It was a fine German-made instrument – so beautifully carved and lustrous, Uncle Moses and Aunt Neesy's initial thought was to sell it at auction. Such a valuable violin would fetch enough money to purchase two Longwool rams ("At LEAST two!" as Uncle Moses often later complained), but Jesse begged and begged to take possession of it.

He was so persistent that his parents eventually relented, and immediately regretted the decision. The noises he was capable of coaxing from that instrument at the start were harsh enough to scour a fleece! One

Eyed Meeker claimed he could hear the screeches and yelps from clear across the river. After a few months of loud, discordant bowing, his parents banished him to the loft in the cow barn, yet even with all three bay doors sealed, painful misfires of 'Hush-a-bye Baby' managed to seep through the siding. Passersby out on the lane were compelled to cover their ears, and we all shuddered to think how the poor beasts trapped inside the barn must have suffered!

But there's one thing I have to say when it comes to the character of my dearest and oldest friend Jesse: His tenacity is epic. When he puts his mind to something (even though instances of such behavior can only be honestly described as rare), he gets the pudding he wants. It is also clear that God endowed him with a gifted ear for music. By the next fall, he had graduated from simple nursery tunes and could play 'One Morning in May' and other tavern favorites with hardly an errant squeak. Somewhere along the line he bought himself an Irish penny whistle, which, compared to wrangling with Uncle Gideon's fiddle, was an easy instrument to tame. His newfound passion for the musical arts was catching, and I was soon carried along by his enthusiasm. While I never learned to play an instrument, I could sing well enough, and had a knack for picking out the harmonies. Jesse and I became a right jolly duo, and found ourselves singing together whenever we could. We couldn't help ourselves. We sang to fill the hours threshing hay, or repairing fences. We sang while walking to and from the schoolhouse, in the cornfields, and up and down the rows of peach and apple trees in our father's orchards. Thanks to the relentlessness of our song making, our friends and family soon threatened to ride us from town on a rail, and who could blame them? On the other hand, who could blame us? I can see now that the reason why we sang so much, beginning in those years, was to vent our growing anxieties, to ease our cares, and distract us from the war. Singing kept the bedlam at bay.

Those Royal Rats

It was a steamy day in July 1779. Jesse and I were drenched in sweat as we poled our skiff across the flats from South Beach, singing loudly as we went. Whaleboat War or no, we were still asked upon to venture out onto the Sound to help find food for our tables, and were thus fishing for fluke near the oyster and mussel beds around Cockenoe Island. Daylight provided us with a certain measure of protection, but even a task as innocent as fluke fishing came with some risks, as Jesse and I were keenly aware. It was not unknown for smugglers to secret their contraband on Cockenoe. Two lads inadvertently stumbling upon such stores would not be viewed favorably. They'd likely be shot first, and questioned only after the musket balls had flown. Adding to our worries, were the rumors that had been growing about an infestation of rats out on that little strip of sand and shrubs – escaped two years ago, it was believed, from the holds of the British warships that had anchored nearby. We attributed such idle talk to the general hysteria of the times, but figured it best not to take chances, and thus announced our arrival at the shoal with full-throated salvos of "Whiskey in the Jar"!

To our great relief, the lagoon appeared as pristine as always, with nary a mouse or bolt of smuggled English silk in sight, and in less than an hour our baskets were brimming with fish. Satisfied our quota had been reached, we plunked ourselves down on the island's stony beach, keeping one eye on the tide that was about to turn from low, and the other eye on a bank of clouds building upon the western horizon. We wouldn't be able to tarry for long, but knowing that an incoming tide would ease our way back to the beach, we allowed ourselves a moment to lay back on the smoothed stones and stretched out our legs for a well-deserved rest. Across the water, as still as a millpond, our beloved Connecticut shoreline from Calf Pasture to Kensie Point lay green and gauzy above the narrow strip of sand. Cows and sheep dotted Compo Hill. To the east, the freshly whitewashed steeple of our West Parish Meetinghouse pointed skywards from a cluster of trees, shimmering like a beacon in the hazy sunshine.

I had just dozed off when I heard a strange scratching noise coming from the baskets. I wondered what on earth it could be, when Jesse, who had stopped singing by then, and had likely dozed off as well, screamed that womanly scream he sometimes does. I lurched bolt upright, and saw what must have been a dozen rats, fat as peahens, crawling about our baskets and chum pots, while others were making off with the leftover contents of our lunch pails. We shouted and stamped our feet and threw stones at the mangy devils, but they were bold as brass and held their ground until we succeeded in beating them off with pieces of driftwood. With our baskets rescued and safely under our arms, we ran for the sea, splashing across the muddy shallows of the lagoon as fast as our legs would take us.

There was no way of knowing on that sun-drenched summer's day, that our fair shores were about to be invaded yet again by the craven enemy encamped just a few miles away, across the Sound. We were yet innocent of those two devastating raids – bringing with them as they did, far more destruction and additional suffering than anyone could have ever imagined, or thought possible. By that summer, in spite of all I had been forced to come to terms with – the horrible consequences of war I had born witness to, the lingering suspicions about Father's loyalties, and all the chaos and near daily depravations we were suffering – I had somehow managed to retain my footing. On that summer's day, Jesse and I were just two hale lads, laughing and hooting about how we had gone splashing across the waters of the lagoon to reach our skiff like a pair of cormorants taking flight. With our baskets safely boarded and tied, we shoved off and began poling for all we were worth towards the shores of Compo. What invincible heroes we felt ourselves to be! Such free and mighty Lords of our realm! The muscles of our sun-browned arms felt as powerful as steel springs, our heaving chests as strong as a smithy's bellows. To celebrate our triumph over the rats, and to set and maintain our rhythm, we began singing one of the working songs Cesar had taught us. It was a glorious moment, however fleeting, when we so heartily sang:

"Purtiest singin' I ever heard

Way over on the hill.

The angels shout and I shout too,

Singin' with a sword in my hand.

Lord! Lord! Lord!

Singin' with a sword in my hand!"

We surely were quite the trubadors in them salad days, we truly was! My, how free and innocent we were before them two tragic fires. And don't it now seem like it were only yesterday when the war was long past and we was huddled in our favorite corner table at Disbrow's, pickled halfway to Peekskill and reliving our misbegotten glory days? Your nose getting lit twas always the sign that we was rum'd and ready, and when the crowd urged us to regale them with one of our ditties, we was allus more'n pleased to rise to the clatterings of their cups!

What'll it be? I'd enquire of the throng.

Soldier, Soldier! came the usual reply — one of our favored standards that never failed to get them a-rolling off their stools with me, a big ox of a feller doing the high bits and you, the little bantam rooster that you was, coming in with the low parts. It's a good song and made them laugh ever time. I went fumbling for the fiddle at me feet and pulled a few bars — all soft and trembly to start, an then quick'n lively the way they likes it. I sung the first two lines in me sweetest soprano: Soldier soldier will ye marry me, with yer musket fife an drum? And then you comes in, yer buttery baritone never sounding no better: how can I marry such a pretty girl as you, when I got no hat to put on? And then, with a wave of yer arm, the entire house joins us like they allus done:

Off to the habberdashy she did go

As fast as she could run,

Buys him a hat the best that there was,

An the soljer put it on!

Know this too. We weren't alone in those days, Haynes an me. There were a handful of the old Guardsmen yet above ground; hale an hearty old brothers of the blade they were, an allus ready to squeeze into our corner an raise a glass to those distant days. Fellows like Gaybril Allen, Josh Green, Jessie Morehouse come by fairly often. On occasion we hears it too from Wake Burritt or Trow Crossman and sometimes find ourselves surrounded by an assortment of Meekers (who look so much alike not even their mothers can tell 'em one from t'other), each ready with their tales and downright lies about them four tumoltuous days in April.

Nowadays they needs to shout at me over the din in that riotous establishment, but you'd be a- toting one a these blasted ear trumpets too, I am quick to remind them, if you'd been sitting in a little echoey springhouse when yer mother discharged a pistol, sending lead hissing down the well and yer eardrums splattering cross the walls! But deaf or not Cousin Haynes, I allus hear yer voice above the throng. I can hear you singing now. — JB

Towns Fired

How eerie it is to realize, after all this time, that Jesse and I were probably the last two living souls to gaze upon our beloved church steeple bathed in summer sunlight, towering proudly above the trees, before it was reduced to a smoldering pile of ashes. Just hours after poling back to shore from Cockenoe, the clouds lowered, bringing periods of fretful rain, followed by a dense fog, and when the shroud finally lifted on the evening of the next day, the British fleet was spotted off Kensie Point. Moments later, warms of filthy Jagers were rampaging through the streets of Fairfield making off with everything that wasn't nailed down and burning the rest. They set fire to the courthouse and the schools, to homes and barns and shops – over two hundred dwellings in all – laying down a swath of destruction that stretched from Black Rock to our church, which was one of the last buildings to succumb, put to the torch almost as an afterthought as the last of the soldiers returned to their ships. Had not a thunderstorm blown through that evening bringing with it torrential rains, I'm sure the Redcoats would have laid waste to even more. A week later, the fleet was back, and Tryon's Hessian hordes hadn't lost any of their taste for pillage and destruction, this time unleashing their fury upon Norwalk to our west. The smoke from these two conflagrations lingered in the sticky summer air and stung our eyes for days. It was more than any of us could bear, stunning us into a kind of walking death. As Cesar put it "de boo hags" had come in the night to rob us of our spirits. When the air finally freshened, the smoldering

181

heaps of cinders and ash left us with a vague, but unshakable sense of dread; a feeling that anything yet standing or neatly stored might at any moment be taken from us, overrun by swarms of Redcoats.

If these ruthless raids were meant by General Tryon to convince Connecticut's Patriots to lay down their arms and relinquish all hopes for independence, his strategy failed. When the Redcoats raided Danbury in'77, they marched through several towns. Some houses were burned along the way, but the ravages were spread across a broad area. In any given location, most of the homes and shops remained standing, and there were plenty of neighbors ready and able to help the less fortunate quickly rebuild. The Danbury Raid also had a clear military purpose. The thousands of barrels of beef and pork and other foodstuffs, all the ordinance, the tents, medicines and shoes kept in Danbury, were vital to Washington's Continentals. Everybody knew that the British, camped on Long Island and in New York City, might at any time endeavor to capture or destroy these valuable stores. A military expedition for this purpose was a logical – some might say inevitable – consequence of the rebellion, a fact about war that in a small way helped to mitigate the horribleness we experienced.

But the back-to-back raids of '79 were different. They were lightning strikes with no justifiable military targets, lest you count the homes and personal property of Patriot soldiers and their innocent wives and children. His Majesty's troops took direct aim upon our peaceful village greens, our courthouses, churches and commercial centers, the very hearts of our communities. The Redcoats of '79 came with no purpose but to terrorize the citizenry. With the men of Fairfield gathered in the hills in the vain hope of staging an organized defense, the women that stayed behind were herded into the square at bayonet point. They were unmercifully stripped of their buckles and rings, and made to watch helplessly as their houses were entered, their closets and trunks opened and looted, their furniture and china cast to the street. They could do nothing to prevent the skulking soldiers, as savage as red Indians, from tossing pine torches through the broken windows, and upon the rooftops of their homes.

I will never forget the nights of these two raids. When Fairfield was burned, Father, Cesar, and I left the house as soon as a loud thunderstorm had cleared. We walked to Bennett's Rocks where several of our neighbors were already gathered. From this vantage point, we could see that the storm had drifted to our east, and while stars were already peeking through breaks in the sky directly above our heads, Sherwood's Island and the town beyond it were yet entombed in a maelstrom so thick and churning it was impossible to discern where the smoke ended and the clouds began. Sheets of lightening continued to flash from behind this ghastly veil, giving momentary definition to individual columns of rising smoke, and to the ghostly crowns of the slowly retreating thunderheads. When Norwalk burned a week later, we only needed to climb to the top of Bald Mountain to get a sense of the destruction visited upon that town. From over the brow of Grumman Hill came a dusky orange glow that seemed to be emanating from the center of the earth. Even at that distance – two miles as the smoke drifts – the heat could be felt as we gazed across the Saugatuck, lapping like the Devil's tongue upon our huddled faces.

A Conversion Come Too Late

Let there be no doubt, the Fairfield and Norwalk invasions were acts of pure evil, revealing that degree of depravity that is the unique purview of fallen mortals. Not even an angry and vengeful God, with His sword as quick and terrible as we know it can be, would have visited so much devastation upon so many innocent souls. These raids were the blows that pushed all but the stubbornest of fence sitters off the rails – even Father was swayed. Just months earlier, he had still been calling for calm. What we needed to end the cycle of violence, he stood to announce one Sunday in church, were not half-cocked schemes hatched over flagons of hard spirits, but a flag of truce. Let us urge the leaders on both sides to declare a ceasefire from Pelham Bay to Montauk! But after these raids, and after receiving word from several reliable witnesses that General Tryon had been observed sitting in a rocking chair on top of Grumman Hill contentedly sipping tea with his aides as the homes and stores in the harbor below were being consumed by the flames, Father had seen enough. He was ready at last to supplicate himself before the Committee of Safety and sign their Oath. He was ready to fight.

Alas, his conversion to the casus belli came too late. What our neighbors saw when they looked at Father in August of 1779, was not an honorable man who had struggled honestly with the issues and turned at last to the Patriot side, but a man who had for so many years turned his other cheek to the dreaded enemy. What they saw was a man whose house was yet standing, and whose fields were not trampled, a man without answers to questions that had been whispered about him for over two years: What sayeth he about his oxcart spotted at the beach? What sayeth he about the rumors so widely circulated of the officer's wig found by his fireplace? And what reason can he give as to why his coat was found covering the remains of a boy at the ford? With the ashes from Fairfield and Norwalk yet drifting in the air, not even Uncle Joseph with all his influence could protect Father any longer. No matter what Father now said about joining the Militia, or paying his one thousand pounds in bond, or swearing his allegiance, he would have to answer for his past. And his past was about to arrive at our doorstep. It would come at full blaze, and it would exact a terrible, terrible price.

Barn Burning

In my waking nightmare, I was being chased through a forest by a red-eyed banshee. The shrieks of my pursuer were so blood curdling and otherworldly, it took a while for my arousing brain to realize that the howls had not come from some strange phantom, but rather from my baby brother Isaac who was downstairs in his cradle. As my eyes opened and adjusted to the light, I could see that Mary was already out of bed and cowering in the corner. Her nightgown was as coppery as a setting moon, her shadow dancing eerily up the wall behind her. I'd seen that particular cast of light before, and sure enough, Esther and Nate were at the window and telling us there were pine torches out by the barn, almost delighted in their childlike way, it seemed to me, at the sudden arrival of yet another wartime adventure. Betty and John jumped into my bed and buried their faces into my shoulders. There were angry voices coming from the yard; men who clearly meant us harm. It was a few days after the Norwalk invasion and we had feared there might be reprisals against us, but I never expected anything as bad as this. We didn't know it yet, but our wheat field, the one up towards the ridge that we planned to bring to market, was already in flames. And that would be the least of our miseries.

The scenes that night remain a blur. So much happened so fast it is difficult for me to recall the events in any sensible order. What I remember most in those first few moments were Isaac's unrelenting and piercing wails over the low drumming sound of what seemed like an army of men shouting from all directions out in the yard – all of that punctuated from time to time by my mother's voice crying "No! No! No! No!" It sounded as if she and Isaac were out by the barn, and they may well have been, but by the time I got downstairs they were on the porch with Father. Mother was holding Isaac in her arms. Someone had thrown a rock through their bedroom window sending shards of glass into his cradle, giving him several small cuts on his cheeks and forehead. Mother was alternately dabbing his face with her kerchief and angrily shaking the bloodied garment at the crowd. Little Isaac, just a few months old and in a nightcap, was not seriously injured although you would not have thought so if you saw how much blood there was. Mother was shouting from over Father's shoulder at the men who were just a few feet away. At one point she broke free and flew to the top of the porch steps. I'm sure she would have gone down them had Father not grabbed hold of her nightgown. She was left spitting into the air above the crowd, cursing them all to hell, calling out by name those she recognized. I could see that most of the men were common tavern rats, but Elijah Abel and Increase Bradley were there, I'm sure of it, standing in the shadows behind the roiling clutch of torches. Father was calling to Cesar for help as Mother continued to struggle against the two of us, her knees thudding into my ribs, with Isaac yet wailing in her arms. From behind me I heard the sharp thumps of a man's boots bounding up the porch steps. There was something about the heaviness of the footfalls; about the particular way the leather soles landed on the boards that caused me to slump nearly to the floor with dread. I took a breath and turned to see the familiar tangle of hair beneath the grimed and shapeless hat. He must have pushed his way to the stairs from the back of the crowd, because Mother surely would have called him out had she seen him, or perhaps she simply failed to recognize him, because for the past two years we believed he was out of our lives forever. But no, he hadn't left for Ohio as Uncle Joseph had assured us. I couldn't believe my eyes, but there he was, looming above me, as big and as hulking as ever, reeling on the top step and full of venom. So close, I could smell the stench of rum on his breath: Ezra Weed. I saw too that Captain Lyman's wig had not been dispatched to the incinerator as promised either, because the frightful man was holding it now above his head at the end of a broken rake handle. He turned to face the crowd and began waving it like you would a battle flag as the men that surged below him took up a chant, "Tory bastards! Tory bastards!"

I looked beyond the crowd for Cesar and saw him pulling Timothy from the barn. He must have already moved out the other draft animals along with the goats and the sheep because I could hear them bleating from somewhere off in the darkness. Why, I wondered, was he freeing the livestock? Out in the pens and free to roam, they're as good as stolen, I thought, and then I saw some men scurrying from the open barn doors with armfuls of straw that they were piling around the outside walls and I realized Cesar was saving the poor beasts from the fire about to be set. With so many men against us there was nothing we could do to stop them. All seemed lost. The entire yard was seething and just as the pine torches were closing around the opposite sides of the barn I heard a man from beside the house shout, "Fire!" followed by a thunderous roar of musketry that made the torches teeter in place as if momentarily stunned and confused. The mob quieted, and a lone man stepped into the circle of light.

It was Uncle Joseph dressed in his ridiculous deerskins and the hunting shirt accented by the golden sash Aunt Sarah had sewn for him. One line of about a dozen of his militiamen had fired a volley into the air, and when they shuttled off to the side, another line stepped forward with muskets leveled directly at the crowd. I looked for William and Jabe and saw that they were standing shoulder to shoulder in this second line – so soldierly the two of them looked, so brave, so resolute.

"Put your torches down!" Uncle Joseph commanded, "or be prepared to feel the lead of your countrymen!"

There was some grumbling, and the torches seemed to waver, but it was too late. Someone must have come with a kettle of turpentine because there wasn't any visible smoke at the start, just a loud whooshing noise followed by a lick of flame that shot into the sky from a side window of the barn. With that, Father leapt from the porch and ran to his brother shouting, "Buckets are in the shed!" and the next thing I knew, members of the Home Guard were strung down to the river, organized into a bucket brigade. Most of the men in the mob, including Ezra Weed, disappeared into the night, but to my surprise a few of them threw down their torches and joined with those who were now attempting to put out the flames. I was in the line directly between William and Jabe, close enough to the barn to feel the intensity of the heat and see everything. We set grimly to our task at hand as the cries of my brothers and sisters on the porch were joined by the awful screams coming from the animals that were safely away from the fire but still trapped in their pens. Father was darting all about the barn, his face blackened and wet with sweat, pointing to the places where he wanted the boys to hurl their buckets of water. For one fleeting moment it looked as if we might be getting ahead of the fire when there was another loud whooshing sound as the hay stored in one of the bays suddenly ignited. Flames were soon curling around the beam over the center door like a red creeper twisting around the limb of a tree and I saw Cesar – uncharacteristically bareheaded – pause for a second at the doorway before ducking down and racing inside the barn.

Father said later he must have remembered his box of carpenter tools that he kept in the back, and I was thinking that too, when I threw down the bucket I was holding and ran towards the door. The heat was so great it was difficult to breathe but I was determined to assure myself that Cesar was all right and that he'd soon emerge safely. I could see that there was a narrow pathway off to one side where no flames had yet reached, only smoke flowing, like a river turned upside down, below the ceiling. When Cesar didn't come out I began shouting his name and feared he may have tripped and fallen and I was plucking up the courage to dash in after him when Father and William grabbed my arms and pulled me away. We stumbled onto our backs a safe distance from the barn just as the beam over the front door fell to the ground bringing with it a curtain of fire. A few seconds later, the entire structure was fully engulfed. Only the posts and beams and rafters remained in place, neatly squared and angled, a black skeleton holding up an undulating torrent of blinding flames.

We sat on the ground and watched as the men and boys gathered around us, their faces upturned and lit, some shielding their eyes from the heat and glare, all of them transfixed and silenced. If my siblings or the animals were yet crying I do not remember hearing them as I was only conscious in those moments of the rumbling and crackling, as first one part of the barn's remaining skeleton fell to the ground, and another, and then another, until it was reduced to a great jagged pile of burning and glowing bones. It was then that Father leapt to his feet as if abruptly awakened from a dream and began running down the rows of men shouting for Cesar and asking if anyone had seen him escape from a back window, but nobody answered or even stirred as they continued to gaze upon what was left of our barn.

"The root cellar!" he blurted aloud, and to nobody in particular, before returning to William and me. "Let's pray he made it there. I've seen barrels of apples survive fires such as these." It was then that Uncle Joseph ordered his men to fall in, and they quietly trooped back down to the beach. The others drifted away as well. Mother must have been inside the house tending to the children, leaving only Father and me sitting on the ground.

"We'll look for him in the morning when things cool," he said, wiping the sooty grime from his face. "You'll see," he continued quietly, "he'll pop out as fresh and sweet as a Pippin."

I don't remember climbing back into bed that night and awoke the next morning to an acrid smell of smoke, lingering still in the air. Father was sitting on the side of my mattress, washed and in a fresh change of clothes. I looked past him and scanned the loft. Shafts of sunshine were streaming through the front windows, telling me it was well past the break of dawn, and yet my brothers and sisters remained tucked into their linens, dead asleep. Nothing was stirring out in the yard. Not a single bird or cricket. A more profound silence would be impossible to imagine. I looked next out the side window, and beheld a strange, disorienting emptiness filling the space where the barn roof should have been – a blank patch of pale morning sky, and such a desolate shade of blue it was! Sitting up caused me to begin coughing so violently I nearly fell back onto the pillow, and when I finally caught my breath, I leaned over, allowing Father to gather me awkwardly in his arms. We sat like that for a long time, until he pushed away, holding me at arm's length, allowing us to see eye-to-eye in what was to be a terrible awoken truth, the words I knew he was about to say presaged by that face of grim necessity I dreaded to my core, and have never forgotten. "Cesar is gone," he told me bluntly, and for the briefest moment I dared to believe he meant that Cesar had escaped from the fire and had run away to find Phyllis and the girls, but I knew that that could not be. A vision of the gentle man I loved so dearly came vividly to mind at that awful moment. It is the end of a summer day. His hat is tipped back upon his forehead, the letter "C" pearls around his eye, his tender smile looks down as I nestle my face against his knee. A puff of cinnamon pipe smoke goes billowing towards the sky. There was no escaping the bitter truth. Cesar was dead, Father had told me, and I collapsed back into arms. This time, I had no strength to resist.

Oh Haynes, I hardly knows how to tell ye this, but there ye goes again, missing the entire point, an too puddy-headed to see how this entire tragedy, Cesar an all the rest of it, could a been avoided! I suppose by now yer in a far far better place, an I prays you are, so probably none a this don't matter to you no more but I'm a telling ye not only for yer sake but for Rachel's sake an all the others who may be a-reading this record of yers and by jingo it's a record that aughta be set to rights, we owes them that so here she goes. Yer making it sound as if Uncle Joe was the hero whats tried to save yer Da's barn! And it makes me wonder, what's with you uppish Bennetts? Didn't ye ever talk to one another? Didn't ye ever think to ask yer own brother about how it actually went that night? Well, our side of the family did talk, and this is what we know is true. They was out on there normal patrol around the Mill Pond and down at the beach on that fateful eve but instead of circling back like they normally used to do to the Mill River, Uncle Joe orders them up the Saugatauk for no good reason that none could see an when they gets to the foot of Bald Mountain he orders them to halt and they rest upon their arms for an hour or more a-wondering what the devil they was a-doing an twas then they hears the ruckus an they goes to investigate and finds yer barn surrounded by that tarnal mob and Uncle Joe orders them to form up in there battle lines just like you says they was, and they fired that volley in the air and tries to stops them from setting the blaze only they got there a minute too late which was the only mistake that that devil Joe ever made on this occasion because he never wanted to lose all of that valuable property he had already assumed would soon be his. All he needed to do was to make your kind hearted father, a man who never so much as squished a hair nit, believe he had no other choice — to make him see that after all the rumors and all the troubles the farm was either going to be destroyed by the mob or seized by the Committee. I'm telling you, the entire escapade was planned as pretty as paper! Uncle Joe and the Committee, that tarnal nest of snoops and robbers, and Ezra Weed and that greasy old wig was all arranged ahead of time so that our very own Uncle, the Captain Pissmaker that he allus was, could a-looked like he was there to do his sworn duty to keep the order, to be the gallant law-upholding Patriot that saved his Tory-minded brother's barn from that tarnal mob, but believe you me, he warn't no hero there to save the barn, no sir my friend, he was there to claim it, an the tire farm to boot! -- JB

Banishment

Once the decision was made to move, we were out of the house on Compo Road in a matter of days. Everything happened so quickly there wasn't time to reflect, much less protest, and I have been haunted, for nearly half a century now, with the belief that none of it needed to have happened at all. Had Father chosen to plead his case in court instead of putting his trust in the hands of his brother, a strong argument in his defense could have been mounted on moral grounds. Many others with better knowledge than mine about these matters believe he would have been acquitted. After the Fairfield and Norwalk raids he responded – honorably I'd concede – to the need to defend our shores and enlisted as a forty-two year-old Private in Captain Nash's company. That also would have weighed heavily in his favor, surely. I also contend that even without a trial, his rights would have been quietly restored, and he could have held on to his property had he merely kept out of the public eye for just another year or so. The war had moved to the Carolinas by then, people in our part of the country had grown weary of the fight, and passions on both sides had begun to settle down. With a little more forbearance and fortitude, he could have outlasted his enemies regardless of which side won the war. All of us were prepared to soldier on, and I still wonder, why not he?

There was nature working against us too, and some hard realities around the farm to contend with, I will give him that. Without Cesar, we were already short-handed when Father was ordered to report for duty, stationed somewhere I believe, in New Jersey. We were unable to get all of the harvest in that November, and then struggled through one of the worst winters in anyone's memory. With the snow piled up to the second story windows, we lived like moles for weeks on end, tunneling from the house to the well and the privies. By early spring our stores had grown perilously low. We were cold, hungry and miserable, but if you want to know the honest truth, I can't remember a time when our family had ever been more full of spirit or tightly knit. Shared hardship makes for strong kinship. Even while Father was away, we were holding up and holding together.

He'd been home for only a few days and was looking even thinner than any of us. It was sometime in March or early April. The snow had mostly melted, and William and I were in the middle of cleaning out the newly rebuilt barn. On this particular day we were bent to our pitchforks in the bed of the honey wagon spreading muck in one of the far fields when we heard the cowbell ringing. Father had told us earlier that he'd be at the granary all morning. We were thus surprised, when we got down to the house, to see him sitting at the kitchen table with Mother. From their expressions I knew immediately that something was wrong, and thought at first we had more downed fences to contend with, or had a dead cat to pull from the well. But when we were asked to sit down and wait for the other children to assemble, I knew it must be something worse than routine reprisals. I feared that there might be some bad news about Gaylee or perhaps about Jabe who had been on duty that night with the Home Guards.

With every one of us gathered I saw that Mother was quietly crying to herself. Father walked over and stood behind her. She reached up and clasped his hands, drawing them down to her shoulders. "There is no easy way to tell you this," he said looking from face to face around the table. "I hardly know where to begin." Isaac wriggled at Ester's knee, and she lifted him onto her lap, shushing him as Father continued. "I've talked matters over with your Uncle Joseph yet again this morning, and we can find no other solution." Mother closed her eyes and took a breath. "I've quitclaimed him the house," he proclaimed.

There was a long silence. "What does that mean?" one of my

sisters asked at last.

William pushed his chair hard from the table and stood staring across it at Father, both fists clenched at his sides. "It means we are moving," he snarled, and stormed from the room. Father called after him, "Tis a bitter pill we must learn to swallow!" The back door slammed. "Yet for the time being!" Father turned and ran to the window where William could be seen running towards the river. "Lest we lose everything," he murmured softly into the glass.

With the advantage of hindsight, it seems impossible to believe that I couldn't see this coming. The Committee and the Selectmen had seized the properties of suspected Loyalists all around us; others we knew had been convicted of Toryism and were sent to jail leaving behind wives to throw themselves at the mercy of the court, begging that they might be allowed to keep possession of their furniture, a few measly candlesticks, perhaps a milking cow. Still others simply jumped aboard the first sloop or cutter they could find, and sailed away with their families to Nova Scotia, leaving their homes and farms and businesses behind. Why should our fate be any less harsh than theirs? Why was I unable to anticipate any of this, and why was I so ill prepared to accept Father's decision? I have no good answers to these questions other than to simply say I believed at the time that Father was somehow magically protected. Protected because he was such a respected member of the community, and because Uncle Joseph had such tremendous influence with the Committee. Most of all, I believed my father was protected because no matter how bad the situation ever became, I knew there was always one sure card he could play to get us into the clear forever: a simple out-of-court gambit that so many others in his position successfully finessed. All he needed to do to was pay his bond and sign his Oath.

But the stubborn old fool refused, too proud until it was too late to do him any good to take this prudent course. He had gambled on an eventual British victory, and put his trust in his brother and lost nearly everything as a result. We found ourselves removed from the house my grandfather built; banished from the farm my grandfathers before him pulled from the wilderness and tamed. Father would never see his apple orchards grow and thrive, and William would never take over for him.

Mother would never again run a respectable household, or see her children dressed in anything but homespun. Plans to send me to Yale evaporated in that very instant, making me destined to become a lowly sail maker's apprentice, instead of studying to become a physician.

On the Sunday after the papers were signed and filed with the officious little clerk in the courthouse, we rode to church in our buckboard. Uncle Joseph had made sure to arrive especially early that morning, and when we reached to the meetinghouse door, we saw that he and Aunt Sarah and the cousins were already sitting in our pew. We quietly climbed the west staircase and found seats in the gallery. Looking down from that unfamiliar vantage point at our neighbors and friends, looking down especially at our pious cousins as they settled into the Bennett pew dressed in their Sunday best, gave me a eerie sense of separateness, almost as if I were invisible, or that I never even existed. As I sat scanning the sea of women's hats, the curly tops of the children, and the powdered heads of the men as they each quietly prepared for worship, I willed them one by one to look up and receive my gaze. To my dismay, nary a one of them raised even a furtive eye. Not one single peek, and I knew our fall was officially sealed. I never felt so forlorn and unmoored, and it comes to me now as no surprise that it was around that time, perhaps that very night, when my many long years of night terrors began.

Night Sweats

April 6th, 1828:

I had a bad recurrence last night, the first in a long time. Some men followed me home from the tavern earlier in the evening, I'm quite certain of it, which must have been what triggered the dream. "Picture Asa," Kessie whispered in my ear when I awoke covered in sweat, gasping for breath. She was lying beside me with her face nestling against my shoulder, her hand gently pressing upon my chest to help subdue its violent heaving. I did as told, and imagined Asa, the little beribboned queues of his snow-white mane and beard encircling his face like the rays of the sun, sitting beside the boy calmly attaching his arm to his shoulder with one of my heavy sewing needles. Instead of red spatters on white serviceberry blossoms, I pictured my own children running down a row of be-pinked apple trees, set against a clear blue April sky. Instead of streaks of red, I visualized the buttery yellow of Asa's poultice covering the wound, and instead of blued fingernails, the young boy's hand was be-tipped with violets, freshly picked from the forest floor.

Over time, and with more and more practice, this trick works now like Billy-o. When I concentrate on pleasant associations, the pounding of my heart begins to subside, and my breathing slowly steadies. I heard the clock in the kitchen strike three last night, and then strike once again on the

196

half hour, and that's all I remember hearing, so I slept well enough. I have been engaged in a lifelong battle with these nightly terrors, but thanks mostly to Kessie, I have, at last, gained the upper hand. They nearly consumed me when I was a young man, and then after Kessie and I were married, and I became busy in my loft, they slowly diminished to once or twice a week. Although my sleep was often greatly disturbed in those years, I was able to conduct my daily affairs well enough. My measurements were accurate and my seams straight; I was finding good work and meeting my responsibilities. But once we began having children, and I grew more and more anxious about our personal finances, of having enough ships to fit with sails and enough bread and cheese stored in the larder, the nightmares returned, and with a vengeance. I grew deathly afraid to fall asleep. I dreaded to see the sun go down, and found myself lingering later and later at Disbrow's – Jesse and I were among the last to leave on some nights – and because I knew Kessie would never permit me to climb into bed with her fully clothed, I'd oft times pick a neighbor's barn and pass out on the straw. She bore so much, and never wavered. It was Kessie who seemed to know when to treat me gently, and when to remind me in her own inimitable way that it was time to dispense with the hysterics, crawl out of bed, fetch my ditty bag and haul my miserable carcass down to the ferry! Kessie was my savior and redeemer. And so she remains.

It's been twenty years since I was in danger of sinking below the nightmare swells forever. I can trace my slow recovery back to the morning Kessie insisted that we take a walk to the ford. It was a Sunday like any other. We had planned on going to church, but Kessie told me as we were getting out of bed that she'd had enough. It was time, she said, for me to take her to the place where my nightmares all began. I hadn't stepped foot on that rutted trail for years and refused to go, and told her she had lost her senses, but she gave me that look of hers that says there's no point arguing. "We'll make a day of it," she said, and proceeded to pack a picnic lunch. I know it must have been at least twenty years ago because I remember she was carrying a wee babe — John Hervey I suppose it was — tucked in a sling against her chest. I pulled Sarah in a wagon, while Lotta and Uriah were old enough to trot along. I remember seeing the two of them climbing on the outcropping of rocks that rise beside the road just before it turns sharply down to the river. The back of Lotta's yellow cotton dress had mud spatters from running across wet ground. Uriah's britches were spattered too, and I thought neither of them knew how lucky they were to have a mother who didn't fuss about dirtied clothes, or ever complain about extricating the thorns and burrs that they so often came home with, buried deep in the elbows of their woolen jerseys. The morning sun struck upon the backs of their heads as they climbed on all fours up to the top edges of the rocks. It was April, which I am sure was part of Kessie's plan. She wanted to bring me to the ford in the springtime, not only because that was when the raid occurred, but also because she knew it would remind me of how beautiful are the woods in Connecticut when the leaf litter thaws and the lower canopy begins to green, and the tops of the trees swell to a rusty red. Behind the children, I could see the shadow made by the steep drop-off towards the river, and when I looked to the road ahead I could see the point – not too very far in the distance – where the wagon ruts abruptly ended, creating the illusion that we were walking directly towards the edge of a precipice. I stopped dead in my tracks. Kessie must have anticipated my hesitancy because she was ready at my side, quickly taking me by the elbow, pressing me forward, telling me to run to the children, to get them off the rocks before they slipped and fell, which I did. When we were all safely assembled on the road, we proceeded as a family down to the fording place. In spite of my apprehensions, the road looked nothing like the one in my dreams. Not only were we heading in the opposite direction than I had headed on that terrible afternoon, which will make any path through woods appear totally different, there was fresh grass growing down the center of the roadway on this morning, with trout lilies and trillium hugging the shoulders. I saw none of the gashed and trampled ground that I remembered, nor any of the raw and gaping smell of it. My breathing was under control. I was gaining confidence with every step down the hill.

We found a dry spot near the riverbank, and put our blanket down and ate our lunch. When we were finished with our meal, Lotta and Uriah took off their shoes and stockings, and tiptoed into the cold water hunting for crawfish. Kessie settled herself on the root of a giant sycamore tree where she could lean back against its mottled trunk to nurse the baby. Sarah crawled around beside me at the water's edge, picking up small river stones that we used to build a village with houses and shops and barns. Before long, both she and John were napping in the pull wagon, while Lotta and Uriah, their feet and ankles pinked with cold, warmed themselves whilst building a stone levee to save our little village from the slowly rising tide.

The Saugatuck spreads wide and flat at this quiet bend where the salt and fresh water currents fuss with one another daily. Kessie and I sat shoulder-to-shoulder watching as stray bits of fluff went floating down from the trees, alighting upon the smooth black surface of the waters. A busy pair of cedar waxwings went crisscrossing from bank to bank, snatching mayflies, pausing to allow a noisy kingfisher to streak upstream, blinking blue to grey through shafts of sunlight. It was well past midday before a lone farmer appeared on the opposite bank to disturb our solitude. He came splashing across the ford with his horse and cart, looking a bit cross – perhaps I thought, for having unexpectedly encountered we strangers – but he turned as he was driving up from the river, acknowledging Kessie and me with a wry smile and conspiratorial tip-of-the hat for being out and about on the Sabbath.

We took this as a sign to pack our things for home. Kessie swaddled the baby against her chest and called to the others, telling them to run ahead and to wait for us at the top of the hill, and when one of them asked her why, she fired back "Because I told you so that's why, now scat!" and she and I rolled up the blanket and started slowly up the embankment. From that direction, the road immediately looked all too familiar and foreboding. I stopped in my tracks. I told Kessie to go on without me, and that I'd wade over and walk downriver to the bridge and catch them up at home, but Kessie gave me that look of hers once again, leaving me with no alternative but to follow her up the hill. When we neared the crest, I looked over and could see where the six-pounder would have been positioned. I paused for a moment. Here, I realized, is exactly where the boy must have been standing, and I confirmed that the line of fire would have been straight down towards the tops of the serviceberry trees on the other side of the cart path which explained once and for all how the spatters of blood could have reached as high as they did, and I pictured the scene through his eyes, just as it oftentimes plays out in my nightmares: I turn to face the fellows pressing up the hill behind me and raise my arm to beckon them forward. The wind rippling through the sleeves of my shirt is the only sound I hear until the flash from the cannon reflects off the upturned faces surging below me, and I feel the thud and see something red pin-wheeling over the road and into the trees, and I go running after it as fast as I can. Kessie took me by the hand and whispered gently, "Now take me to the place where you found the boy," and so she and I made our way down the road, ducking through the underbrush and stepped into the clearing and sure enough, there was the tree he was sitting against. The first thing I noticed as I approached, was the red ribbon affixed to his hat, just where it was meant to be, on the left corner, closest to his heart. I was cheered to think he was one of us – a strapping lad who looked to be asleep, holding in his lap what I thought was his musket, but as I got closer, I noticed the blue-tipped fingers, calmly curled as if poised to pick a lady's slipper, and thought, how odd. That is not a natural angle for someone's hand to be resting, and I dropped to my knees and told Kessie how I had called to him "You there!" and was reaching out with my hand to jostle him awake before I noticed the white splintering of bones where his shoulder should have been, and I told her what made it all the more horrifying was the comprehension that in one moment here was a boy about my own age sleeping peacefully against an old tree, and in the next moment, here was a pallid and mangled corpse. "Just imagine," I sputtered, "the poor fellow had run over a hundred feet in search of his own arm!" What agonies must have been going through his mind once he retrieved what he was after? What horrors did he feel as he sat alone on the ground with it resting in his lap? I told Kessie how I grabbed the first rock I could find and ran back to the road, falling hard upon Father, beating him with it about his face, calling him a traitor and a coward. "You are nothing but a cold-blooded murderer! You damned bastard! YOU sent the devils to the ford! YOU deserve to be the one lying dead on the ground!" I confessed to Kessie, had I not been hobbled by my broken ribs and bandaged eye, and had not Jabe been there to pull me away, I might easily have killed my own father right then and there, and what I cannot ever erase from my mind, what is worse than all the disrespect I showed, worse even than all the blows I landed, is the desolate sadness I saw etched on Father's face after Jabe had pulled me free. I can't ever forgive myself for all the things I said to him, and I told her how those feelings of shame became co-mingled with everything else: the torches in the yard, the memory of Private Betts, the Cowboys beating me with their musket butts, Cesar running hatless beneath the burning timbers of the barn – all conflated with the sickening horror of the red-ribboned boy, that valiant young comrade-in-arms, who made my years and years of nightmares all the more vivid, all the more unbearable.

Kessie and I stayed beside the tree; it must have been for several minutes, without saying anything more. I was on my knees with Kessie kneeling quietly beside me. She tucked down her chin and pulled back the sling at her breast, and when we both saw that John had somehow managed to remain fast asleep throughout this entire ordeal, we couldn't help but smile. From in the distance we heard Uriah calling to us. "Are you ready to leave now?" Kessie asked me quietly, and I told her yes, and so we stood and brushed ourselves off and walked back to the road to find our children. Lotta was dancing away on the rocks at the top of the hill – the six pounder would have been rolled onto the ledge at the very place she was playing – with Uriah standing just below her on the path, his fists planted on his hips and with a face like thunder. Sarah, meanwhile, was sitting contentedly in the pull wagon. Lotta ran down from the rocks, and Uriah wrestled her to the ground, angry with her for not helping to pull the wagon. Their clothes, having gotten wet at the river, were now thoroughly blackened in spots. "A pair of river rats you are," Kessie tisk'ed as they ran ahead of us, scrambling over a stone wall and disappearing into someone's apple orchard, their happy cries receding as they chased one another beneath the pink and white blossoms. Kessie carried the baby; I pulled Sarah in the wagon, with the sun nestling warmly over our shoulders. The evening air was filled with the smell of fresh mown grass and sweet, live earth. From somewhere high in the trees came the echoing knocks of a lone woodpecker. A bobwhite whistled nearby, and we ambled along the road towards home.

Try as they might, those men from the tavern will not get the better of me any longer. Let them taunt me all they wish, let them skulk menacingly in the shadows, let them come in the night with their crowbars and torches. Seeing the doors open to the Weston School For Free Negro Girls will be my vengeance!

Father's Bath

A fireball came hurtling across the predawn sky in and out of the clouds, and illuminated the countryside below. "It sounded like a six pounder," Father told my sister, followed by the running roll of musketry in the distance. My sister Betty and her husband Taylor were living at the time with our elderly parents on a small rented farm near Uncle Thaddeus's gristmill outside of Gilbertown. Betty and Taylor were roused from their bed by the sound of the blast and ran outside to look for Father, not knowing what on earth could have made such a frightening noise. They found him slumped by the open barn door clutching his chest. It was only after taking a few draws from Taylor's flask that he was able to describe what he had just seen flying overhead. The fireball had come from the north, streaking directly over the barn – a ball as big as the moon and the color of the sun, trailing fire that turned the darkened barnyard to day. Before it disappeared over the distant treetops, the percussive boom came so loud, and so close, it knocked him to the ground. All of them were in a state of unbearable anxiety – concerned of course to see Father crumpled and pale, but mostly deathly afraid of the unexplainable noise that had awakened them. Taylor's first words over the caterwauling of the livestock were something about it being yet another sign of Mercy's curse, which was utterly inane to even suggest, and Betty admitted how Father managed to grumble something about Taylor being even a greater superstitious old fool than anyone had ever thought. No matter. Whether you believe that the earth-rattling visitor was a natural or supernatural phenomenon, there is no denying the fact that the terrible shock of it weakened the old man's heart, and confined him to his bed, and that within three months after witnessing the now famous Weston meteorite, he'd be dead.

I received a letter from Betty towards the end of February informing me that she was debilitated by ague. Our sister, Mary, she reminded me, was away for the winter visiting her children, and that Mother had broken her shoulder, leaving only me to tend to Father. He was bedridden, yet holding firmly to the belief he'd soon be right as rain, insisting that he be given his spring bath early this year. Would I please drive up from Compo, Betty pleaded, to help them just this once? The thought of drawing the bath for my Father, whom I hadn't seen for years, filled me with horror. I couldn't think of anything I'd rather do less, but Kessie prevailed upon me, and in spite of pressing affairs at the loft, I made the necessary arrangements to be away for a few days and proceeded by sledge to Gilbertown.

Nothing could have prepared me for the scene that awaited me at the drafty old farmhouse. Mother welcomed me at the door looking tired and frail, her bad arm wrapped tightly to her side. "Thank God you've come," Betty cried wanly from a bedroom inside the house. Taylor was nowhere to be found. Drunk already, I correctly assessed, even though it was not yet noon. The kitchen was in a right tip. There was hardly any wood laid by, and so my first order of business was to fill the firebox. It wasn't until after sorting out some of the mess and helping to get our dinner going, that I ventured to look in on Father. Mother followed behind me, her good hand placed upon my shoulder, and there he was, propped on a bolster, eyes closed in a shrunken skull haloed by his great head of hair, grown snowy white, but thick as ever.

"Dell," Mother announced while guiding me to a chair at the head of the bed, "Haynes has ridden up from Compo to help us for a few days. Pray, open your eyes and say hello to your son." On the nightstand on the other side of the bed was a stack of his books, a pair of his spectacles, a pitcher of mulled cider. When he roused himself and caught sight of me sitting beside him, he managed a faint smile, and then signaled with his hand for a drink while nodding towards the pitcher.

"How are you feeling, Father?" I asked.

"A bit breathless," he replied with effort, and we sat together in awkward silence, not knowing what to say to one another next.

"Will you eat some dinner?" Mother asked Father at last. "There's a pot of bean porridge going," but he didn't respond, intent instead upon getting down his sips of cider. "At least some rye 'n 'Injun bread?" she pleaded.

The agreement was for me to stay for three days. Enough time to help Taylor split and stack next year's firewood in the mornings, while spending the afternoons helping Mother with the backlog of household chores that needed doing. Betty's fever broke on the second day, but she remained greatly weakened, so I promised on the night before I was due back at Compo that if Father was still insisting upon his spring bath I'd help get him into the tub in the morning.

At first light, the old man began to bellow; he had waited patiently for as long as he could stand it. "Get me up and get me washed! For goodness sakes get me out of this infernal bed and into some proper clothes!" he cried. I heard Mother in the kitchen boiling the water, whilst Taylor and I went outside to drag in the tub and find the soap. When the tub was filled, Mother sent Taylor away and asked me to help get Father out of bed. His look of thunder when I first entered the room turned to an expression of grim resignation when he saw me standing next to the bed, looking as if I had no idea of where to begin, which was of course true. "Come son," he said to me, "let's get on with it," and he leaned forward from the bolster, allowing me to untie his collar and remove his nightshirt. As I pulled the garment away, I nearly gasped to see how loosely his skin was hanging from the bones of his upper arms. He took no notice of my reaction and placed his shriveled arms around my neck, his skin as dry as ashes. He smelled faintly of soured cider and urine, and when I leaned back to pull him over to the side of the bed he whispered in my ear, "There's a good lad."

"Pray, give me a moment," he said quietly, catching his breath whilst sitting at the side of the bed. There was no color to his face save for some red and grey blotches across his forehead. Had I walked in just then, I don't believe I could have recognized the man beneath all the wrinkles. Mother secured a flannel around his waist, and with both his arms draped around our shoulders, he was able to stand. We took his full weight and slowly guided him into the kitchen where, between us, we managed to get him over the edge of the bathtub and into the warmed water. He immediately complained of the cold. Mother went for the kettle, and it was when she was tipping in the steaming water that I saw the large, polished scar that stretched from the middle of his back, covering the whole of one shoulder.

"Where did you get this?" I asked, having never before in all my years seen it.

"From the fire," he replied matter-of-factly, as if reminding me of a piece of information I ought to have known.

Thinking he meant the fire that killed Cesar I said to him, "But you never went into the burning barn."

He corrected me. "No, these scars are from the house fire before you were born. The one that took my grandparents."

"What happened?" I asked, placing my hand gently upon the scar, and he leaned forward – no, I believe he recoiled – or began to, and then he must have thought the better of it because he grew motionless, allowing my hand to remain where I had placed it for a moment longer. Mother knelt on the other side of the tub, the sleeve to her good arm rolled up. She picked up the wash flannel and reached into the water for the cake of soap as Father proceeded to tell me the story, including parts of it I had never heard before. He told me that he and Mother were newlyweds, living temporarily with his grandparents while the farmhouse intended for them was being built at the head of Compo Road. "I was heavily pregnant with William," Mother interjected cheerily, as Father continued. They had been awakened in the middle of the night by the smell of smoke. They grabbed for their shoes – and ran outside.

"That's right," Mother broke in, "there was a hard frost." Half the house was already fully engaged in flames. Everyone was accounted for except for the Grandfather Deliverance and Grandmother Mary. Father recounted how he ran through the front door and into the parlor and tried crawling on his knees down the hall, but the heat was too much, and the smoke too thick, to get to the bedrooms. He came back outside where the others were now huddled beneath blankets Happy had found for them. The flames were by then licking through the upstairs windows, but he went back into the house to try again and when he came back out the second time, his nightshirt was on fire. Moses and Joseph had arrived by then, and began pelting him with their coats as he went rolling about on the ground. They reproached him, angrily, for not going through the cellar door in the back of the house, which is where they now dashed. They managed somehow to get to the bedroom, pulled the two of them out, and laid their bodies on the frozen ground. Grandmother Mary was already gone, but Old Dell was alive and lingered a few days, his lungs choked with smoke.

"I failed them," Father whispered to me, his throat catching with emotion. I could see tears welling in Mother's eyes as she continued to gently wash his chest with the soapy cloth in her one good hand.

"No," I said to the back of his head, my hand still resting on the terrible scar. "You did all you could" – and Father cut me short. "You are wrong!" he snapped. "I could have saved them! Joseph and Moses believed as much, I know they did. It is only for the sake of harmony that they have kept all such incriminating thoughts to themselves, but I have had to live with the truth for all these years!"

Mother dropped the cloth and put her hand alongside of Father's face. "Shhh," she whispered.

"No Molly," he retorted, "Haynes deserves to hear this!" He then tilted his head towards me, lifting up his chin so that I could see the side of his wizened face as he continued to speak, barely above a whisper. "When I entered the house that second time, the parlor was pitch black and filled with smoke. There were flames falling all around. I knew exactly where I needed to go. I was able to identify them in the pitch darkness by the mere feel of their spines – and I grabbed all that I could carry. So you see," he said with a pitiable moan, "I didn't go back into the house to try and save my grandparents. I went back to save the books."

The three of us remained silent as Mother continued swishing the water in the tub. I know Father was waiting for me to say something – anything, one way or another, but I could not speak and cannot explain why. There was so much the two of us could have given voice to just then, but when our moment finally arrived to speak – and actually listen – to one another, we chose instead to keep our own counsel. I so wanted to hear from his own lips: How did those British soldiers on our porch know his name? I so wanted him to explain: Why on earth did he sign the loyalty oath only after it was too late to do him, or us, any good? If he couldn't provide answers to such questions, or give some sort of explanation for the decisions he made and the actions he took, then at least an acknowledgment of some sort would have been dearly welcomed! Something. A simple utterance that showed that he cared, that he took responsibility for the heartache he caused. Had he only spoken up, it would have freed me to make my own peace, to beg for his forgiveness, to let him know how much I wished I could take back what I said and did to him at the ford, to say how much I regretted the bitter wedge that kept us apart for so many years. I was ready at that moment to surrender my pride. I was ready, even, to tell him how much I loved him. In that long stretch of silence, save for the quiet, swish ... swish of my mother's hand in the bathwater, so much could have been resolved between us, and yet, when the moment to speak finally arrived, all I could think to do was to walk away.

I went through the kitchen and stepped outside where I was greeted by a white wafer sun suspended in a grey paper sky. A single row of trees an earlier farmer must have planted years ago traced around the side of the barn. His trees had grown tall, marking a lane no longer used, choked now with dead weeds poking through the snow. Deep woods covered the ridgeline that curved from around the back of the house, receding into the distance, like a finger lying upon the snow-covered fields, pointing south towards the Sound. The whole world was painted in greys and gauzy whites. The only sign of color were burnt yellow leaves clinging to the birch tree saplings that dotted the understory, tracing up and over the ridge like a scattering of sentry fires. An unseen hinge squeaked as the wind blew through the trees and rattled hard against the side of the house. Taylor was in the barn banging furiously at some piece of iron equipment with a hammer, cursing at full purple. Mother's kettle whistled from inside the kitchen, and I hugged my arms against the cold.

207

Father owned twelve books in all, a few I think that he purchased later on, but most were those he saved from the fire. He kept them close within reach wherever he resided his entire life, and must have read each of them several times. They were part of the furnishings in our house in Compo when I was a boy, and I made note of the titles. They were: Buffon's Natural History; The Horse Hoeing Husbandry, by Jethro Tull; Two Treatises of Government, by John Locke; The Anatomy of Melancholy, by John Burton;; Cicero's de Republica, and a pamphlet called A Sermon on Religion, by A Natural Man. Some of the lighter works in his collection were Tristram Shandy; The Vicar of Wakefield; Gulliver's Travels; The Adventures of David Simple; and of course, his most beloved Complete Works of William Shakespeare.

When Father died and his paltry estate was settled, he had no real property to convey and very little money to pass on to his widow or any of his children, but he left to me all of his books. After the solicitor's waiter delivered them, I put them in a crate and pushed the lot beneath the bed. I wanted no part of them. They reminded me too much of all we had lost. "What use could these heavy tomes be to any of us now?" I asked myself. Gaylee used to complain that they were blasphemous if not downright Satanic, and said we'd have all been better off had they been left in the house to burn. She never accused Father of not acting quickly enough to save Deliverance and Mary – nor did Grandfather William or anyone else for that matter – but she did occasionally rue the fact he risked his life for these books, but never thought to save the family Bible. In her mind, if any sin had been committed on the night of that terrible tragedy, that was it.

Father died a fortnight later, in early March 1808. I went back to Gilbertown and drove his body back to Compo where we buried him in the West Parish cemetery. It's been nineteen years.

Oh, you two! All yer lives you went an flapped yer tarnal bone boxes when you should ought to keeps em shut, an clamps them shut when you should ought to pries em open! And what do you mean, pushed them books beneath the bed? What a bale a goods! I've seen you reading them books with my very eyes, an if I had a penny for ever time you quoted 'the Bard' (especially when you was a might obfuscated down at Disbrow's) I'd be richer'n God! You and yer Da was cut from the same bolt of cloth, which to my way of thinking mostly means high an bloody minded! Why were you both so tarnal stubborn? I can't for the life of me answer that one – it's a hubble-bubble if ever there was one! Listen Haynes, heed me now. You was overly rough on yer Da. I mean, stroke too hard on any fiddle string, an it's gonna screech! The only sin that man ever committed in them wartime days is that he loved you more than he could ever say, an he loved William too, and simply couldn't bear the thought of yer heads getting blowed off! That's all there ever were to it. I swear. It's the bottom fact. – JB

Promise

April 12th, 1828:

Dagger Barnes leaned over and said, "Stop the wagon." This happened one morning last week after meeting him at the ferry. We were headed north on Compo Road on our way to bring his son Eldridge home. The boy fell off a ladder, which was the word Platt had earlier sent to my attention, although we all knew it was more likely that he had been pushed from the roof by one of his fellow workers. As sure-footed as he is, it's hard to imagine him falling by accident, and it's even harder not to suspect that the other boys working with him on the roof might have deliberately given Eldridge's ladder a kick. Of course, we'll never know exactly what happened because the last thing he would ever do is inform on his workmates, but I do know that their offenses upon his person have been relentless over the past year, relentless and escalating in their viciousness, and I feel at least partially responsible. I was the one who had arranged for his apprenticeship, fully aware of the potential risks, and I've known for some time what was going on. I am well acquainted with these boys and their families, and feel I should have interceded months ago.

In any event, we were making our way up the road whilst Dagger, in his customary manner, sat beside me without speaking. I too was lost in my own private thoughts, imagining what I'd say and do if given the chance to confront those nasty devils. I wanted to tell them what vile cowards I thought they were. I was so angry, and if I could find a way, I'd hunt down every last one of them and hang the little imps to the roof by their thumbs. If those thoughts weren't troubling enough, there was something else weighing upon my mind as we rattled along in the wagon. I was agonizing over how to broach the delicate subject I had promised my daughter and son-in-law I would raise forthwith to Dagger about Eldridge and his obvious interest in their daughter Rachel. This, in fact, was the pretext for why I had volunteered to accompany him on an errand that he could have easily and no doubt would have preferred to handle on his own. Eldridge's leg was broken and in a splint, but from what Platt had reported in his letter, his injuries weren't severe enough to require an extra set of hands to get him situated in a wagon bed. I was also quite certain his tormentors would be feeling contrite by this time (they had, after all, been raised Christians) and would, therefore, not be inclined to create any further trouble. There was simply no good reason for me to be driving Dagger to Platt's, a plain fact that I knew he knew too.

Dagger and I didn't speak about any of this in the wagon – or about anything for that matter – and here is the nub: all of it now feels utterly beside the point. Had I not been so preoccupied at that moment, I may not have been quite so utterly stunned by what unfolded next. I am reeling still. It's as if yet another chapter in my life's story must now take a different tack. Call it Providence. Call it written in the stars. Call it what you will, this revelation is going to require far more time to properly digest.

"Stop the Wagon," Dagger said, and I looked up from the reins to see that we were passing the old homestead. I didn't think anything of it. I no longer feel especially angry, or sad, or regretful whenever I have occasion to travel past the old place these days, and thus Dagger asking me stop at that particular stretch in the road didn't feel noteworthy in any way. My first thought was that perhaps the wind had blown off his hat, or that he had suddenly realized he had left his money belt on the ferry. He got down from the wagon and took a few tentative steps towards the house, and then planted his fists upon his hips. "I know this place," he said with a sweep of an arm "The Dutch roof ... the well out front ... the servant's quarters off to the side with its red door."

He looked thunderstruck. "What of it?" I asked. "This is my cousin's farmhouse. Surely, it seems familiar to you merely because I have spoken of it."

"Nay," he insisted. "You've never told me about this house – t'was my mother what told me about it when I was a boy." Dagger was looking straight at me now. "Is there a walnut mantel inside with a sunburst carved on its front piece?" he asked, and my eyes revealed what I didn't need to put it into words.

He turned to look at the house and its grounds. His voice thickened. "This is the place where my mother and her twin sister were christened."

I've never known Dagger's age, or much at all about his personal life. Like so many of his race, his past was a murky one, and a subject I was happy enough to leave well alone. I never even thought to question him about his parents, or the circumstances of his birth. I did have a vague notion that his father had been a hired hand working for a Mr. Barnes somewhere near Groton, but that was all I needed to know. Such matters were of middling importance to me, and now, I sat in the wagon feeling every bit as dumbstruck as he looked, my mind began spinning with numbers, counting back the years. Could it be possible?

"What was your mother's name?" I asked at last, and he told me: "Promise."

Compo Yet Abides

April 16th, 1828:

From the kitchen window of the firetrap we've called home for the past decade or so I can look over the roof of Jesse's barn and see the pasture that covers the crown of Bald Mountain. It has recently greened, and Sherwood's Blacks and Reds are grazing at the very spot where I once stood all those years ago, and saw the gans'ls of the Halifax drifting behind the dunes of Saugatuck Shores. It's the place where all of us gathered two years later to witness the night sky glowing red from the fires in Norwalk. The stone wall we started at the base of the hill never got any further, but before we were forced to give up the farm, Father did manage to plant a few apple trees up the slope, Northern Spies if I remember correctly, and from where I sit, I can see their upper branches. The trees have been allowed to grow tall and leggy. They aren't good producers, but are nonetheless in full blossom. They look lovely in the morning sun, which comes up directly over the midpoint of the ridge at this time of year, a reminder that while generations come and generations go, the hills and dales of Compo yet abide. Nothing any of us humans can bring to bear, neither with our warships, nor by the alchemy of our greed and passions, has the power to alter the underlying bones of this place I call home.

I can also see down to the ferry. It's been a while since I've boarded that scow often packed with sheep and goats and God knows what else. There were long stretches in my life when I was crossing over and back daily, making me one of One Eyed Meeker's most regular of regular passengers. I once knew every inch of that creaky amalgamation of timbers, every nail and splinter. The old man is tying it now to the pylon, and I can see the opposing columns of day laborers and tradesmen, the one filing on while the other disembarks; the two sets of folks hurrying past one another without so much as a friendly tip of the cap, without even raising their heads. One boy is leading a milk cow, another is concentrating on a twist of goats, and a few men are laden with bundles. Here comes a journeyman wearing a carpenter's belt ... there's a Negro seamstress with her carpetbag, each walking intently, lost in their own vain shew. There's One Eyed Meeker, leaning on his ferryman's pole, as ornery as ever, in the midst of his daily harangue with no one in particular that his passengers have long since learned to ignore. As best I can remember, Meeker has run the ferry for the Disbrow's for as many years as they've held its charter. His single peacock-blue eye and the unpainted scow he operates, are as much a part of the landscape around here as are the bitterns and egrets tiptoeing across the tidal flats. I suspect the old man (and by the bent-over look of him, soon his progeny) will be ferrying people and their valuables across and back from Compo to Norwalk until the Sound runs dry.

The Meekers are among the Stayers. The Stayers are the ones who haunt the wharfs and warehouses on either side of the Saugatuck at all hours of the day, willing to work when there's work to be found, but free of the restlessness that runs like an electrical current through so many of the others I see hiving at the landing every morning. These are the Goers. They are the restless souls with a twitchy bounce to their step; people too numerous to know by name – I wonder even where they all come from – saving whatever extra money they are able to squeeze from their employers to put towards their dream of heaping riches one day in places far away. No doubt they will be striking soon for the latest Promised Lands: the Western Reserve, or perhaps Indiana or Illinois – places where I hear the soil is black, and the land spreads flat and wide for as far as the eye can see. This is the fabled American frontier, where in just a few short years a man with a mechanical threshing machine can turn surpluses of wheat into towering stacks of Liberty Dollars.

Just as on the day I started this epistle one year ago, Kezzie is walking from the shed with a bag of seed potatoes. Spring has returned, and she is ready once again to break ground in our kitchen garden. Her face is set with that look she has whenever she's gearing up for the hard work she complains about, but secretly loves. I will join her soon to cut and dust the seeds, and we'll talk as is our custom about our ever expanding brood – our girls Lotta, Sarah, and Mary and our sons John Hervey and Uriah, all grown now with children of their own. How do you think Lotta will cope with a third baby, Kessie will ask, with Zack not four years old and Betty still in nappies? They'll manage fine, just as we once did, I will assure her. Do you think Mary and Thomas's leaky barn will have to come down? No, not likely. Will John Hervey get his riding chair and peacock himself around the square? How could it be, she'll tisk, that one of our children should want to purchase such a frippery? Because he's more a Wright than a Bennett, I'll reply, handing her the next seed potato to place in the row.

I've taken advantage of these warming days to make good progress on this memoir, getting most of my best work done when there is just me and the stove and my oil lamp to contend with. Much has happened in the intervening decades since the war. It saddens me to report that William and I have lost touch completely. He moved to Pennsylvania with his wife and children, not long after the war ended, where he bought a small farm. I haven't seen him since, and our correspondences by post have recently trickled to a close. I also regret to report that as soon as Uncle Joseph took over the place on Compo Road, he allowed the farm to fall into ruin just as we all expected he would. He bought a Negro named Timothy to replace Cesar, and in addition to putting him to work in the fields and in the barns, he dressed him up in livery, and had him serving meals at the table and welcoming guests at the door. What a pointless extravagance! I heard it said that Uncle Joe spent many an evening when he first moved into our house digging through the ashes of the old barn in search of Cesar's money. He was convinced Cesar had stashed it in a safe box that he kept buried in there somewhere. "There could be no other reason a man would risk running into a burning barn," I heard him once say to Aunt Sarah, "than to retrieve his life's savings." The greedy fool may very well have kept at his nightly excavations until the ground froze solid that winter – I wouldn't put it past him. It wouldn't have mattered one way or another because only I knew where Cesar had that box hidden. He had it buried under a large rock at the base of the stone wall in the corner of the rootstock orchard. I shouldered over the rock myself on the morning after he died, and Father and I took the safe box on that very day to Phyllis, presenting her with the

Spanish dollars Cesar had managed to save. Heaven only knows what happened to all the money, although I know the Judge freed Phyllis. And yet, to my lasting distress, he never freed the two young girls, Promise and Gift, deciding instead to sell them at auction. I blame Father for this. He held Cesar's cash, and could have attached certain contingencies to its transferal, demanding that the Judge use the money to fulfill ALL of Cesar's wishes. But the Judge was in no mood to consider such liberal terms. He told Father that due to his grievous loss of property in Tryon's fire, he could no longer justify the use of the two girls, nor in any way afford them. "We must all learn to live with less," he lamented as we were climbing into the wagon, and ere we drove through the gate he added his final summation with a wave of his arm. "I'll be taking the wenches to Black Rock tomorrow!" he avowed, and that's the last I ever heard about either of those little girls … until last week.

When Uncle Joseph died a few years ago, he conveyed the property to his eldest son, Sherwood, who shares both his father's weakness for hard spirits and an indifference towards the rigors of farming. As far as I can tell, he's made his living mostly by selling a few acres of his property to various neighbors every other year or so. At the rate he's going, he'll be out of land to sell by the end of the decade. Most of the other Compo Bennetts are spread to the winds these days. My daughters still live nearby, as does my brother, Isaac, the sea captain, who lives in a house just up the road. He and his wife have but one boy – a man he is now – named John Benedict, who also makes his living at sea. As far as the Norfield cousins go, young Jabez removed to Nova Scotia immediately after the raid, and his parents, who were never formally accused of any untoward behavior during the war – how they escaped any incriminations I will never know – lived out their years in comfort. I occasionally wonder if Aunt Sarah's recent interest in the girl's school has something to do with atonement. Who can know? And then there is Jesse. There will always be Jesse. The old widower and I remain loyal friends. He and I have seen it all.

The Last of the Night Stirrings?

April 20th, 1828:

I yet again interrupt this remembrance of days long past to sadly report on the tumult of my life in the present. The louts from Disbrow's called upon us again last night, but were nowhere near as menacing as they have been in the past, assembling this time out in the yard without any torches, bricks or crowbars in hand. They seemed content to merely awaken Kessie and me with their drunken jeers, to revel in the news that all plans for the academy for Negro girls have been placed in abeyance. What a bitter defeat our Anti-slavery Society has suffered! In spite of all our good works – the money we have raised, the care we have taken to enlighten our fellow citizens, the eloquent appeals to their better angels, all seems lost. It is utterly impossible to deny that ignorance has prevailed in the end. The opponents to our cause were successful in raising so many irrational fears. "Picanninies" from all over America would soon be flooding into our community, they cried. These lower orders of human beings were sure to "elbow out" our own young women from the education they deserved. Their sly, licentious proclivities would "contaminate" the morals of our young men, and lead to interracial marriages. Educating a mere handful of free Negro girls would not just disrupt the social order of our little corner of the world; it would bring about the ruination of our entire nation! These sentiments are so widely felt and deeply inbred, I doubt we will ever prevail in ridding our state, and our nation, of the stain of slavery. Alas, the vote was nearly unanimous at the special Town Meeting convened yesterday. What the mob was unable to achieve with its violent acts of intimidation, the so-called respectable men of Weston have put to rest for good and all with a simple raise of their hands. When I heard the bastards drifting away last night, it broke my heart to suspect they won't ever be coming back. There is nothing left for them to rail against. There is simply not enough support in the community at large for the school we planned. I doubt there ever will be, which is a tragedy, even if it must certainly be a deep relief to our dear Jesse.

Rachel's Sampler

May 3rd, 1828:

Writing is a lonely business. I sometimes wonder if anyone besides Kessie (who gushes over every word I read aloud to her) will find what I've worked on for so long even the slightest bit interesting. My brothers and sisters surely won't. They would rather leave our history buried in the cellar, and have taken great pains to never even ask me about my musings. And my children, who came of age in a world so very different than mine, are much too busy with their own affairs to care about the tumult that shaped the life of their rather ordinary, often irritable sail maker father. Besides, they know me all too well. They have seen me in my cups, howling at the moon. I can't blame them for not wishing to share in my deepest thoughts.

On the other hand, my grandchildren may in good time prove to be willing readers. This is what I am hoping for, and believe there is at least a small chance that this next generation of Bennetts will one day favorably receive this missive. After all, they haven't had to contend with my failings, nor have they ever felt the sting of my switch. There is a kind of unspoken once-removed-ness between us that in a strange way makes for a comfortable place for us to meet. A place where the very gulf between our ages doesn't add distance, but helps somehow to bring us closer together. It's a wonder to see how readily their little hands take hold of my big, gnarly finger, or how unfazed they seem to be of my wild, and I should think, rather frightening ogre's eyebrows, or how they never take umbrage over my poorly shaved chin, or disparage my crooked stoop and failing eyesight – and not once has any one of them ever lodged a single complaint about my food-stained shirtfront! And while their parents show impatience from time to time over the fact I am no longer able to split a cord of firewood between breakfast and supper, my grand children never express even the slightest twinge of annoyance towards my diminishments, and seem, to my astonishment, to have as much pure filial affection for me as I have for them. They call me "Henny" of all things, so Kessie and I are "Henny and Kit," and I like to imagine that many years from now one of them will stumble upon this journal in the attic, or in the bottom drawer of some desk, and will blow away the dust from its cover to take a few hours on a winter's eve to skim through its pages. Goodness knows they owe me at least that much. Oh, how they have conspired against me! Pilfering my quills to make Indian headdresses, spilling my inkpots, scattering papers, shouting at all hours beneath my window with their games of shadow tag and blind man's bluff! Don't children have chores to do these days? With such devils careening about, it's a miracle I've gotten anything at all down on paper!

It's been over a fortnight since I last sat at this desk. There was, as expected, quite the rumpus over the Dagger Barnes connection, but now that the initial shock has worn off, I believe it's safe to say we are all beginning to get used to the revelation that my closest business associate for so many years has turned out to be Cesar's grandson. It is, after all, nothing more than a coincidence – a cold quirk of history. Of course there is still the matter of the Eldridge and Rachel connection, but with all the catching up we've needed to do, all the questions Dagger has naturally wanted to know about Cesar and the Judge and all the rest, it hasn't felt like the right time to talk about the difficulties those two youngsters will surely face should they ever decide to become engaged and marry. Besides, Eldridge's broken leg is keeping him at home in Norwalk, giving all concerned the perfect excuse to sweep the matter under the rug, at least for the time being – an act of self-preservation for which members of my family in particular are always ready to undertake with great alacrity.

The sticky little problem with Rachel and her beau notwithstanding, our grandchildren – a baker's dozen at last count – give us such pleasure. In spite of all their noise and inherently chaotic natures, they are ever a welcome distraction. We love that Lotta and Mary's children live just up the road, and come by our house almost daily to play their games and stage their pantomimes. We love also to travel round to visit the others in their houses in Norwalk and Weston, and do so as often as we can. I've lived a good life and have known many of its pleasures, and here is one of the great abiding truths I have come to appreciate these past few years: there isn't anything better in all the world than a young grandchild fresh from the wash basin smelling of soap, wrapped in warm flannel, presented to you by its mother for a good night hug and kiss as you sit by the fire at the end of the day digesting your grog and stew. I find the love that wells up at these quiet moments far too formidable to resist, leaving me with no choice but to unfasten the binds of my usual reserve, and happily surrender to it.

I am joyed to see that all thirteen of them are blooming fair, each blessed with good health and promising futures. None, thank goodness, show the least inclination to become a sail maker. I imagine most will find farms (or farmers to marry), some may become seafarers or learn a trade, one or two might even find a patron and be able to attend college in order to become a lawyer or a physician, perhaps even a clergyman. They are all without question bright enough, and have the requisite breeding to enter the ranks of the professional classes, which would be wonderful, and a vindication of sorts for me, but truth be told, I don't really mind what any of them become, so long as they remain as vital and as curious and as kind as they are today. What else matters?

Rachel is the only one among them who gives me any reason to pause. And it's not only because of the blush that comes to her cheeks whenever she sees the dashing, yet ill suited Eldridge Barnes. I am concerned about her rebellious and willful nature in general – traits she has displayed in one way or another since the day she was born, tendencies that if not kept in check, could easily make her life more difficult than one's life needs to be. These characteristics have been made even more manifest of late, ever since she began work on her decorative sampler assigned by her grammar school matron. This is an endeavor meant to hone the needlework skills she will need to keep her future family well clothed and provided with marked linens, and while she is well aware of the practicality behind this domestic custom, she comes to the task reluctantly, with her independent spirit on full display, especially if you know where to look for it. Others might perceive a young girl dutifully working on her coming-of-age sampler, but I see the aforementioned rebelliousness expressed silently in every furious stitch she makes. Take for example, the matter of what verse to stitch along the bottom of her design. She has dug in her heels, refusing to inscribe anything that expresses what she calls "insipid piety," nor will she agree to any aphorisms that mention a woman's "duty" or "obedience." Blake is her favorite poet, and she is campaigning hard to use a few lines from his works. Even I said to her, "Rachel, be reasonable! Think about what you are suggesting! Remember, dear child, this sampler is being done as much for your mother's sake as it is for yours. Why not compromise and borrow lines from a more suitable, less controversial poet? Alexander Pope, for example!"

Meanwhile, her thoughts this morning seem far away, pursing her lips with each stab of the needle through the cloth on her lap, knitting her brow as she pulls it out from the other side. The precision of her stitches on the cloth is everywhere impressive. The numerals and letters of her alphabet are finely drawn, the floral design of her border is as lovely as it is intricate, and there, as the centerpiece of the sampler, in the place where some girls might depict their loving parents standing beneath a grape arbor, or the house where they were raised, or a perhaps a vase filled with their favorite cut flowers, Rachel has decided to stitch an apple tree. Why? I wonder. There is nothing special about the handful of apple trees on the farm where she lives. Her father is no orchardist. He grows mostly onions! And as far as I know, nobody has ever talked to Rachel about the apple orchard that her great grandfather had once planned to establish. That part of our family's past is dead and buried. It is never spoken of.

Seeing the design she has chosen suddenly brings to mind a dream I must have dreamt just the other night: I am leaning over the bow of a fine, two-masted gaff-rigged schooner captained by my brother Isaac, hired on as an idler on one of his trading voyages to the West Indies. My main purpose is to observe first-hand how the sails I had sewn for the ship's owners would hold up against a strong ocean wind. We tack down the East River and glide through the Narrows. We soon find ourselves beyond Sandy Hook, out on the open ocean with a fresh westerly blowing, sailing fast to the southwards. Dolphins go jumping over the waves while ghostly schools of manta rays swirl beneath them. It is a crystal blue-sky day – "church steeple clear" as Father once described it – with the swells striking rhythmically against the bow. I gaze transfixed as foamy white diamonds skitter across the dark blue surface of the sea, and in the next moment, I am not a man, but a boy, and instead of looking down at the ocean, I am looking upwards, where the be-sparkled splashes of foam have suddenly transformed into apple blossoms, blown from the treetops, fluttering across a clear blue Connecticut sky. I am lying on my back in the old apple orchard beside our house on Compo Road, and the next thing I know, it is no longer spring, but a crisp autumn day. It occurs to me that I was supposed to be picking up windfalls, so I jump to my feet and look down the long row. There's my brother William, perched atop of a ladder, leaning into the heart of an apple tree, with a canvas bag slung over his shoulder. Just below him, I can see my father, busily lifting baskets of apples into the back of a wagon. The two of them at that distance appear as mirror images of one another, save that one is fair and the other is grey, and when Father senses that I am looking at him, he turns in my direction. He gives me a wide, toothy smile, while proudly presenting me with the bushel basket he is holding, tilting it towards me, so that I can see that it is brimming with golden Roxbury Russets.

I watch as Rachel bites off another length of golden thread from the spool. She readies for another stitch. There is something about the tilt of her head and the cast of her finely chiseled profile as she perches on her footstool in the lamplight that strikes me deeply. She has for certain a strong family likeness, but there is something more about her very presence that I am sensing just now. It's that stubbornness – that's part of it, along with the careful planning so evident in the design of her sampler, her assiduous attention to every silken detail. There is also a hint of sadness that I see, or an emotion more akin to resignation, lurking behind her frequent flashes of willfulness that lay just beneath the surface of the dreams I know she is dreaming. I can only pray that her expectations for how her life should be in a perfect world will not keep her from one day joining with the other children at play outside my window, or prevent her from finding a boy – the right young man – who will prove every ounce her match. But that's not quite what is touching me so deeply either. What's touching me the most – what I have just this moment realized, and can hardly bear to

223

put to paper lest she were to look up just now and slay me with a smile, is that when I gaze upon this wisp of a girl, this fellow free thinking yet confirmed Stayer, I see a living echo of the proud and defiant man I battled with for all those many years.

I see in her my father, Deliverance Bennett. A recognition, and yet another surrender too.

Eldridge Barnes

June 6th, 1828:

His leg has healed; I notice he's walking with a slight limp, but beyond this minor impediment, he looks to be as strong as ever, and is back at work for Mr. Platt. His workmates ------------------------

October, 1836:

Dear Rachel, and anyone else who might be reading this. As you've probably already gone an figgered, I were the one to find yer old Hennie slumped upon his desk, ink spilt everwhere. He was layin on his side with his one good eye gazing out the kitchen window and an empty vial of ladnum in hand, so you can rest assured he went peaceable. Poor Kessie couldn't quite glom the fact of his sudden, unexpected demise and went wandrin off like she was doing more an more in them days. I stuffed this journal neath the bed an forgot all bout it for years an years – not until your old Kit went an wandered off once'n for all. One of them Meeker boys found her among the rocks out on the Shores, washed over by the tide. Poor Kessie. She'd become so sorely forgetful. I done my best to allus fetch her back, I truly did, but she were jest plain determined to go off.

Clearin out the place to make room for the new boarder, I had a decide what in tarnashin to do with all her belongings an such. You're married an all, and with hardly any more a our direct line left in town, I threw it all away, cept acourse for the few pieces of silverware which I gave to yer Uncle Isaac. I was set to give him this journal too, then I figgered I autta finally read the tarnal thing, which is what I done, an as you can see, I left my comments when I figgered comments was needed. I tell you what. Now that I been pouring over this here diary I don't want no more part of it! No offence or nothin, but yer old Hennie may a bin smart an bookish an all of that, but he were sorely bone headed bout certain subjects! He wrote down some things that was better left un-wrote down. Certain memories are still too raw when it comes to certain folks round here, folks who knows someone what nearly died on one a them prisen ships, or who might a had there house burnt down, or who lost a brother or a father to them tarnal Tory raiders. There was plenty a awful sufferin an plenty a dodgy-doins to go round in them days, but here's the true fact a the matter when it comes to what we Bennetts done, an what we didn't do. Uncle Joe an Uncle Jabez – an even sweet Aunt Sarah – was scoundrels through an through, an my own Da went along for the ride with little account to show for his trouble, God rest his sorry soul. Yer old Henny had his whirlygigs in such a twist about that oath Uncle Del signed too late, an about all that liberty stuff, he couldn't allus see straight. He knew Uncle Jabez and Aunt Sarah was bad all right, but I don't believe he ever fully come to grips with how deep in it they truly was, an specially Uncle Joe. He was slyest of em all by far. An here's the saddest part. Them miscreants seen there chances, an they took em, an they came out the other end a things smellin sweet as clover, but not poor Uncle Del, yer great grandfather. He done everthing right for all the right reasons an all he got left with was nothin more'n a few sorry cows. Tain't fair I tell you. Plain tain't fair!

So here's what I figgers. I figgers we Bennetts ain't off the hook jest yet, so I'm givin this book now to Isaac. Let him decide what to do bout it, an if'n he asks me, I says burn the tarnal thing! Them Disbrow drunkards a been more or less mannerly these days lately. What's the sense'n stirrin em up?

Meanwhiles, here's what I have to say to my old friend an boon companyen. In case you aint noticed, that Eldridge feller kinder drifted off an Rachel married her man Tom, so there weren't no Bennett chimney tops runnin round the place after all, an thank God fer that! But not everthin's on the up an up in Compo. There's some furniture been moved round, that you can't help but notice. I wandered up to Tipping Rock the other afternoon jest to sees what I could see. Our little monument's a-sitting there still, but there's nary a candlewood pine to be found, just the bedrock, making it hardly worth a tinker's cuss as a hiding place no more. I swear Haynes, you can climb up on our rock an see clear down to the river's mouth! So there I was, braced against the wind, with me cap pulled round me ears an you won't believe what I saw! Smoke! Great white puffs of it blowin in the sky on the other side a Bennetts Rocks and a-chugging eastwards, one of them filthy steamers stuffed to the gills with trumperies, bound for Boston. An there's something more I wish to say, an I hesitates to say it on account of how you allus used to get so maudlin drunk at times. It's this, an don't let it go to yer head. When I was settin on that rock of ourn with the sun going down behind the Shores an I got to remembering about when we was young, and about how in spite a all yer occasional darkling moods, what a trusty trout you allus was. Oh Haynes, taint hardly a Guardsman left in Disbrow's except for me these days. Old Trow aint had his brow rubbed in years! Sure, I gets out me fiddle whenever they calls upon me, an I gives the crowd a spirited go at whatever standards they wishes to hear, but what I'm trying to say is that as pretty as this old fiddle of mine ever sounds, taint the same without yer buttery-tones to back er up. No by jingo, it truly aint the same. — JB

Epilogue

Every single detail of Nathan's Minuteman ensemble was spot on. The magical transformation from ordinary suburban kid to Revolutionary War hero began when he donned a shimmering white blouse ornamented by frilly do-dads down the front, a silk garment that once belonged to a long forgotten dead aunt. The thing reeked of mothballs, the chemical swirl of which nearly gagged him, and probably would have, had the fabric not also been imbued with, as best as he could place, the friendly fragrance of that synthetic syrup trapped inside a wax pop bottle. The blouse had been exhumed from the sea captain's chest in the attic. It was, in fact, a fine example of high Victorian feminine haute couture, but to Nathan's eyes at least, it looked both Colonial and manly. Over top of this shirt he wore his brass-buttoned Sunday school blazer (last year's model and thus a little short in the sleeves) accessorized by his canvas Safety Patrol belt and crisscrossed by one of his mother's leather purses with an extended shoulder strap. For leggings, he wore long johns underneath a pair of khaki jeans with the legs rolled up to just below the knees. The crimped edges of a Swanson's TV dinner plate were cut and fashioned into silver buckles for his shoes. His mother made a few nips and cuts to a dishtowel, tied a ribbon around it to make a ponytail, and centered this terrycloth contraption upon his head. For a hat, he wore one of his father's commuter train felt fedoras pinned into three corners. When all of the component parts were fully assembled and he got his first look at himself, the image staring back from the full-length mirror in his parent's bedroom was that of the best Minuteman ever! There couldn't have been a more authentic-looking Son of Liberty, and the costume's final touch, the coup de grace that completely sold the look, was his firearm. A few years earlier, when his parents had torn down the dilapidated shed in their backyard to make room for a flagstone patio, they discovered an old flintlock, rusted, and nearly split in two at the stock. This antique was the genuine article, but hazardous to say the least. When Nathan first shouldered it in front of the mirror, the end of the barrel banged into the ceiling, making a dent, before strafing across the wall behind him, sending a row of framed pictures crashing to the floor. There's no way he should have been allowed to even touch such an unwieldy relic, but after days of beefing and moaning, his parents finally relented. They allowed him to carry it, just this once, for Halloween.

It was 1963, and he was but eleven years old. The movie *Johnny Tremain*, that masterpiece of Disney schmaltz, had been released a few years back. Nathan had managed somehow to see it several times. He loved everything about the flick: Its inspiring depiction of the Boston Tea Party; the rugged Son's of Liberty making fools of toffee-nosed Tories; Paul Revere's ride; and of course, all those thrilling battle scenes with muskets poking out from behind bushes and stone walls, picking off hapless Redcoats. At that point in history, his great grandmother, Gigi, had told him the family story. He was fully aware of Deliverance Bennett (her third great grandfather and his fifth) and he knew that some sort of a minor battle had been fought near their house on the northern end of South Compo Road. He knew too that a few British soldiers had been "given succor" in their kitchen, but if anybody had ever mentioned that this ancestor of theirs harbored Royalist sympathies of any sort, it never sunk in. Such an inconvenient historical fact was utterly incomprehensible, and thus, in Nathan's mind on that Halloween night, Deliverance Bennett was as true-blue as any other red-blooded American Patriot that ever lived. Deliverance was his go-to Minuteman, and as he and his cousin Bud went careening through the neighborhoods that night, it was Deliverance who Nathan imagined himself to be. He became that same brave hero, that same embattled farmer answering freedom's call – swooping across the manicured lawns, ducking under clotheslines, leaping over jack-o-lanterns, weaving through clutches of fellow trick-or treaters – into clouds of gun smoke he charged, with flags unfurled and grapeshot whizzing through the rhododendrons, running step for step to the cadence of the song from the movie ("we are the sons, yes we are the sons, the SONS of lib-er-ty!"), ever attacking, never yielding, giving it ball for ball to row upon row of lousy Lobsterbacks.

Their battle plan was carefully mapped with a single objective in mind: maximum yields of candy. They started their campaign around Nathan's house, heading over to Park Lane, a brand new development near the Post Road where the neat, three bedroom colonials were squeezed tightly together. After picking that high-producing enclave clean, they were transported by automobile down to Bud's house, which was closer to the beach and more to the point, situated in the midst of several densely packed neighborhoods. Down Compo Parkway they raced, up Minute Man Hill and through some backyards to get to the gazillions of bungalows that packed the far side Compo Hill, overlooking Old Mill Beach. They went at it nonstop, filling their pillowcases with loot until nearly nine o'clock. By the time Nathan got home and stumbled up to his bedroom, he was completely tuckered. He got out of his costume, relieved to be free of the thermal underpants and terrycloth wig that had made him so sweaty. He clunked the distended pillowcase onto the top of his chest of drawers, carefully spilling out its contents. The mountain of candy before him was magnificent to behold.

"Nate!" his mom hollered from downstairs, "Get to bed. It's a school night!"

"Alright already!" he hollered back with a wave of his hand, transfixed before the joyful feast.

"Hey!" his mother snapped, louder than before, stirring him from his reverie. She was now at the foot of the stairs to show that she really meant it. After a sigh, he turned reluctantly from his hard-earned delights and stumbled into bed.

The Minuteman costume lay in a heap in the corner, smelling faintly of mud and grass and salt air, of home. The flintlock was leaning in the corner too. He reached for it. As he reclined against the headboard with the firearm resting on his lap, he took a few moments to reflect upon what turned out to be the most epic Halloween of all time. What a killing he and

Bud had made! And what a terrific Minuteman costume he had worn! Sure, the musket weighed a ton, and there were moments when he felt like chucking it, but he had soldiered gallantly onwards. The Redcoats he encountered along the way never stood a chance against such a brave warrior armed with such a fearsome weapon. He turned out the light and nestled back against the pillow, cradling the flintlock against his chest, gently thumbing its hammer. In a few moments, his eyes adjusted to the dark, and he gazed reverently upon his faithful gun. The light spilling in from the hall was just bright enough for him to notice that there was a design etched onto its brass firing plate, a peaceful scene of what looked to be of a deer, bounding forward, enwreathed with oak leaves.

Trying now to prepare for sleep, he ran his fingers across the intricate furrows left by the gunsmith, quietly contemplating their scoops and curves. With the broken musket across his chest and his fingers still poised upon the firing plate, he drifted off to sleep and was soon deep into a dream, a wondrous romp, filled to the brim with Zagnuts, Baby Ruths, Fire Balls, Bit-o-Honey and Pez Dispensers, all arrayed upon a distant hilltop. There came approaching the sound of fifes and drums, as if a marching band at a Memorial Day Parade was about to round the corner. Suddenly gun smoke swirled into the sky. There came also the sound of battle cries rolling down the wind from across a broad patchwork of fields he remembered from somewhere long ago but couldn't quite place, the gentle undulations of his dreamscape inerrant, right down to its granite bones, its sloping pastures greened by the coming of spring, its shadowy hollows pinked by the sunlit crowns of apple trees.

Jonathan B. Walker was born and raised in what is today, Westport, Connecticut, living in the area of town and on the very same road first settled by his family in 1664. He currently resides in Pennsylvania where he blogs about books, (www.jonosbookreviews.com.) His short stories have appeared in the on-line literary magazine, BioStories (www.bioStories.com.)

41518286R00135

Made in the USA
Middletown, DE
16 March 2017